Y0-AFX-208

HIS MOUTH
WAS OVER HERS . . .

and she was lost. Belinda was unable to think of anything, unable to fathom the consequences of what was happening between them. She was so innocent of a man's needs that the hot and cold sensations pebbling her flesh seemed unreal, as if she were in some lovely, incomprehensible dream.

Then he was no longer there—his warmth and passion were gone. She blinked, tottered on her feet, not understanding what had happened until she opened her eyes and saw him standing a few feet away from her. He muttered something low, filled with longing. Her mouth still throbbing from his demanding kisses, she could only stare up at him in the dreamy-eyed confusion of a woman having her first experience with passion.

"I can't do this," he said, his voice hoarse, tortured.

Belinda tried to think straight, tried to comprehend what she had done to make him pull away in anger.

"Get away from me," he said.

She fled. . . .

Forever, My Love

by
Linda Ladd

A TOPAZ BOOK

TOPAZ
Published by the Penguin Group
Penguin Books USA Inc., 375 Hudson Street,
New York, New York 10014, U.S.A.
Penguin Books Ltd, 27 Wrights Lane,
London W8 5TZ, England
Penguin Books Australia Ltd, Ringwood,
Victoria, Australia
Penguin Books Canada Ltd, 10 Alcorn Avenue,
Toronto, Ontario, Canada M4V 3B2
Penguin Books (N.Z.) Ltd, 182–190 Wairau Road,
Auckland 10, New Zealand

Penguin Books Ltd, Registered Offices:
Harmondsworth, Middlesex, England

First published by Topaz, an imprint of Dutton Signet,
a division of Penguin Books USA Inc.

First Printing, April, 1997
10 9 8 7 6 5 4 3 2 1

 REGISTERED TRADEMARK—MARCA REGISTRADA

Printed in the United States of America

Forever,
My Love

Prologue

Gliding as silkily as water over a slick stone ledge, the haunting refrains of violins and cellos and violas drifted from the sparkling mirrored ballroom and through the lavish corridors of the Greenleigh mansion. Like a slow-moving, melodious ground fog, the soft music eased past the magnificent five-foot, eighteen-pronged silver candelabra that guarded the entrance of the rear wing and overtook Belinda Scott as she hurried down the deserted hallway toward Sir John's oak-paneled library.

Straightening the white linen mobcap atop her black curls and patting down the folds of the long apron over her slate gray skirt, she paused before cream-colored double doors inlaid with gilt-edged panels, inhaled one time, deeply, to calm her nerves before entering her randy employer's most private sanctuary. Sir John's constant, overly familiar, highly unwelcome attentions appalled her each time she encountered him, but there was little she could do to combat it.

Unfortunately, she had been forced to endure such behavior for eight long weeks now, since she had been purchased into indenture by his household. His gaze continually latched upon her wherever she went, roved insultingly over the bodice of her servant attire—which luckily, was staid and maidenly modest—then down the length of her body as she passed him, even in the dining room when he partook of the evening repast with the mistress directly across the table!

Resentment was born and spread in a slow, fiery burn inside her breast. His Lordship's actions made her feel like chattel—as if she were some fancy trinket he had purchased for personal pleasure instead of the honest employee she was. Until this moment she had been able to avoid solitary encounters with him, at least for the most part, but now she had no choice. Lady Greenleigh was hostessing a grand party in the ballroom, and Mrs. Hyslop, the housekeeper, had ordered Belinda to answer the persistent ringing of His Lordship's summoning bell. With head held high, she prepared herself for his humiliating inspection, then tapped lightly before she twisted the brass door handle and entered the room.

Inside, she found a trio of elegantly attired gentlemen gathered around a black teak card table, its surface covered with soft green baize. Lord John Greenleigh was adorned in a black satin evening coat, the white linen stock around his meaty neck artfully folded and edged with lace. The younger of his guests was similarly attired, but the other man, an older, much more portly figure, wore the scarlet, gold-epauleted jacket and white breeches of the British military uniform. As Belinda bobbed the shallow, compulsory curtsy, she wondered why the gentlemen were closeted here together when there were so many lovely ladies laughing gaily and enjoying the elegant steps of the minuet in the festive ballroom.

"Fetch a new bottle of brandy from the cabinet in the blue parlor, girl, and be quick with you. Only yesterday I ordered Mrs. Hyslop to see my library cabinet replenished, and I bloody well don't like being ignored."

Pleased that Sir John was too intent on grumbling about the housekeeper and studying the ornate black and red gaming cards he held in his hand to barely take note of her, Belinda moved hastily to obey his command. She left the room and hurried down the quiet back wing to the dark, cold parlor. Shivering, she opened the glass-fronted cherrywood liquor cabinet and retrieved a new bottle of brandy, then took another, so he would have no need to summon her again.

The card players paid her no heed when she returned and carried the bottles to the teak liquor cabinet on the other side of the library. She unstoppered the cork on the brandy, observing through the gold-framed mirror hanging in front of her each man sitting comfortably in Sir John's deep, maroon leather armchairs.

They gambled at the game of whist—one of Sir John's passions, a fact she had learned early in her tenure at his estate—and her employer scowled now at the hand dealt him with not a little consternation. Only one man sat facing her, and he appeared calm and confident, a good deal younger than the others, though his longish brown mane had begun to thin at the pate, receding in faint half-moon indentations above each black, heavily delineated eyebrow. It was to him that Sir John addressed his remarks.

"Bartholomew, old friend, drain the last of your drink and allow the wench to refill your cup. By thunder, man, you've been a surly soul this night," he said peevishly, shaking his hoary head with obvious annoyance. "Despite the fact that you rob us blind with your damnable luck."

She watched the balding man, the one called Bartholomew, as he shrugged off his companion's complaint, grinning affably as he tossed down the last of the amber liquid pooled in the bowl of his brandy snifter.

"If you had spent the last three years on Manhattan Island, my friend, where your fellow New Yorkers brand you villain for your righteous support of mother England, I daresay your own spirits would not be of so jolly a bent. In patriot eyes, we, who do the honorable thing and remain loyal to the Crown are spat upon and pelted with horse dung if we are fool enough to turn our backs on the baser populace."

"Ah, so 'tis the rebellion that wears so mightily on your usual high spirits," interjected the heretofore silent British officer as he spread out his cards faceup on the table. He grimaced when Bartholomew easily bested him with a winning hand.

Raking more gold coins into the considerable pile in front of him, Bartholomew's frown deepened. "Aye, Jack, and such ugly abuse 'twould work against any man's nerves. Especially with patriot sabotage running rampant both in the thoroughfares of Manhattan and on English ships in the harbor. Hell's fire, I witnessed a mass hanging of rebels at the Battery on the day before I set out upon this very journey, which sickened even me, for all my loyalty to George. Every day it continues, and do not forget that, though misguided, these are fellow Americans, my own countrymen."

"Aye," agreed Jack, the military man, as he leaned back and folded his hands across his trim waist, "but nevertheless they are traitors to their rotten cores. You cannot expect His Majesty to turn a blind eye upon defiance and open rebellion."

Bartholomew shook his head. "In any case, 'twas enough to send me here where English sentiment, and present company, are far more to my liking."

"What keeps you, wench? Hurry it up, I say!"

Sir John sent a black countenance in her direction, sputtering about the ineptitude of colonial servants, but Belinda preferred that abuse to his usual lecherous leers, even when he continued his harangue as she wrapped the full bottle in a brown linen towel.

"I say, these bloody indentures are lax in their duties. Why Colleen insists upon having such to serve us I cannot fathom. They are poor baggage, indeed, set up next to Mister Stanley, the butler who presides over our English staff in Sussex with such proper decorum. 'Tis yet another burden we bear, forced to serve His Majesty in the midst of this godforsaken frozen river. My poor maimed leg already dreads the coming winter." He lounged further down into his chair as Belinda turned toward the table. He used his fingers to massage the old battle wound in his right knee—of which she had heard him complain often since her arrival.

"I have worse problems than inept staff," Bartholomew murmured without glancing at Belinda as she approached the table. His remark brought Sir John back to the subject of the American war waging somewhere to the south.

"You must keep your faith, Bart, for the major here under Lord Cornwallis and the Lords Howe will crush Washington and his rebels before the year is out. In the meanwhile, a few nights spent in Quebec among good friends will surely ease your sorrows. I shall insist that you stay here with Colleen and me until you show more cheer." He paused, apparently noticing for the first time that it was Belinda who had answered his summons. His hanging jowls slid into a sly visage that made her tense. "Perhaps a cozy night held in the arms of a wench as comely as Belinda here would ease your suffering soul."

Belinda stiffened with insult as she waited silently for permission to pour, clutching the bottle tightly, but her jaw clenched so hard it ached, for, even though she did not dare a look she knew both the officer and Bartholomew the American were no doubt measuring her as bedmate.

Rigidly controlling her humiliation over being treated like some deaf and mute creature standing forth for their masculine pleasure, she replenished the glass in front of the man named Bartholomew. Never looking at him, she made to move away but could not, for he reached out and caught her wrist with his fingers. Startled that he had detained her by force, she turned to look down at him.

His grip tightened, and she watched his face register an expression that could only be identified as shock, as if some hideous, misapportioned gargoyle had suddenly appeared before his eyes. Frightened by the way he stared at her, she could do naught but wait while he took his leisure examining every inch of her face. As moments passed, a warm burn of embarrassment rose underneath her sculpted cheekbones and flushed her pale skin crimson.

"Have I offended you, my lord?" she offered at last, hoping to end the rude scrutiny.

At her hesitant inquiry, Sir John lifted his eyes from contemplating his cards. He stared curiously at his guest, but Bartholomew quickly released his restraint upon her person, allowing Belinda to set down the bottle and flee the encounter.

Outside, she pulled the door shut and rushed down the corridor, afraid of what import the young American's interest in her might have. She glanced behind her and increased her step, having seen the heated glow before. When a man looked at her in such a way, he usually meant to take liberties with her.

Similar incidents had happened more than once since her family had lost all, first in London where they were forced to accept contracts of indenture, then again during the endless weeks aboard the British frigate that had brought them across the Atlantic Ocean. Now in the house of her new mistress where she thought she would find refuge, she found the same perils stalked her. Slowly, with burgeoning anger, she was beginning to detest all men, with their burning gazes and roaming hands that she constantly had to evade.

When she slowed and glanced back again, the man, Bartholomew, had not turned the corner of the wing in pursuit of her, as she had feared he would. Relaxing a bit, and thankful she had misjudged the situation, she hesitated for an instant, well aware her orders had been to return immediately to the hubbub of the kitchen and transport yet another heavily laden silver tray of petit fours and dainty pecan tarts into the ballroom for the revelers. She peered down the intersecting hallway to the closed door that hid the servant stair which led upward into the vast attics where she and Annie shared their tiny room.

Her little sister had felt poorly today, and Belinda was ever grateful that the mistress had been kind-hearted enough to allow Belinda to relieve the child of her duties in the scullery, at least for the evening. Still, Belinda worried about Annie, all alone on the servant floor. She was only four years old, and so high up in the garret where no one would hear if she should worsen and call out.

Aware she could very well be punished by the mistress if caught shirking work so early in her indenture, especially after the master's displeasure over the forgotten brandy bottle in the library, she hesitated for a few moments, then made up her mind. If she hurried and made certain that her visit to the attic was brief, she would not be missed.

Time was of the essence, and she lifted her petticoat and skirt and ran the length of the hall. She took the enclosed stair with great haste though her tiredness was edging on exhaustion.

She had risen at dawn to ready the ballroom and performed all of Annie's chores as well as her own. It was well nigh after eleven now, yet still no end to her toil was in sight.

Belinda loathed the life of a servant; worst of all was being ordered about like a slave. She found it took all her internal restraint to stand obediently and weather without retort the often undeserved verbal lashings she received from both mistress and housekeeper if she was not quick enough to attend their bidding. Their attacks bore not a candle to her damnation of each and every one of them, and often she was forced to lower her gaze to hide her contempt for their pompous, haughty manners. If it had not been for Annie, she would have run away long ago and taken her chances at the thrashing she would receive if caught.

Her father had had no choice. She could not blame him, she told herself again, as she always did when unspoken anger thickened at the back of her throat. It was her grandparents' fault—they who sat in their great, landed estate, lord and lady of the manor, and all the gold coin in the world. They had been the ones who had disowned Belinda's mother when she had run away and married beneath her rank.

How she hated them both! She would never forgive her grandparents that, nor the terrible treatment of her dear father when they had ruined his well-established printer's shop in London, forcing him to indenture himself and his two daughters. Her grandparents' evil revenge had killed him as surely as if they had taken shears and cut out his heart, for he had caught the bloody flux aboard the awful, foul-smelling ship in which they had made the voyage to Quebec. Not only had he succumbed to its vile ruin of his body, but little Annie now lay weak and frail in her bed from a bout with the same malady. Only Belinda had been strong enough to fight off the myriad infections running rampant in the hold of that horrific vessel.

No one was in sight when she reached the quiet third floor where the twenty-some-odd servants kept their rooms. She and Annie shared the one at the back of the house, under the slope of the eaves, with so low a ceiling that she had to bend over to climb into the lumpy cot she shared with her sister. She hastened down the hall and soundlessly entered the room. Annie lay on the narrow bed, fast asleep, thankfully not plagued at the moment by the awful cough that shook her thin body and brought up tinges of blood from her lungs.

Belinda crossed the narrow space and sat down on the edge of the bed. She smoothed back a dark strand of Annie's loosened hair. Her sister was about to turn five years old, but she looked younger, so thin and pale that her skin seemed as delicate as old paste. She had suffered so since their mother had died from fever two years earlier. Their grandparents had rejected Annie and Belinda as thoroughly as they had their daughter's husband.

Bitterness again overwhelmed her when she remembered the one time their mother had taken them to the vast ancestral estate of Lord Burnside, and the vivid recollection of the pain on her mother's face when the great carved door had been slammed in their faces had been etched indelibly upon Belinda's heart.

A sound behind her shook her out of her sorrowful memories, and she jumped up, fearing discovery by the mistress. But it was the dark-eyed American named Bartholomew who appeared in the threshold. Terrified to find him inside her room, she watched him shut the door and lean against it. He stared at her in the same way he had in the library, as if she was some morbid creature he intended to trap inside a cage.

"You should not be here, my lord," she whispered timidly, twisting her fingers together as she glanced down at Annie.

"Nor should you, wench. You neglect your duties."

He stood still, and so did she, every nerve jumping, ready to flee him. Since Annie slept peacefully, she took a step away from the bed, gingerly edging along the wall away from the intruder.

"My sister's very sick. I was checking to see if she was in need of laudanum. I must return to the kitchen immediately."

"I have no intention of awakening the little girl. I wish only to talk with you." He had kept his voice distinctly low, but his intent coffee-brown eyes never left her face. She was completely unnerved by the strange way he kept examining her.

"What do you want?" she asked stiffly, fearing that she already knew. What would she do if he groped at her, here so far away from the other occupants of the house—with Annie asleep in the same room?

His chuckle was low, but sounded loud in the heavy silence. "Don't distress yourself, wench. I'm not in the habit of ravishing servant girls if that be your fear."

Belinda was not sure she should believe him. Why else would he have found his way here to the servants quarters with such stealthy tread?

"The truth of the matter is," he informed her a moment later, "I've climbed all those bloody stairs to offer you a proposition."

"I'm a good girl, my lord. Do not think I am some cheap dockside tart you can have for a sixpence."

One dark eyebrow arched a degree. "I offer you much more than that, girl." He paused then continued softly, a knowing smile tugging at one side of his mouth. " 'Tis your freedom from servitude I can give to you. And that of your sister, too, if you wish it."

"Freedom?"

Astonished, her eyes locked on his face, her

breath lodged tightly in her throat. Could he really mean it? With nearly the full seven years of indenture stretching out before her?

"Aye. Sir John has already offered me your contracts in return for his gambling losses this evening. If you agree to my proposal, I'll be taking both of you to America with me."

To America? she thought, excitement burgeoning like wind under a hoopskirt, *the land where men fought to be free, where she might have a chance at a decent life once she was released from indenture?*

"Why would you do such a thing?" she inquired, cautious enough to realize there would no doubt be an ulterior motive involved. "What would you expect of me in return?"

Suspiciously, she watched him lower his lean body onto the ladder-backed chair beside the door, but her heartbeat quickened to staccato as he casually crossed his legs and took a deep drag upon the slim cigar he carried with him. She hated her life of servitude with every ounce of her being.

On the other hand, Lady Colleen had shown herself to be a fair, if exacting, mistress. Would this arrogant-acting American be a harder taskmaster? Silently, she watched blue smoke float upward from his cigar in a meandering wisp that curled back onto itself before it vanished into nothingness. The acrid odor of the tobacco, pungent and overpowering, filled the cramped attic room.

"The American colonies are revolting against the king. Did you know that?"

Belinda nodded, but said nothing. She had kept abreast of the war tidings in the London newspapers while she worked in her father's printing shop on Regent Street, but she would not reveal the extent of her education to this man, nor to any other person, for fear that they might separate her from Annie, who was just learning to read. It was rare for a woman to be as learned as a man, here or in England, but her father had not believed such to be right and had taught her well.

"Then you'll know also that the Tories align themselves with the Crown. The patriots, on the other hand, are traitors, and those loyalists among us work diligently at ferreting them out of the dirty holes from which they preach their insurrection."

She had heard the patriots were brave men, ready to face death before enslavement, a decision she could understand now that she had spent time as a chambermaid. Bartholomew was obviously a Tory. Why else would he be so friendly with Lord Greenleigh and the British officer? But what did she have to do with the internal problems of the American colonies? The man answered her question almost before it entered her mind.

"I want you to help me prove that one of them isn't the loyal Tory he purports to be but a patriot spy in our ranks. He is guilty of the worst kind of treason, and I want to prove it to the English authorities."

"Why would you have need of me to help you?"

"I've my reasons. You've no need to know the details at present."

Belinda frowned at his cryptic reply. "What would you have me do to this man? I am but a lowly serving maid."

"I want someone working for me who is living inside his house. Someone who knows his business. Where he goes, and when, who visits him and what they discuss. He travels a great deal, purportedly on business, but I think differently. All these things could be readily observed by an alert servant in his employ."

"You would give me my freedom for merely serving as chambermaid inside this man's house?"

"I'd give my life to see him uncovered for what he really is. He holds what belongs to me, and I would have it back." The man's voice had grown harder, edged with bitterness. His dark eyes assumed a distant look for a brief moment, then he returned his regard fully upon her. His face remolded before her eyes, the angry sneer fading into a casual, nondescript mask. "Is that not a good barter, wench? Your freedom for keeping your eyes open and your mouth shut?"

"How long will I have to work for this man?"

"However long it takes. I daresay it won't be for a length of seven years as it would be in this house. Once he is arrested by the English, you go free—you and your sister both. You have my word upon that. I will put the terms in writing if you so wish."

Although afraid she could not believe him, she found that she wanted to take him up on his offer, more than anything. She did not like this frigid place called Quebec. Were the American colonies not known as a place where people could get ahead without the advantages of nobility or wealth? She and Annie could build a new life there, and if she did this job well, they could be free, possibly within a year or two. Free to live their lives in any way they wished!

"I will not leave Annie alone. If I enter his house, she must go there with me."

He smiled. "Of course. In truth, she may very well prove to be the deciding factor for him. How old is she? Three or four?"

"She's almost five, but why would she make a difference to this man?"

"All you have to worry about is doing exactly what I tell you."

"How do you know he will even have need of help?" she pressed him, well aware of the evasiveness of his last answer.

The Tory looked at her momentarily, and the chuckle that followed suggested supreme confidence. "Have no fear, my dear, he'll hire you and little Annie on the spot. I have absolutely no doubt on the matter." He sobered and suddenly showed impatience with her questioning. "What

do you say? Will you come to America with me
and do my bidding?"

Hesitating a fraction of a second longer, Belinda studied his features, now completely bland
of expression, trying to detect any hidden
agenda in his eyes. Was it worth the risk to go
with him? She glanced at Annie, at the way the
child's chest was heaving with labored breaths,
at the grime under Annie's fingernails from
scrubbing soot off the kitchen hearth.

"Aye, my lord, I have always wished to
visit America."

Bartholomew's thin lips stretched slowly into
a wide, self-satisfied grin. He stood, bent forward in a deep bow, as if she were a lady, then
let himself out the door.

One

"I'll caution you again, Belinda. Gabriel Elliott is nothing if not deadly. Don't be so foolish as to succumb to his charm as most women are wont to do, because—and you can trust me in this regard—he is a crack shot with a pistol, and would not hesitate to shoot you dead if he discovers you're a Tory spy."

At Bartholomew Smythe's frightening prediction, Belinda's clear blue eyes widened considerably, and she fearfully turned her gaze down the cobblestoned thoroughfare called Broad Street to the residence of the notorious American. A shiver started somewhere deep inside, pebbling the skin of her arms and legs, as if a deadly viper had been held against her breast. For weeks now she had thoroughly regretted her decision to come to New York. The more details she heard about the clandestine treachery required of her, the deeper her foreboding became.

"What if he doesn't need a maid?" she asked

Bart hopefully, her fingers squeezing Annie's hand. The little girl stared mutely up at Bartholomew, her brown eyes wide and frightened.

"I told you not to worry about that. He'll hire you, especially if you've got the child with you."

Perplexed, Belinda wondered why that would make a difference, but Bartholomew continued nodding with absolute certainty. "Don't return to my house until I send word to you. He could have you followed until he decides if you are trustworthy."

Belinda was pleased that she wouldn't have to see Bartholomew Smythe any time soon. Never would be all right with her. "What if I can't find out anything for you?"

"You will. Until you do, perform your duties and do precisely what he tells you. I'll make an effort to approach you when I feel the time is right."

His straight thick eyebrows came together in one long, black slash, revealing the displeasure she had grown to recognize since he had brought them from Canada. She had witnessed firsthand how quick and violent his temper could be upon those who disobeyed him. He had slapped a maid just the day before, hard against her face, and sent her weeping back into the kitchen. Belinda was well pleased to take Annie out of his reach.

"He's just returned from one of his so-called business excursions to Boston, so hurry along before he decides to leave again. Do you remember the story you are to tell him?"

Wondering how she was ever going to get through this day, Belinda nodded.

"Remember, you don't know me. You have never met me. Do you understand?"

"Yes."

Bartholomew gave her a short shove at the small of her back to propel her on her way, and Belinda led Annie slowly down the cobblestones edging the great bricked houses built along the east side of the street. Utter dread gripped her chest, squeezing, constricting so hard she felt she could not draw another breath. A young boy attired in the simple brown homespun shirt and breeches of the colonial servants appeared, carrying a wicker food basket, then hurried past her toward the intersection below the house. A dray rumbled past as she glanced back one last time at Smythe and found that he had concealed himself behind a stone wall near where she had left him.

During the last few weeks under the roof of Smythe's own large house on Water Street, while he prepared her for her secret encounter, she had ascertained that his interest in Gabriel Elliott was more personal than mere suspicion of disloyalty to the Crown. There was bad blood between the two men—apparently Elliott had inherited what Bartholomew considered his birthright—though Belinda still did not know the particulars of how that had happened, or why.

Her swallow went down hard, convulsive enough to lodge dangerously in her gullet for a moment as she realized that, by Mr. Smythe's obvious respect for Gabriel Elliott's intellect alone, she was about to face a man who would be difficult to best in a game of wits. Unwillingly, her footsteps slowed as she approached the big house at Number 29. She looked back at Bartholomew Smythe again, stopping where she was, until a sharp thrust of his arm motioned her forward in no uncertain terms.

"I'm glad that we don't have to live with Mr. Smythe anymore, Bee. I don't like him much."

At Annie's scared whisper, Belinda squeezed the child's hand and tried to smile reassuringly. Annie looked much better now; her cheeks had regained some color. "Yes, darling. Perhaps our new master won't be as frightening as Mr. Smythe."

Annie nodded, seeming very pleased at that notion, but Belinda wasn't at all sure what Mr. Elliott would be like. His mansion rose before them in red-bricked elegance against the blue sky, a full four stories tall. Set flush against the sidewalk, the portico was supported by two Doric columns and surrounded by richly carved ornamentation bearing a family crest.

On either side of the heavy crimson front door, tall windows, four in number, displayed gleaming glass and lavishly draped velvet curtains dripping with gold braid. Her eyes traveled up the towering facade and found five windows on both the third and fourth floors, similarly adorned, then higher up, three dormers with a railed widow's walk crowning the tiled roof.

The home looked deserted, however, and as she searched for movement behind the lacy panels peeking from under the velvet and hiding the interior, she prayed in her heart that no one would answer the door.

"It's a grand house, isn't it? As grand as Mistress Greenleigh's." Annie looked awed as she gazed up at the mighty facade.

"It's very big." And very intimidating, Belinda thought, with a new rush of fear.

"Like the place in the country where Mama took us? Where she lived before she met Papa?"

Annie's reference to their grandparents' estate brought up the old hatred inside Belinda, but she only nodded, though she knew that Lord Burnside's ancestral mansion would have dwarfed the city townhouse before them.

An egg cart drawn by an old, sway-backed white mare clopped slowly past them, and the farmer in the seat tipped his straw hat to Belinda as she continued to loiter hand in hand with Annie on Gabriel Elliott's front curb. Could she go through with this? she wondered, still hesitating uncertainly and fighting her desire to turn tail and run.

A hitching post topped by a solid brass pineapple stood at the edge of the street, but no sad-dled mounts were tied at the iron ring. No visitors, at least, she thought, relieved. A bricked driveway stretched behind a six-foot wooden gate leading to the rear of the house.

A deep breath fortified her march up the four fan-shaped steps, set on each side by ornate black railings. She paused again, her hand rest-ing on the intricately detailed wrought iron ban-ister. Confronted by the task at hand, the Greenleigh employ in Quebec City no longer seemed so dire. No matter how egregious the faults of the man who lived in the prosperous-looking mansion before her, she had no business involving herself in Bartholomew Smythe's espi-onage activities.

What had she been thinking? She should never have come here, much less embroil Annie in such a dangerous ruse! What if the man named Elliott figured out she deceitfully misrep-resented herself? War waged here in the Ameri-can colonies, and if he was a secret patriot as Bartholomew suspected, her actions could be deemed as treason. She could be imprisoned, or even hanged! What would happen to Annie if that happened? Tempted to back away, then flee at a hard run, she nevertheless took a step for-ward because they had come too far to turn back.

Once they finally stood upon the porch, she found herself before an eight-foot-high front door set with panes of stained glass. The scene portrayed in the brilliantly colored door window was a sleek, three-masted ship upon cerulean blue ocean waves, its sails billowing white against a lighter blue sky. On a shoreline behind the sea a single golden light shone forth from a black-and-white striped lighthouse. Bolstering herself once more with a deep-drawn inhalation, she twisted the bell ring and heard the jangle sound inside the house.

At least Annie would be with her. As long as they could stay together, she could endure their plight. And the sooner Belinda could ferret out incriminating facts about the man named Elliott, the sooner they would be free again. That knowledge would have to sustain her courage.

As she stood waiting with Annie's hand clutched firmly in hers, she tried to revisit every detail that Bartholomew Smythe had drilled into her—though quite sparse in nature considering what he expected her to accomplish—about the man on whom she was to spy.

According to him, Gabriel Elliott was rich, powerful, and extremely well established in New York society. Though Elliott had apparently lived and worked as a Tory throughout the war, was even trusted by the British high command garrisoned in the city—Bartholomew had branded him a liar and rebel to the core. Elliott was purportedly shrewd as well, and a hard man to best, which added to the fear clutching at her heart and putting such quivers in her breath.

If he did uncover that Belinda worked for his

enemies, she had been instructed to escape his house with all due haste. But, she mused with newly blossoming hope, perhaps he would refuse to hire her in the first place and send her merrily on her way. How could Bartholomew Smythe be so positive that Elliott would even need their employ?

While the bell sound died away inside, she smoothed the folds of her full blue skirt, but her fingers were trembling so she formed a fist. Her mother had set aside a handful of the gowns she had brought when she had fled her parents' estate. She had saved them for her two daughters.

Though the dark blue velvet afternoon dress was old-fashioned, and even threadbare in spots, the lace collar was hand-tatted and not yet faded yellow by age. Belinda had never worn the dress before, but she had kept it with her through all their troubles because the fine garment somehow gave her courage to face their uncertain future. The dress made her feel like a lady of quality, as her mother had been.

As Belinda tugged the cuffs and fluffed her full sleeves, the door swung open. Her jaw dropped when she found herself staring up at a tall Indian who loomed before her on the threshold. Annie hid behind Belinda's skirts when she saw the savage, though they had encountered a few of the red natives during their time in Canada. His black hair was fashioned into long braids, liberally wound with white feathers, his face coppery brown with high cheekbones and a broad brow. His attire was peculiar, some sort of fringed, knee-length tunic of brown deerskin and strange moccasin boots that reached to the knee. His black eyes regarded her with no reaction whatsoever.

"Good day," Belinda began hesitantly, aware that Annie was pulling the back of her skirt as an encouragement for them to leave. When the Indian remained mute and unsmiling, she cleared her throat, a hoarse squeak that caused her face to flood with embarrassed color.

"We are here to see the master of the house, Mr. Gabriel Elliott. I have a letter of introduction from my previous employer."

She withdrew the folded parchment from her pocket and held it up for him to see. The Indian stepped back in what she assumed was a silent entreaty for her to enter the house. She did so, dragging Annie with her, who still clung to the back of her dress.

"Gabe is working in study." The Indian's English was accented but a good deal better than she had expected. What really shocked her was the familiar way the man addressed his employer. "I will take letter to him."

Belinda handed over the paper Bartholomew had given to her. The Indian's face remained inscrutable as he moved away without a word, slid open a set of double doors to Belinda's right, and disappeared inside.

Growing a bit more calm now that she was

inside, Belinda seated herself and Annie on a small black brocade settee beside the front door and comforted the child with her arm around her shoulders as she examined the interior of the house.

The entry foyer was spacious, stretching to the back of the mansion. Paneled in glowing polished oak, it sported a wide, elegantly carved staircase that ran up the left side of the entry and curved out of sight. A lamp stood on the newel post, a beautiful piece of marble fashioned in the form of three Grecian maidens holding a lantern above their heads. A tall ornate case clock stood in the alcove of the stair, its huge gold pendulum swinging behind the expensive, etched-glass door. She adjusted her breathing to the slow, steady movements, hoping to appear self-possessed when she was summoned by Gabriel Elliott.

Her attention was diverted from the fine furnishings when a young Negro woman pushed through a swinging door at the back of the hall. The woman did not see them at first, but when she did, she stared, started visibly, then completely astounded Belinda by letting out a short shriek. The hairs on Belinda's nape stood upright. Annie hid her face in Belinda's lap as the maid collapsed against the wall as if a rug had been pulled out from under her feet. The woman went strangely silent then, eyes huge, round, and white.

"What in the blazes is the matter with you, Dulcimer?"

Every muscle in Belinda's body went rigid at the sound of the angry masculine voice inside the chamber where the Indian had disappeared. Gabriel Elliott? she presumed with not a little trepidation, realizing that things were not going as well as she had hoped. She came to her feet, holding Annie close against her side, then swung around to face the door just as a big man appeared in the threshold.

Seemingly all shoulders, he wore a long brown leather waistcoat over a white linen shirt with a neatly folded stock at his throat and tight black riding breeches that reached just below his knee. Glossy brown leather boots reached to his knees instead of the usual stockings and silver-buckled shoes that most gentlemen commonly wore. Her first impression was that he was bigger than just about any man she had ever seen, both in height and build, his masculine physical presence seeming to overpower everything else in the room.

His frown was not one to be trifled with either, for his dark blond brows were drawn into a fearsome glare, his face so darkened by the sun that it nearly matched the teak complexion of his Indian friend. His fair hair was longish, but cut stylishly, short on top but nearly touching his collar at the nape, clean, well-groomed, and heavily sunstreaked, which made the contrast of his dark skin even more striking. He held Belinda's reference letter in one hand, but didn't notice her as he set his full attention on the cowering maid.

"God's blood, Dulcimer," he said with unhidden impatience, "what the devil are you screaming about?"

"Master Gabriel, look, look at them . . ."

Her trembling finger came up to point out Belinda's position just behind him, and Gabriel Elliott swung around in one swift movement as if expecting attack from behind. Belinda gazed back as bravely as she could, affecting a tremulous smile that she hoped would hide the awful tension swirling along the floor of her belly. His mouth dropped until it hung agape, and she watched with astonishment as his face drained of color. He said nothing, however, staring at her before his gaze moved, locking on Annie where she cowered at Belinda's side. The clock ticked on relentlessly, accentuating the silence hanging like a dense cloud over the room.

Belinda somehow worked up the wherewithal to speak. "Mr. Elliott, I'm most sorry to disrupt your household this way." She paused, but when he still stared wordlessly at her, she hurried on. "I was sent here to seek employment. I fear I have arrived at an inopportune moment."

The sound of her voice seemed to motivate him to movement. He came closer, towering over her, though she was fairly tall at five and a half feet, and she realized how very large he was, standing taller than her father, who had been nearly six feet.

"You are English?" was his first query, uttered during a thorough examination of her person. Surprised, she shifted uncomfortably as his eyes, dark blue and fiercely intense, roamed her features.

"Yes, sir. I was born in London."

Faintly shaken by the way he loomed so close and scrutinized her—What on earth compelled these Americans to stare so rudely?—she hugged Annie closer and went on quickly with the story Bartholomew had drummed into her head night and day.

"We have been indentured in Quebec City, but our master had too many maids already so we have been sent here to finish out our employ, hopefully in the house of one of his friends. He gave me a list of gentlemen who might have need of our services here in the city."

She looked down at her lap and realized that she was twisting her fingers together, an open revelation of her apprehension. She stopped at once, but still squirmed uncomfortably under his keen scrutiny. His eyes delved into her— sharp, intelligent, very dark blue, and brimming with strictly controlled emotion. He had a few lines at the corners of his eyes as if he had often squinted against bright sunlight, and his jaw was clenching then releasing—she could see quite clearly how the muscles of his jaw worked. Why was he so agitated? She rushed on, gesturing to the sealed letter he held. "That's the letter of introduction from my previous employer."

"And who would that be, mistress?"

"Lord Greenleigh of Quebec City."

With that revelation, his intensity suddenly relaxed, as did his manner. He lowered his gaze to the letter so she could not judge a reaction from the expression in his eyes.

"John and Colleen sent you here to me?"

"Aye, sir."

Wondering what connection he had with the English lord, Belinda concentrated on getting her rehearsed statements precisely correct, already intimidated by the sheer force of Gabriel Elliott's presence. He was as dangerous as Bartholomew had intimated, she felt that instinctively.

"We have been to several houses here in New York, but no one currently has need of staff. Please, sir, you are the last name on my list, and we are very tired, especially Annie."

"This cannot be your child," he said flatly. "You are too young."

"She's my sister, and she hasn't been well of late. But we both are hard workers. You would not regret taking us into your household."

Gabriel's face had regained its composure, but his powerful blue eyes delved incessantly into her own. She avoided visual contact, afraid he would see through her lies, and hear the way her heart was thumping intolerably hard. Oh, dear Lord, there was no possibility that she could successfully dupe this man!

Already she sensed that he was much too smart and wildly intimidating to be fooled by someone as inexperienced in subterfuge as she. Even worse, she was not a good liar. She was a terrible one, in fact, and always had been. Gabriel Elliott would suspect her if only by the way her mouth was trembling. Her panic began to rise, so she pulled her bottom lip between her teeth to hold it still.

"Perhaps I should come back another day," she suggested nervously, backing toward the front door with Annie in tow. She made it only a step before he strode forth and blocked her retreat.

"No need for that. Please come into my study. Actually, I do happen to have need of a servant or two." When Belinda glanced at his maid, he explained further. "Forgive Dulcimer's reaction to you. She's had a slight shock."

Belinda glanced uncertainly at the maid, who was now fanning her face.

"We'll have our interview now. Dulcimer, you may return to your chores."

"Yes, sir. 'Twas the shock of seein' them standin' there that shook me in the knees . . ."

The woman's words petered away as Gabriel preceded Belinda and Annie into his office. She hesitated just inside as he closed the door behind them.

"Please, sit down." He gestured at the chair in front of his desk. "What is your name, mistress?"

"Belinda Scott."

"And the child's name is Annie?"

She nodded as Annie perched atop a velvet upholstered bench near the window, and she took the indicated chair.

"Please make yourself comfortable while I read what Greenleigh has written." She could ascertain no telltale dislike in his tone for the man, nor any other emotion. He seemed almost indifferent now as he rounded the desk and seated himself in the high-backed black leather chair. He glanced across the desk at her as he broke the wax seal with his thumbnail, but his gaze moved to linger longer on Annie.

When he lowered his eyes and began to scan the contents, she had her first opportunity to thoroughly examine him without his knowing. Rugged, manly in his appeal, he was handsome with attractive, even features, and a large-framed, well-conditioned body. In truth, strength seemed to describe every aspect of him. She wondered if that same strength invaded his will, his character, and integrity, or was he a traitor as Bartholomew insisted?

His arched eyebrows were furrowed now with concentration as he skimmed the neatly scripted note, and she realized that, for all his fierceness, he had absurdly long golden lashes. His nose was a strong, straight line—there was that word again, she thought—and his mouth generous in a pleasant way. She guessed that he would have a most agreeable smile when he was not caught up in the somber mood of the moment. Somehow she felt him to be a serious man who rarely summoned up his lighter emotions. He appeared to her studious and sober, as if he dealt with important things and had no use for trivialities.

"Why did Greenleigh send you here to me? I have not seen him in a great while."

The question was so wholly unexpected that she could only stare at him as her mind sorted through a barrage of answers for the most appropriate response. She realized with self-mockery that she was already over her head with this man, and now at a loss of how to handle even the simplest of his questions. She was not going to make a good spy. She attempted to swallow down her fear. "I do not know, sir. He only gave me the letter."

Gabriel observed her silently. "I suppose you and Annie can work with Dulcimer. One person is not enough for a house this size. She will be glad for the help."

Belinda waited, trying desperately to read something behind his impassive face, but to no avail. "I would be grateful for employ, sir. Both Annie and I are used to kitchen chores."

"You are quite well spoken, Mistress Scott. Why were you forced into indenture?"

Belinda felt the usual burn of humiliation, and was reluctant to tell him, or anyone else, the travails of her family. She shielded her feelings by dropping her long black lashes and stared at her hands where they lay folded upon her lap. Bartholomew had told her to keep to the truth as much as possible, and she sought to do so. "My father fell on hard times and was forced to indenture us to avoid debtor's prison."

Keeping her eyes downcast, she could almost feel his gaze roaming over her like a trail of hot sunlight. She hoped he could not sense how uncomfortable she was.

"And your father? Is he still with Lord Greenleigh?"

"No, sir, our father died during the voyage from England."

"I'm very sorry to hear that." Suddenly, he became more brusque as if ready to be done with the interview. "All right then, it is settled. I will take you both on until your indenture is served. Dulcimer can acquaint you with your duties." He rose and moved to the bellpull. It was then Belinda caught sight of the Indian who had answered the front door. He hunkered down in one corner of the room, staring silently at her. Somewhat unnerved, she wondered if he had been there during the entire interview.

Moments later, Dulcimer arrived, still staring at Belinda with the same astonished expression. Gabriel spoke quietly to her for a moment, out of Belinda's earshot, then turned back to Belinda.

"Dulcimer will show you to your room, then explain what duties will be expected of you. If you have any questions, you have only to ask her."

With that he dismissed them both with a casual nod. Belinda thanked him, then followed the young woman out and up the elegant stair, which rose in spirals three floors above, each step taking her deeper into the huge brick house, and deeper into Bartholomew Smythe's plot to destroy Gabriel Elliott.

Two

"The Englishwoman is lying, Namasset."

Gabriel swiveled around to face his Oneida blood brother as soon as Mistress Scott was out of earshot. He leaned back, braced his elbows on the arms of his chair, and thoughtfully steepled his fingers as he watched Namasset rise from his haunches.

The Indian's footfalls were as completely soundless atop the plush scarlet-patterned Persian carpet as they were upon pine needles of the forest floor. Even more than his stealth, however, Gabriel valued his friend's intuition, which Gabriel had learned to appreciate in the wilds along the Bronx River when they were little more than boys. Earlier, before Gabriel had laid eyes on the young English girl, Namasset had warned him to be wary, for he sensed she held secrets behind eyes the color of the sky.

"Her eyes dart like silver fish in the shallows," Namasset remarked as he reached the desk and perched a fringe-adorned hip on its edge.

"She's as nervous as an alley cat, and for good cause, I'll wager. Twenty shillings says my old friend Greenleigh has sent a Tory wench to spy on me, and if my memory holds, I recall LeClerc mentioning seeing the man here in New York during the summer."

Namasset made no response. His eyes were black and deep, unreadable. Gabriel, too, had learned long ago to hide his emotions in the way of the Oneidas.

"She is much like your woman. And the child is like Jessie."

Gabriel feared that his eyes did show his pain now, so he angled his chair to where he could stare out the window. Through the rectangular panes he could see a few children playing in the vacant lot across the street. They ran to and fro, scattering the leaves on the ground. He could hear their laughter in his mind even if he couldn't hear it in the air. It was tag they played, and memories of his only child streaked like a whirling storm through his mind, guilt falling like an anvil behind it, heavy, black, cold enough to chill his soul. Not for a long time, not since the war had begun four years ago had he dwelled on thoughts of Patsy and Jessie.

He had been such a fool then, young, eager, stupid. He should never have taken them to the mill house, not a decade ago when enemy tribes lurked in the dark forests. Patsy had been a gentlewoman, a lady born and bred in genteel society, more accustomed to candle-bright drawing rooms and lavishly appointed tea tables than wilderness cabins where roving Mohawk bands took American scalps for British coin.

The ancient sense of horror slithered alive inside his gut, like angry snakes, striking at him over and over. The thought of what she must have suffered before she had died sent him rigid, and Jessie, his poor baby daughter, he would never forget how he had found her. Revulsion sent his stomach heaving, and he forced the horrific visions out and bolted them inside the room he had carved into his heart for them. *Don't think about them.* Think about Belinda Scott and what she was doing here.

"Perhaps we can use this girl for our own ends," he mused aloud, appalled at the beads of sweat across his brow brought out by the memories of his family. *Don't think.* Determinedly he cast his gaze on Namasset and awaited the Indian's response. The Oneida agreed mutely, with one short nod of his head. Gabriel sighed, then sat upright, decided.

"Then go, my friend, back to Willamette and your boys. But before you leave the city, summon LeClerc here for the dinner hour. We'll see if he shares our suspicions about my new serving wench. He spends more time than I in the dockside taverns as well as Tory drawing rooms. Perhaps he's heard mention of the girl being put into my house. My instincts tell me the redcoats have finally had the sense to put me under surveillance." *And thank God, if that were true*, he thought with something akin to relief. He was damn sick and tired of remaining behind British lines in the Tory-infested city while loyal patriots fought for America's freedom.

Without further conversation Namasset faded out the door and into the hall. Gabriel had no doubt the Oneida would complete his task quickly and well. He trusted Namasset implicitly, as he did the Frenchman, Henri LeClerc. Neither would fail him: nor he, them. He had to admit, however, that sending an English serving maid was a bit more ambitious than the usual clumsy Tory endeavors meant to entrap him. If Greenleigh was involved, he wondered where he had happened upon Mistress Belinda Scott. And how would he have known her uncanny resemblance to Patsy?

For nearly an hour he sat still, watching the children play and contemplating just what his Tory adversaries meant for the Scott girl to accomplish while in his employ. Afterward, he scanned the newspapers he had brought back from Boston for coded advertisements that contained hidden information about the British military. General Washington counted on him for intelligence as to troop strength and movements. The commander of the Continental Army was an old friend of Gabriel's father, and only he could have persuaded Gabriel to remain in New York after the British occupation began. For years now he had forced himself to sit idly

among the Tory turncoats and pretend to be a
part of their loyalty to the Crown. But because
of his presence in the city, there were now several patriot spy rings operating successfully on
both Manhattan and Staten Island, with many
contacts on the Long Island shore.

Reluctantly, Gabriel played the important role
assigned him, but with every passing day he
resented his enforced daily contacts with the
British officers running the city. And now that
General Sir Henry Clinton had made Major John
Andre his adjutant general and head of British
intelligence, he was compelled to court the
friendship of Andre in the hope of eliciting
information.

Unfortunately, as he pored over the papers
spread out before him, he found little that he
had not already passed on to Washington and
his command. Perhaps Henri would have more
to tell him tonight.

Rising, he found himself restless enough to
pace from window to window. He stopped at
the one overlooking the driveway. He immediately hid his presence behind the swagged drap-
ery when he saw Belinda Scott wielding a
broom near the covered portico that led to the
coach house.

Gabriel observed her closely as she went
about her task with concentration and diligent
effort. From this distance she looked even more
like Patsy than she had at close range. He had
been shocked upon first glance, of course, but

when he really looked at her, he could see the differences were many. They shared the same blue eyes and dark curly hair, but Belinda was taller, healthier-looking than Patsy had been. Her eyes blazed azure and were widely spaced, where as Patsy's had been the deeper color of cornflowers.

In his mind's eye he saw her body the way he had found her, the pristine snow stained crimson by her blood. He blocked out the picture, clamping his teeth together. When he did allow himself to think about her, he preferred to remember her the way she had been here in New York where she had been hostess at his table and met him at the door with a smile. Their union had been arranged by their parents, but he had grown to love her. They'd had five years together before she died. She had given him Jessie, and he had gotten both of them killed.

He had not been involved with a woman since, not genuinely. He had not wanted one. He had needed women physically and had taken a few into his bed, but never for long, and never for any kind of true involvement. Since Concord his passions had been focused entirely on the war and driving the British off American shores.

As he watched Belinda, she completed her chore and disappeared around the corner of the house toward the rear entrance. He turned away from the window and left his study. By the time he had dressed for dinner and an evening out

with more unsuspecting Tories, the Frenchman
had already received Namasset's summons and
was awaiting him in the drawing room.

When he slid open the doors, Henri LeClerc
stood beside the fireplace, one hand propped on
the mantelpiece. He turned, smiled his engaging
smile, obviously in his usual good spirits as Gabriel quietly shut the doors behind him. Though
a product of a French father and a heiress from
Charleston in the Carolinas, Henri had spent
most of his youth on the Continent and spoke
English with a heavy Parisian accent. He was a
handsome man, his blond hair glinting gold and
tied back into a bagwig. Like Gabriel he had
little use for the powdered wigs sported by the
British officers and the Tories trying to impress
them.

"So, *mon ami*, you have taken on a Tory spy
in your household?"

Gabriel scowled at his remark and motioned
him to silence with a forefinger against his lips.
"We cannot speak as freely as before, Henri. Be
on your guard and say little when she's
around."

"Is the fair mademoiselle cupping her ear at
the door panel even as we speak?" Henri's grin
was as contagious as always with the easy affa-
ble manner of the carefree blade he had become
since the war had begun. Such personal affability had wormed many uncensored revelations
from his ale-swilling companions, both Tory
and British.

"No doubt she will be, if given any opportunity to eavesdrop. 'Twould be best if you kept her duplicity in mind when you're in my house."

Henri sobered instantly, silently observing Gabriel as he moved across the room to where a bottle of sherry sat atop a silver tray. "Namasset told me the serving wench resembles Patsy. And that she's brought a small child with her."

Gabriel splashed sherry into two glasses. "Aye, she bears a slight resemblance, but after the first shock one can see the differences." He turned and handed Henri a goblet. "Did you not see her when you arrived?"

"Afraid not, my friend," he answered, taking the glass and drinking from it. "Dulcimer admitted me, so I've yet to come face-to-face with our mysterious spy." Henri paused, his hazel eyes narrowing upon Gabriel's face. "Do you think they chose her because of her resemblance?"

"It would be quite a coincidence if they had not," Gabriel answered. "I suppose they thought I would immediately bare my soul to her if she looked like my wife." He frowned and changed the subject. "Have your agents heard anything about the British recruiting a woman to expose me? It could be one of Andre's plots. They say he's crafty."

"Nary a whisper of such a ruse. I still find it hard to believe the British suspect you. Your cover here is perfect—you're a mainstay in all their parties and parades. I daresay if she's been put here, it was by a Tory."

"Possibly, but she came from Lord Greenleigh's employ, and he's been an acquaintance of mine for years. He bears me no grudge that I'm aware of. And I doubt he would sign the letter of introduction himself if he had something underhanded in mind."

A soft tap sounded at the door, and they both quit their discourse and waited until the door opened. Belinda Scott appeared, hesitating on the threshold. She looked as if she were entering the gates of hell, and her voice betrayed her even more, trembling noticeably when she spoke.

"Dinner is ready to be served, Master Elliott."

"Thank you, Belinda. We will retire to the dining parlor shortly."

"*Oui*, she looks a bit like Patsy," Henri murmured softly after she was gone, "though not so much as I thought she would. She is very beautiful, no?"

Gabriel agreed with his friend's assessment, but he didn't say so. "Remember, Henri, don't forget to curb your speech around her. She can't be trusted."

Leading Henri into the large dining room with its high ceiling and white walls stenciled near the ceiling with swags of pine and golden pineapples, he motioned for him to sit beside his own place at the head of the table.

Long white tapers burned in a six-pronged sil-

ver candelabra between them. Silence rested
heavily upon the occupants of the room as Belinda carried forth an engraved silver soup tu-
reen made at a silversmith shop in Boston.
Gabriel had picked up more than the ornate
bowl when he had visited there a week ago.
Paul Revere was a loyal patriot who often gave
him invaluable information to pass on to the patriot army.

As she carefully placed the heavy dish before
them, Gabriel scrutinized her delicate profile. He
did find her attractive, but more surprising was
the quiet elegance about her, both in her speech
and movements, a genteel air that one usually
did not find in so young a woman, and especially not in a kitchen maid.

A perfect selection for Greenleigh to choose to
work his ugly business, if indeed it were
Greenleigh who stalked him. For the first time
he realized that she might not be a true indenture but a woman trained to portray one. If that
were the case, she would have little choice but
to do whatever she was told. Or could it be that
she did not know her true purpose in his house?
And what of the child, Annie? How did she fit
into her plot? They certainly looked like sisters.

Belinda carefully ladled into two white china
bowls the thick fish chowder, a culinary dish he
had not known Dulcimer to prepare in the past.
Every movement Belinda made was graceful, re-
fined; she performed the menial task as if she
had performed it many times before. Questions

badgered him as he watched her serve Henri. She was not very old, he decided, probably in her early twenties, but certainly not much more than that.

"She is indeed of English birth," Henri noted when Belinda had returned to the kitchen for the next course, "and by her accent, I would say she is more cultured than most girls in servitude."

Henri's remarks followed Gabriel's own thoughts and acted to heap more fuel atop his suspicions. "I know little of her past, except that her father nearly went to debtor's prison. I daresay it would be unwise to question her too fully so early in my employ. If she is a Tory spy, we can use her to feed the enemy whatever tales we want them to hear."

"And if she is not?" inquired Henri, dipping his spoon into the delicious-smelling soup. He tasted it, then closed his eyes in an ecstatic show of appreciation. "Ah, but this is superb, this wonderful bouillabaisse. You have a prize in Dulcimer, Gabe. She has outdone herself, for this fare rivals that made by my *grandpère's* chef."

With an uninterested shrug Gabriel showed little interest in the cuisine. Belinda Scott was his primary concern at the moment. When she entered the room again, this time carrying a serving tray with golden brown buttermilk biscuits, he involved himself in a benign conversation with Henri concerning the rain now drumming against the roof. As if an after-thought, he complimented the soup.

"Thank you, sir." A pleased smile tugged shyly at her lips, but still, she avoided his gaze. " 'Twas one of my mother's favorite recipes."

"You made this?" His own surprise brought out his remark before he thought.

"Aye, sir. Dulcimer was busy with the roasted lamb and sweet potatoes and bade me try my hand at the first course."

"It is quite wonderful, mademoiselle. Gabriel has found a prize in you," Henri told her with suave Gallic charm. The latest addition to Gabriel's household staff blushed and lowered her eyes.

"She does have a charming way about her," Henri commented as soon as they were alone. "I fear that lovely smile is deadly to gentlemen who receive it. She will tease secrets from your lips, if you are not careful, Gabriel."

"I know what she is. You had better watch yourself." Annoyed at himself for admitting a devious girl into his household, he frowned. He would have no trouble remembering who she really was and what she wanted from him.

"Do you have anything noteworthy for me to pass along to our friends?"

Henri's low-voiced question referred to intelligence to be taken out of the city to Gabriel's network of spies. Henri often made the journey in the dead of night, enjoying the thrill of evading the British sentries. Gabriel spoke in an undertone. "I have a message for William Leary in Brooklyn Heights, and he'll have information for you to bring back."

"I'll return two days hence, I suspect."

Gabriel looked toward the door, wondering if Belinda lingered outside. He lowered his voice still more. "See what you can find out about the girl. Greenleigh's not the most clever of men. If he's involved, sooner or later he'll boast about placing her here. I want to have proof before I accuse her of anything. Meanwhile I'll keep a close eye on her and see what I can discover."

"I say, *mon cher*, you've a much pleasanter task ahead of you than do I," Henri murmured, pouring himself more madeira and slicing into his tender portion of lamb. "Now let's finish our repast, for we're to meet Annabelle and her friends at the theater. Bloody Tories, one and all, and never likely to hold their tongues, especially after a night of wine and carousing."

When they stepped into the hallway a short time later, Gabriel caught a movement out of the corner of his eye, but when he turned, found no one in sight. Belinda Scott, no doubt, already at work with her sabotage. She would soon find there was nothing incriminating in his house to hand over to the Lord Greenleigh.

And there would never be. Not until Gabriel found something he wanted the British to have. Belinda Scott could very well become his most valuable resource through which to feed false information to the enemy, perhaps even better than his lovely, Tory-loving Annabelle. In the coming days he would find out just what the Englishwoman was capable of, for in truth, the idea of using her against Greenleigh and his lobster-back friends was growing more and more appealing to him.

Three

"Lawsy, Belinda, don't dawdle with the tray, Master Gabriel insists on his morning coffee without delay."

Belinda obeyed Dulcimer's instructions with all due haste, nudging open the swinging door with one slender shoulder while precariously juggling the silver serving tray heavily laden with a plate of biscuits and ham kept warm by a silver dome, and the steaming coffee in an ornate silver pot. Her jittery nerves caused the white china cup to rattle on its saucer as the door swung back and she hurried through Gabriel Elliott's magnificent home to his private bedchamber.

Yesterday she had kept to her room after she had served Gabriel and his guest and then helped Dulcimer with the kitchen chores. She had kept Annie with her in the incredibly comfortable room they had been given, certainly not wishing to encounter him after Dulcimer had retired to her quarters. She could have, should have, used the time after Gabriel left the house—she had watched him from the shadows of the lavish front parlor as he departed with the Frenchman, both gentlemen still attired in the elegant evening clothes they had worn at dinner—to explore the multitude of empty rooms in the mansion. Bartholomew had ordered her to do so as soon as possible, but she had not dared, terrified that someone might catch her snooping through Gabriel's personal belongings.

Instead, she had striven, despite extreme fatigue, to sit vigil at her window to observe when, and with whom, he would return. By the wee hours of the morning she became too weary to keep her eyes open and had fallen upon her bed in exhaustion, not stirring again until Dulcimer banged forcefully upon her door just before dawn to summon them to the kitchen.

There, she and Annie met the pitiably few servants who worked in the house on Broad Street by day—Lizzie, a scullery maid barely past twelve and her younger brother, Tommy, who was the stable boy, and Paulie the gardener, old and wizened and hard of hearing—all of whom good-naturedly took turns letting her little sister help them with various tasks while Belinda was kept busy as Dulcimer's assistant. At precisely seven o'clock, the bell from Gabriel's bedchamber had jangled insistently on the wooden board over the kitchen door that held a long line of chamber bells.

As she negotiated the sharp angle halfway up

the enclosed servant staircase and came out upon the second-floor rear landing, she marveled at how few employees Gabriel Elliott engaged in service. Never had she known a man of such substantial means to keep so conservative a staff. Why, even her own family, in their better days before they had lost all they owned, had kept two downstairs maids, one upstairs maid, a cook, and two stable boys. Little had she known when she was brought chocolate upon a tray at first awakening that she would soon be the one carrying the breakfast tray for others. Like a wet dog drying its fur, she forced herself to shake such memories from her mind. She had learned long ago to accept her plight. No good came of reliving her past.

Pausing long enough to shift the tray and balance it atop her left palm, she tapped a knuckle on the oak panel of the master's door. His deep voice called out from inside, and she filled her lungs with a bracing, deep-drawn breath, turned the brass handle, and entered, praying he would not still be lying in bed, as Lord Greenleigh sometimes had been. To her surprise, he was not only already up for the day, but dressed immaculately in white linen shirt, charcoal gray waistcoat, and breeches. He wore tall riding boots as seemed to be his preference and sat behind a cluttered desk centered in a curved window alcove of the sitting parlor that adjoined his bedchamber.

"I've come with your breakfast and morning coffee, sir."

Gabriel looked up then, her appearance seeming a distraction, then gestured at the one cleared corner of the large desktop. "Good day, Belinda. Put it down there, if you will."

As Gabriel returned full attention to his work, Belinda carefully lifted the dishes off the tray, arranging them in a place setting, and lastly pouring his cup full of Dulcimer's strong, fragrant brewed coffee. She unwrapped the hot biscuits and arranged them with pats of fresh-churned butter on the edge of the plate beside the thick slice of smoked pork in the exact way Dulcimer had taught her. As a final touch she folded the thick napkin in a triangular shape beside his plate, one made from the most expensive weave of white linen she had ever seen, and embroidered with golden threads in the Elliott coat of arms that emblazoned his front door.

"I'll come back later to attend to the chamber, sir," she murmured, dipping the perfunctory curtsy, more than pleased that he was paying her no mind. She had already found that when he looked at her, especially if he smiled and treated her kindly, guilt rushed up like a spring torrent and stained her face with a scarlet confession.

"No, you may stay. I've no objection to you going about your chores while I work."

More than a little startled that he would want

her to busy herself when he was having breakfast, she nevertheless turned and obediently
crossed to where his huge four-poster mahogany bed stood against the far wall. She began to
make it, smoothing the white linen sheets and
retucking them securely at the end and sides.
She glanced often at him while she straightened
the heavy burgundy velvet bedspread, but he
seemed oblivious to her as he sipped his coffee
and scribbled notations on the papers in front
of him.

She took the black feather duster from her
pocket and began to dust the marble-topped
bedside table. Everything in his chambers was
quite neat and orderly so her work had little
impact on the polished wood surfaces. Gabriel
Elliott was a well-ordered, precise gentleman, all
his books between heavy brass bookends, his
possessions neatly arranged on shelves and
tabletops.

On a mirrored highboy in the dressing chamber, separated from the bedroom by swagged
velvet draperies, she caught sight of a collection
of silver frames. She crossed casually to them,
fearing that Gabriel was surreptitiously noting
her every movement. She lifted one at a time,
in a show of cleaning them, though there was
not a speck of dust to be seen. She found them
to be miniature portraits, painted by an artist of
great talent. The first, encased in heavily engraved silver, portrayed a family. A very pretty
woman, a mother, stood with a man just behind

her, his palm resting possessively upon her shoulder. She held a swaddled infant on her lap.

But it was the second one that attracted her attention, for it was a portrait of Gabriel standing with a young lady. She stared at the woman's face, her mouth parting with a slight gasp. The feather duster fell unknowingly from her fingers, and she stared at a woman so like herself in appearance that she could not believe her eyes.

"Now I suspect you realize why Dulcimer was startled when she came upon you yesterday evening?"

His voice came from very close behind her. She spun around in alarm and found that he had bent over to retrieve the feather duster. Disconcerted by his proximity, she stepped backward and bumped into the highboy hard enough to overturn the other frames. He did not retreat, but merely reached around her and righted the miniatures.

"I'm sorry if I startled you. You look very much like my wife, don't you think so?"

Belinda nodded without answering. More aware of how he loomed over her, so large and powerful, this stranger whom she was to betray to his Tory enemies.

"She died nearly ten years ago."

Belinda stood very still, feeling her face begin to burn with both anger and embarrassment. So that was why Bartholomew had chosen her. Horror soon followed when she realized how cruel such a ruse was to a widower. She never would have agreed to put him, or anyone else, through such a shock, even if he had lost his wife many years ago. They had to have been very young when they wed. For the first time, she looked into his eyes and wondered how old he was. Most certainly not more than thirty years old, though she dared not ask him personal questions.

Gabriel seemed to be waiting for her to speak, for he was examining her face again, as if comparing her anew to his dead wife. She wanted to shiver under his impassive scrutiny, but even more, she wondered what he was thinking. "I'm sorry, Master Gabriel, if looking upon my face has caused you pain. I would not have come here if I had known about your wife."

His expression was impossible to decipher, but he finally shook his head and gazed again at the portrait. His voice was quiet, emotionless. "She's been gone for a long time."

Belinda worked up her nerve to ask a question, though she knew she was overstepping her bounds by doing so. "Were you married long, sir?"

"Five years," he answered, his manner growing abrupt as if dismissing the subject. "She and my daughter died at the hands of British-led Mohawks."

"Daughter?" she parroted, shocked again that he had had a child, though she should have suspected a man like him would have a family.

"Jessie was about Annie's age when she died." His voice grew gruff and she felt he was hiding his pain from her—that it had not diminished over the years.

Now she knew why Bartholomew had thought it a good idea for Annie to accompany her to Gabriel's house. Killed by Indians. The hairs on her forearms rose in a shiver.

"Yet you employ an Indian, the one who opened the door for us."

"Namasset is an Oneida. The Mohawks are the savages who sell scalps to your countrymen."

Had they been scalped? she thought, her stomach rolling with absolute revulsion. A hundred questions erupted in her mind, many things that she wondered about him but could never ask. She had to remember that she had come to spy upon him, not to become his friend. She had a feeling she would like him, if she could let herself. But she could not, and she could not raise his suspicions with a barrage of nosy questions. Already she felt like a felon being inside his house under false pretenses, and he seemed a better man than Bartholomew Smythe ever had. Nothing could have kept her there except for the promise of freedom.

"I'm terribly sorry if I have disturbed your work, sir. I'll try to be more careful with your belongings in the future." She moved away from him, busying herself with straightening the toilet articles beside a rose-sprigged bowl and pitcher.

Her employer arranged the pictures to his liking, then recrossed the room and reseated himself at the desk. But she felt his dark blue eyes upon her as she went about her work; she could see him watching her in the mirror over his bureau. Very little time had passed before he spoke to her again.

"Tell me about yourself, Belinda. How did you happen to come to New York?"

"As I told you, sir," she answered, turning toward him, chagrined at the detectable quiver in her voice. He had to hear it, too. Oh, Lord, she was so terrible at this! He was an astute man; he was going to know she was up to no good! "Lord Greenleigh had no further need of Annie and me in Quebec city."

"What about your family? You mentioned your father, but what about your other relatives? Are they still in England?"

"I have no other family. Only Annie." That was the lie Bartholomew had insisted she use. No complications to explain away, he had instructed, and the falsehoods came easily because she didn't consider her grandparents as kin anyway. She was a truthful person, had always been taught to hold honor and honesty as the highest of virtues, but her freedom remained a powerful incentive to dupe this rich American stranger who questioned her about her former life. But what if her duplicity eventually put a noose around Gabriel Elliott's neck? And sent to prison Dulcimer and the other servants who had welcomed Annie and her so kindly that very morning? She pushed such thoughts away, unable to think about such dire consequences to her actions.

"Where were you born in England?"

Why was he probing at her past so mercilessly? Did he already suspect? She refused to elaborate.

"In London, sir."

"Indeed? I know London quite well. I have a house there near Kensington, as a matter of fact. In which part of the city did you reside?"

Belinda had not expected so many questions from him, nor ones requiring such detailed answers. Though Lord Greenleigh had leered and groped at her, he had certainly revealed no interest whatsoever in her personal life. She was treading on shaky ground at the moment, especially if she told him the truth.

"My father had a shop on Regent Street until he was overwhelmed with debts and forced into bankruptcy."

"What sort of shop?"

"A printing establishment. He was a master engraver."

"And his name was?"

Belinda began to wonder if he already knew exactly who she was and what she was doing in his house. The idea was terrifying. Perhaps it would be she swinging from the gallows, not he or his staff.

"I do not wish to offend, sir," she said quickly, "but it pains me greatly to speak of Father since his death was so recent." That was so true. She missed him dreadfully, and her feelings must have shown on her face because Gabriel was instantly apologetic.

"Forgive me. I had no wish to upset you."

She was shaken, but not for the reasons he thought. She had to get away from him before she slipped and revealed herself for the villainess she was.

"I am finished here, sir. Unless you have further need of me, I beg your permission to return to my duties in the kitchen."

"Of course." She turned to flee, but he stopped her before she could escape. "Oh, and Belinda, please tell Dulcimer that I've decided to host a small party two nights hence. Tell her to begin to prepare for the evening. I'll provide her with a list of refreshments and libations. Also, I'm expecting a man by the name of David Matthews to arrive within the hour. Show him into the library and apprise me immediately of his arrival."

Belinda left the room as quickly as possible, but she tucked away the visitor's name to give to Bartholomew. On her way to the kitchen she checked around the library in search of a good spot to eavesdrop on the two men. And after she had seen this Matthews, she would sketch his likeness and send it along for Bart's perusal. She wanted to find something quickly to take to Bartholomew so she could get out of Gabriel Elliott's house and the terrible plot against him. She didn't want to get to know him any better, didn't want him to get to know her. No matter how she proceeded now, one of them, either Belinda or Gabriel, was going to be destroyed.

Four

By ten o'clock on the night of November tenth, Gabriel's party was in full swing. He moved casually among his glittering guests as they mingled and chatted with friends throughout the ground-floor rooms of his mansion. At the same time he was careful to keep a constant eye on Belinda Scott. At the moment she wended her way gracefully through the dining room toward the parlor, offering up a tray of sweetmeats to several British officers congregated in the doorway.

Gabriel frowned at their obvious admiration of her. They were not the only ones who had noticed her beauty; more than one gentleman had turned to watch her slim figure move away after being served by her. Even now she was being ogled and flirted with by the three soldiers. Though she surely could not help but be aware of the sensation she created in her black gown and frilly white apron, she seemed oblivious to anything but her duties as she passed as unobtrusively as she could among his guests.

"Gabe, my darling, you must tell me where you found your new servant. The gentlemen seem to find her quite extraordinary to look upon, and I cannot help but notice her resemblance to poor Patsy."

Annabelle's voice was unexpected. Unfortunately, she caught him watching Belinda with the same interest as the others she had mentioned. He smiled and foisted off her queries with a nonchalant shrug. A verbal row with Annabelle did not appeal to him at the moment, not in the midst of a social gathering, and he recognized the jealous twinge underlying her words only too well.

The way her scarlet-painted mouth tightened downward at each corner pinched the black beauty patch she wore on her cheek, an unmistakable sign of her ill-content. If she was not so important to his own intelligence gathering, he would be pleased never to see her again. The truth was that she was an integral figure in Tory society, and he needed her. It was imperative to remain on her good side.

"Come now, Gabriel, don't be coy. Tell me where you got her."

"Got who, Annabelle? I have no idea what you're talking about."

"You know precisely who I mean. The chambermaid with all that curly black hair falling out of her cap. And don't pretend you haven't noticed how much she looks like your wife."

Inwardly Gabriel winced, then had to marvel

at her lack of tact. He leaned a shoulder against the pillar framing the doorway. "I thank you for drawing my attention to that, my dear. Her name is Belinda Scott. She's an indentured servant whom I recently acquired from her previous employer in Canada."

"Is she living here in your house?"

Irked by her possessive-sounding questions, all of which were no business of hers, he assumed a noncommittal grin. "She's indentured to me, so of course she lives here. If you must know, I felt sorry for her so I took them both on."

"Them both?"

"She has a sister. There she is, over by the credenza, receiving coats from new arrivals."

He was amused at the relief that revealed itself so readily on Annabelle's painted face when she realized Annie was a child. Annabelle had feared she had two rivals in his household and did not bother to hide it. Of late, any woman Gabriel found interesting infuriated her.

"Will you keep them on?"

"I suppose, providing they continue to perform their duties to my satisfaction."

Annabelle tilted her head coquettishly, appraising him with narrowed eyes. Not a ringlet in her enormous, white-powdered wig wiggled. No wonder she envied Belinda's soft black hair, beautiful despite being completely devoid of adornment. He thought the fashion of wearing wigs pompous, and too English for his taste. He never wore them.

Annabelle's eyes were following Belinda as she moved about the room. "She doesn't look much like a servant to me."

Gabriel had to smile. "Indeed? Are servants no longer allowed to be fair of face?"

"She's far more than fair, and you know that full well. What is she like? Do you find her agreeable?"

Annabelle turned her pretty, heart-shaped face up to him, her huge black eyes full of open jealousy. They had known each other for years, been lovers on and off after she had become a young widow, but now she was dead set on an engagement between them, an eventuality that would never happen. Gabriel had no wish to wed, not her, not any woman. He would not go through again what he had endured the day he lost his family, what he still endured when he allowed himself to think about them.

"The truth is that I've hardly noticed her," he lied smoothly, hoping to put an end to her petty jealousy. He nodded politely to a passing British lieutenant with whom he had spent some time at the King's Stag Tavern the previous night, but he was bored with Annabelle, both her conversation and her company.

He had given the soiree in order to meet Major John Andre, Sir Henry Clinton's new adjutant general and head of British intelligence in New York. Gabriel was eager to make his acquaintance, then use their friendship to his advantage. Unfortunately, the man had not yet arrived. He decided to give Annabelle the answers she wanted to hear, if only to rid himself of her.

"She's only been here a day or so, and I've been much too busy down at the shipyard to think about her. Dulcimer says she and her sister are settling in well enough."

"Does she have a room in the servants' quarters?" This time she didn't even try to hide her jealousy.

Annoyance rose inside him, and with some effort, he tamped it down, reminding himself how important Annabelle was to his spy network. "I'm weary of this conversation, Annabelle. I don't tell you whom you can and cannot employ, and you're sure as the devil not going to tell me. Now if you'll excuse me, I see Henri in the foyer."

Annabelle's lovely lips settled into their familiar pout of displeasure, but he knew her disgruntled mood would not linger long, not with so many young officers hovering about with whom she could flirt. She had been the belle of many a ball since the death of her rich, elderly husband several years back, but Gabriel was still her primary target for wedlock.

Eager to escape her presence, he moved off through friends and acquaintances, greeting them alike with warm regard, be they Tories whom he detested, or patriot friends who manned his own clandestine spy ring. Sometimes it was hard to know from one day to the next, which was which and who was who. Turncoats were plentiful in this endless war of rebellion.

Although he was surprised Henri had returned so swiftly from his mission behind American lines, he was glad to see him back safe and sound, though he feared the early return did not bode well.

"*Mon ami*, I am glad to see you." Henri greeted as Gabriel reached him.

The Frenchman pulled his white silk scarf from around his neck and handed his black felt tricorne to little Annie, then ruffled her curls as she bobbed a curtsy and rushed it into the cloakroom. The child already looked better than she had when he had first seen her inside the foyer. Happier now, it seemed, for she was usually smiling and running about the house. Much more so than her older sister, who invariably avoided his gaze.

"It seems you have a jolly group here this evening, Gabriel, my friend. Any sign of Andre?"

"Not yet. Feel free to mingle to your heart's content." He drew Henri aside where they would not be overhead, then added in a low voice. "Did you learn anything regarding the matter we discussed?"

"Only that she is completely unknown by our side, but a query's been dispatched to our people in Quebec. We'll hear soon enough if she told you the truth about her previous employer." Henri looked up into the taller man's eyes. "Has she done something suspicious?"

"I have a feeling she's too smart to do anything too soon. I daresay she's been thoroughly coached by whoever sent her here."

"If she has ferreted out anything about us, she has an impressive selection of Tories this night to whom she can pass off the information, eh, Gabriel?"

"I've been watching to see if she spends time with anyone particular. She's nervous and showing it, but she hasn't made an overture toward anyone, at least none that I saw."

Henri suddenly smiled and nodded when he glimpsed an acquaintance across the room. "Lady Annabelle does not look particularly happy at the moment. And she sets her frown upon you. I suspect you are in her bad graces this night."

Gabriel gave a tight smile. "I'm no longer sure she's worth the effort of putting up with her temper tantrums."

"The general seems to think so. Her close relationship with Clinton alone has given us information we could never have attained elsewhere."

Gabriel knew his friend was right, but still he was damn sick and tired of the woman's vanity. They had been lovers, true, but more for convenience than because they cared about each other. The truth was she was too shallow, selfish, and vindictive, not to mention self-absorbed. It sud-

denly occurred to him to wonder if she might
have planted Belinda with him. She was fanati-
cal in her loyalty to the Crown, but he discounted the idea almost at once. She was too
possessive to plant a beautiful maid in his
household. Annabelle would have chosen an
ugly crone for such an assignment. He smiled,
but without an inkling of mirth.

His eyes sharpened when he saw Bartholomew Smythe wander through the foyer in his
usual half-intoxicated state. His wife's cousin
was, and always had been a reprobate, a dis-
gusting man both in habits and in allegiance,
but hardly worthy of Gabriel's concern. Bart was
too caught up in his own self-gratification and
boot-licking of the lobsterbacks to cause the patriots too much trouble.

His analysis changed instantaneously when
he realized that Bart was heading toward the
kitchen—in Belinda's wake. Thinking it more
likely that the drunken man meant to subject
her to his unwelcome attentions than anything
else, Gabriel followed him. When he gained the
entrance of the kitchen, he saw them alone inside. Bart had hold of her arm, and Belinda
looked terrified.

Gabriel stepped forth to rescue her. "Cousin
Bart, I've been looking for you. Come, join me
for a drink in my study."

Belinda paled and scurried away as if the
hounds of Hades nipped at her heels, completely forgetting to refill her empty tray.

"Gabe, my man," Bart returned with a hearty slap on Gabriel's back, "quite a party you've thrown here, but I've need of a glass of wine instead of that watered-down cranberry punch you're serving. That pretty little maid of yours just promised to fetch me a real drink."

"I have a bottle of fine Jamaican rum I can offer you instead." He turned Bart's direction with an arm around his shoulders. "Come, we'll toast the king's health."

He paid Smythe's mumbled answer little mind, realizing the fool was too drunk to make much sense. He was more interested in a young British officer who was passing them in the corridor. He invited him to join them for a drink, and once inside his private study Gabriel strode to the liquor cabinet and poured them all liberal libations of the potent brew.

"It's been a while, Bart," he said with casual interest as he relaxed into one of the deep wing chairs beside the crackling fire. "Have you been out of the city?"

"Now and again. In truth I've been contemplating a voyage to England to visit my kin in Yorkshire. I'm bloody sick of this war."

"As are we," said the officer, a bearded, smallish man by the name of William Quarme, a British lieutenant off the H.M.S. Halifax. Attired in scarlet coat and full military regalia, Quarme lounged down in a chair and crossed his boots at the ankle. "But it won't be long before we subdue these colonial buffoons. They fight in rags and without even proper boots on their feet. It's like shooting fish in a barrel, and they run like rabbits when they hear a musket shot."

It was extremely difficult for Gabriel to sit still for such outrageous slander and force a smile in answer to the insults of the prissy young officer, a man whom Gabriel knew spent more time adjusting his lace cuffs than fighting patriot soldiers. He spoke to Quarme, keeping his voice carefully innocuous.

"And have you fought many battles of late, Lieutenant?"

"Aye, Mr. Elliott, we skirmished with the shabby devils a few days back, near Beekman's Inn on the New Jersey shore, but they ran like cowards as the mangy curs usually do."

He lied, and Gabriel knew it. The Continentals had led Quarme's guard into a trap because Gabriel himself had given over information garnered from this very same boastful lieutenant. He had gotten it to Washington's headquarters in time for the general to ready his troops to meet the British before they reached the inn. Young Quarme had been in his cups the last time Gabriel had seen him, nearly a fortnight ago at a large party at Annabelle's house. Despite his prideful talk, Quarme's own loose tongue had lost that skirmish for his British command.

"Are you here on Manhattan for a while, Quarme? Thought you might enjoy the gaming tables down at Corbie's Tavern. You'd be a welcome addition to our party if you've a mind to join us."

"I'll be here until Thursday, then we're back on the march."

"Chasing the gutless cowards across New Jersey again?"

Quarme took time to down the contents of his whiskey, then shook his curly bewigged head and offered up more information for Gabriel's use. "In truth, we're heading south this time, scouting for signs of the wily Nathanael Greene. We've heard he's on the move toward Virginia."

It never failed to astonish Gabriel just how accommodating the foolish young British fop could be. And there were many others who were equally undiscriminating with whom they discussed their orders. Did they not know yet that the inhabitants of Manhattan were split in their loyalties in this war? That spies were everywhere, that every man, woman, and child should be suspect? Not only would the idiots talk among each other as if they stood in a London drawing room in true-blue England, but they did the same here in New York, openly, with not a whit of circumspection. No wonder Andre was near to pulling out his hair, and General Washington insisted Gabriel stay in the city as the eyes and ears of the patriot army.

"Bart, I hear rumors that you're about to form a Tory regiment," Quarme was saying now, standing up and pouring more rum into his cup.

Now that is interesting news, thought Gabriel, raising his own glass while he watched the stupid English officer partake deeply from his own cup. Plying the enemy with liquor was working well this night, he decided, refilling Bart's glass again. Through the open door of the foyer he could see Henri moving easily among different groups, smiling and joking with his boyish charm, but listening and watching for any tidbit of pertinent information.

Nevertheless, now that Gabriel knew Bartholomew was forming a unit, he would need to know which men would ride under his banner against the patriot army. Before that moment, he had not considered Smythe capable of any sophisticated act of war, but perhaps he had been wrong. Perhaps Bart was not the gutless weakling he had previously thought.

In any case, Gabriel would pass on his suspicions for Henri to take off the island tomorrow. He would use the special disappearing ink he had been given so that his message, written between the lines of a book, would pass inspection by redcoat sentries. It seemed his social gathering was going to be a great success after all, even without Major Andre deigning to appear.

And as for the lovely Mistress Belinda, if she was in collusion with the British, she was being extremely cautious this night. And if her mission was to reveal him to the British as a patriot spy, he would have to make sure to turn the tables on her and hand her over to the patriots first.

Five

"**B**ee! Bee! Bet you can't catch me!"

Still holding the sketch pad on which she had been drawing, Belinda jumped up from the iron garden bench and chased after Annie, thrilled to see the little girl able to run and play again. Annie squealed with childish delight when Belinda grabbed her around the waist and swung her off her feet. Annie broke free and skipped away again, and Belinda watched her race off after a scampering squirrel.

"No, Annie, come back! We've got chores to do!"

She laughed despite herself because her feisty sister was crawling on the ground now, into a thick stand of bushes where her little bushy-tailed friend had disappeared. Looking around, Belinda espied a garden swing that neither she nor Annie had noticed before. It had a wide plank for a seat and was securely attached by ropes to a gigantic limb of a huge red oak tree. She moved toward it, realizing they hadn't seen in because it was half hidden by a boxwood hedge, toward the back corner of rear lawns, near where the stables faced New Street.

Annie is going to be ecstatic when she sees this, Belinda thought with her own rush of pleasure, fully aware how much her sister missed their London garden with its swing and goldfish pond. She called to Annie again, but the child was out of sight now, still stalking her squirrel. Belinda lay her sketch pad on the ground and tested the ancient rope with her weight.

The swing was not frayed and seemed sturdy enough to hold her, and glad to have a few minutes to herself, if only to rest her weary feet, she pushed herself into motion. Her father had put up a swing for her when she was little, and then Annie had used it after her. She smiled at thoughts of those better days when they were a family. She could remember her mother pushing her, higher and higher, and for as long as she wanted her to.

Pushing off with her toes, she strove to think about something else. The party held several nights ago came to mind, and though she had enjoyed watching the ladies in their beautiful gowns, the work had been exhausting with so few servants manning the household. Even past midnight, after Gabriel and most of his guests had left for the theater and a late dinner, she had been up for hours with Dulcimer and the other servants, righting the rooms and clearing the buffet tables.

Despite her trepidation at facing Bartholomew

Smythe again, she had been relieved to see him and give him the man's name who had visited Gabriel. He had not been pleased, because the man was apparently a friend of Bart's and a loyal Tory, and she had known by his first words that he had been drinking too much. A very stupid mistake, she feared, for she had been aware how Gabriel had watched them both. He had followed them to the kitchen, she was sure of it. Did he believe the excuse Bart had thrown out to him? Or did he suspect the truth?

Around her the wind picked up, cool and soothing as it blew softly against her face. It was remarkably mild for November, and as she pulled off her white mobcap and shook out her bound hair, Belinda felt as carefree as a child again. She closed her eyes and pushed herself higher, leaning back as she soared back and forth. Leaves rattled and rustled in a dance across the ground below her, and she could hear Annie's laugh somewhere far away.

This is a good place to live, she thought, but the realization brought only sadness to her heart, heavy and awful, because it was not, and she knew it. She should never have brought Annie to a war-torn city, where no one could trust anyone else, where anybody and everybody could be an enemy pretending to be a friend.

Even she played such a role, *she*, who had no real interest in the rebellion. What a terrible way to live! So sinister and secretive. She wished now that she and Annie were back in Quebec City, safe and secure under the sponsorship of the Greenleighs. At least there was no danger in their household.

The crackle of feet scattering the dry leaves brought her out of her reverie. Gabriel Elliott stood directly in front of her. First she stared in openmouthed astonishment, then she put down her feet and brought herself to a skidding stop. She jumped guiltily from the swing.

"You looked like a little girl swinging so high like that," he said.

To her relief, he smiled, then bent to pick up her discarded tablet. He was dressed as he did when he visited his shipping offices at the wharf, in a brown frockcoat and breeches, with an embroidered black silk waistcoat underneath, his usual spotless white stock tied neatly at his throat. She watched as he flipped through the pages of her drawings.

"Have you been looking for us, sir?" she asked quickly, well aware he had every reason to think they shirked their duties. In truth, they did. "Dulcimer told us to enjoy our luncheon fare in the garden. She said she wouldn't need us for a time, but we should be getting back now, I suspect. I'm sorry if you've been calling for us."

He cut off her apologies with an abrupt motion of his hand. "No, no, nothing like that. I just happened to see you on my way to the stables. Where is Annie?" He glanced around, just as Annie appeared at the corner of the hedge. The child stopped when she saw him, but her face lit up when she saw the swing, still swaying to and from Belinda's hasty exit.

"A swing, Bee, just like the one at home!"

Annie wasted no time scrambling upon it, despite their master's presence. Fortunately, Gabriel laughed, then shocked Belinda by striding around behind the swing.

"Would you like me to push you, Annie?"

"Oh, yes, sir, Master Elliott, that would be grand!"

Horrified, Belinda interjected quickly, "No, no, sir, that won't be necessary. We really should get back to the kitchen."

Her protestations went unheeded.

"Nonsense," Gabriel insisted, handing her tablet to her. "Allow me, if you will. It's been a long time since I pushed a child in a swing."

Completely astounded by this side of her hitherto serious, even taciturn employer, Belinda watched him pull Annie back then release her. The child squealed with utter joy, and a smile tugged at Belinda's mouth, though the scene was both touching and sad. Did he push his own little daughter here beneath this very tree? Had Jessie laughed with glee, too? How full of sorrow he must have been when he lost both his wife and daughter at the same time. She wondered again how they had died. Had the savages scalped them?

The idea made her knees go weak, and she

sank down on the nearby bench again, watching Gabriel push Annie. When Annie began to pump her legs to propel herself, Gabriel walked back to where Belinda sat.

"May I sit down?"

Belinda nodded, made self-conscious by his polite request, then marveling that he was actually there with them at all. After all, they were merely his servants, bound to him by contract.

"I saw you sketching yesterday while Annie played on the stoop."

Belinda had had no idea that he had been anywhere around, much less watching them. She flushed with embarrassment when his gaze moved to the loose curls around her shoulders before he turned back to the tablet and her charcoal etchings.

"You're very good," he said at length. He searched her face. "The drawings of the house and the east portico are impressive. You've quite the knack of portraiture, too. You've caught Henri and David Matthews remarkably well."

Feeling as if she had been caught in the act, Belinda tucked the piece of charcoal in the back of the book and tried to act as if she misunderstood his comments. "I don't shirk my duties when I draw, sir, please believe me."

"I'm not accusing you of shirking anything. In fact, Dulcimer told me that you worked harder than anyone at the party. She's pleased with your work. And I think it's good that you spend time with your sister."

Somehow his kindness flustered her. Never since she had become indentured had any master sat down and spoken to her as an equal like this. She didn't know what to say.

"Where did you learn to draw so well? You've caught the dimensions of the structure almost in the way of an architect."

"Father was an engraver. He taught me the basic skills." While she spoke, she watched Annie soar ever higher into the air, thinking what her little sister lost by not knowing their father.

"Indeed. Can you read, too?"

"Yes, sir." Belinda was proud that she could tell him her family was so enlightened. "My father believed ladies should be educated. Now I'm teaching Annie to read and write."

His gaze rested speculatively on her. "I'm pleased to hear that because I happen to be in need of a clerk at my shipping office. My personal assistant recently decided to join the rebels. Perhaps you could do his job."

Shock stole her tongue, then she stuttered, "But sir, what about my chores here? What about Annie?"

"Dulcimer and Lizzie can supervise Annie. Tell them I have need of you at the docks. Hurry now, take Annie to the kitchen and fetch your cape. I'll wait for you here."

Gabriel watched Belinda take her sister's hand and head off toward the house. He had been

watching them longer than he had intimated to
her, hoping to catch her in some kind of incriminating act. He had not found her snooping
among his belongings other than when she
showed interest in the miniatures that first
morning, nor had he caught her in contact with
British agents. When Gabriel was at his offices,
Dulcimer watched her for him, but Belinda had
not slipped up yet.

Now that he had decided to pass fake information to her through her work at his office, it
would be easier to keep her under surveillance.
He glanced at the house and saw her kissing
Annie good-bye. He shook his head, wondering
how much she had told him was the truth. No
matter how hard he tried to remain oblivious to
her charm, he could not help but consider her
an unlikely spy.

He remembered how disappointed he had felt
when he'd rushed outside after she had disappeared behind the hedge, thinking she was off
to meet a Tory contact. Instead, she had been
swinging like a child, her long hair streaming
out behind her, eyes closed, a smile on her face.
He had been struck by the scene, feeling certain
she must be innocent.

Then he had seen the sketches of his home,
of Henri, of Namasset and Dulcimer, and even
one of David Matthews. Were those sketches
destined for British hands? He had a bad feeling
that's exactly where she meant them to end up.
Why else would she make such detailed draw-

ings? He sought to harden his heart against her while he watched her make her way back to him.

She had swept around her shoulders one of the woolen charcoal-colored cloaks that he provided for his staff, and she had modestly retucked her flowing hair into her servant's mobcap. Her staid appearance took nothing away from the perfection of her face, especially now after the fresh air had pinkened her cheeks and brightened her eyes.

"I thought we might walk," he said as she joined him. "I often do in such pleasant weather."

"I would enjoy seeing the city. I have been out so little since I came from Quebec."

As he led her to the front gate and turned south on Broad Street, he wondered how long it would take for their Quebec agents to get information back about her. The Greenleighs had many contacts on Manhattan. Which had placed her inside his home?

She seemed very small, not quite reaching his chin, and he shortened his stride to match her step. She was quiet again which seemed to be normal for her. She had been the most chatty a few moments ago when she had told him about her education. Had those been lies, manufactured for her own reasons? He decided to try to get more out of her about herself.

"What do you think of America, Belinda?" he

asked, stepping aside and tipping his brown cocked hat for a passing matron.

"I think it is a wonderful country."

Was that bait for him to agree, to revel to her his disloyalty to the Crown? "Actually, we're still a colony of England, you know, and will remain one once the rebellion is put down."

She would not look at him. "Of course. It's just so different here from London."

"Oh? In what way?" He took her arm and helped her across Stone Street. She answered as they continued on toward the Exchange Market between Water and Front streets. His office building was on Delafield's Wharf alongside the Exchange Slip, not far from his home. They had not much farther to walk.

"It seems very big here. The streets are wide, and it seems there is room for everyone who needs a place to live."

"There are huge forests to the north and west of here, vast reaches of land never seen by the eyes of white men."

"Have you seen these forests yourself?" she asked with what seemed genuine, innocent interest.

The question seemed harmless enough, so he answered it. "I have traveled the banks of the North River a good distance toward Fort Niagara. It's vast and uncharted. And beautiful."

"Were you in the army?"

"For a while when I was younger. Before I took over my family's shipping enterprises."

Their conversation was interrupted when they came to the intersection at Front Street. Down the avenue where Whitehall ran along the edge of the Battery, they could see a large crowd gathering. His jaw tightened because he knew there was only one reason for a congregation at the artillery park. The steady beat of drums suddenly filled the air, but Belinda gave him a rare smile.

"Is a parade coming?"

"I'm afraid not," he said, trying to hide the anger burgeoning inside his chest. "The British are hanging traitors."

Her face registered shock, and she peered fearfully down toward the mob of people. He followed her gaze and saw the gallows looming like skeletons against the choppy gray waters of the harbor. He could even see Richmond, the mulatto executioner hired by the British to hang patriot heroes.

"Oh, no, look how many there are," she cried as perhaps a dozen men were herded onto the wooden platform. Nooses were dropped to dangle before each man, and he saw her avert her eyes.

"What have they done to deserve execution?"

"They fought for what they believed in."

"Must we watch this?" she whispered, still not looking.

"No. I have little stomach for watching brave men die."

They turned back toward the wharf, but the

moan of the crowd followed them as the first man gave up his life for his cause. A lone wail pierced the air. The wife of the condemned?

"I've never seen an execution," Belinda muttered, putting her fist against her mouth, as if revolted by the sight.

"Turncoats and traitors die every day. On both sides."

Gabriel had made the remark to gauge Belinda's reaction, and the way her face blanched assured him that he had hit his mark. She was no doubt having an attack of conscience, or self-preservation, if she feared he suspected her. In any case, she had her uses, and he meant to make the most of them before he turned her over to the patriot forces.

Six

The offices of Elliott and Smythe Shipping were located at the corner of Front and Broad streets. As Belinda and Gabriel approached the building which stood within sight of the frenetic activity at the Exchange Slip, she listened while Gabriel informed her that the partnership between the two families had been formed at the time of his marriage. *So that was the reason Bartholomew Smythe felt Gabriel had stolen his inheritance,* she thought as they approached the two-story building that fronted a large shipbuilding yard which stretched all the way to the waterfront of the East River.

Gabriel took Belinda's elbow and assisted her up the front steps. She stood quietly beside him once they were inside the front office. A receptionist was working at a slanted desk set against the wall, a slender young man not much older than she, with thick tan hair tied at his nape. He stood respectfully on sight of his employer. He had shed his frockcoat and wore a plain brown vest and white linen shirt. Black sleeve protectors, such as Belinda had worn in her father's printing shop, covered both his arms against the inevitable inkspots garnered from working on the lined ledgers stacked on a table behind the desk.

"Good mornin' to you, Mr. Elliott, sir," he greeted brightly, but his large brown eyes kept glancing at Belinda as he listened to his employer's instructions for the day.

"Oh, yes, Milton, Mistress Scott is here to assist you with the clerking. Please help her get started."

Milton's ruddy young face clearly registered shock. "Here, sir? As a clerk?"

He did not vocalize his objection, but it was there, and heard quite clearly by all. Belinda lowered her gaze as Gabriel looked up from the paper he was holding and pinned his hapless employee with a cold, hard stare.

"That's right, Milton. Do you have an objection to my decision?"

The youngster did not. He shook his head vigorously and dared another look at Belinda. She smiled encouragingly, not offended. She had witnessed far worse objections by the gentlemen who frequented their shop when she helped run her father's printing press.

"Good. She's had a great deal of experience with both printing and engraving, so I intend to set her up at the desk in the conference room that adjoins my office. Do you have a list of my appointments this day?"

"Of course, sir," Milton said in a voice that told Belinda he was proud of his efficiency. When he presented a neatly scripted list, Gabriel handed it off to Belinda.

"Please show Belinda to her desk, Milton. I need to speak with my overseer down at the yards."

"Yes, sir, of course."

When Gabriel took his leave, Belinda and Milton stood in a moment of awkward silence before he gave a small bow. "I hope I did not seem rude, mistress. I was mightily surprised Mr. Elliott hired a new assistant. He has been most particular that only a few of us remain with him here in the office. Most of the clerks and other employees work down in the yards."

"I wasn't offended. I realize it's a bit unusual for him to bring me here. I assure you, Milton, that I will do whatever tasks you assign me. I worked as my father's apprentice, and he taught me well."

Milton smiled for the first time. "Please come this way."

Young Milton led her through a glass-paned door and passed several closed rooms as they made their way down a long hallway to a narrow back stair. She followed him up the creaky steps, and once atop the landing, she could see that the entire second floor was divided by glass partitions through which one could see all the other rooms. She did note, however, that curtains had been affixed on most of the room divisions, in case privacy was required.

"There, the one with all the windows overlooking the yards is Mr. Elliott's private office. He prefers no one to go inside unless he is at his desk. I warn you because he is quite adamant about that. Not too long ago he let a clerk go because he found him in there without his permission."

Belinda nodded. *Was that where he kept documents he wanted no one else to see? Incriminating ones?* She looked into the spacious office as they passed and observed the large teak desk, neatly cleared of work, but her interest focused on the worktable in the corner where papers and documents were stacked, some casually strewn around. Those would be easy to scan if she could find a time when she could do so without being seen. But what if she did find something criminal in them? What if he were involved with the rebels as Bart insisted?

The drums from the mass hanging came beating back through her mind with their eerie, haunting cadence. The woman's scream of grief rang in her ears, and fear swirled like acid through her belly. She turned and looked through the east windows toward the gallows. She could see a portion of the crowd down at the Battery. Could she turn in someone to the British for such a brutal execution? Could she betray Gabriel who had shown her nothing but kindness?

"Mistress Scott? Is something amiss?"

Milton was looking at her askance, and she was quick to reassure him. "I'm sorry. We passed the hangings in Artillery Park on our way here, and I found it quite upsetting."

"Aye." The expression inside his eyes turned hard for a moment before he hid his feelings. "New Yorkers die there every day. Many without a trial. It's a disgrace to the Crown."

Belinda did not ask him more about it, especially not where his loyalties lay. She did not want to know. She wanted no part of this dirty business into which she had been forced. Didn't every man have a right to his own beliefs? Why should one have to die because of them?

"This is the area that Mr. Elliott was talking about," he told her a moment later, leading her into a small room that adjoined Gabriel's private sanctuary. "There are sharpened quills there in the drawer, and the sand shaker is on the table. I was going to copy the orders and prepare reports this afternoon, but since you're accomplished at the skill, please go ahead and begin on them. They're stacked there on the corner of the table, and Mr. Elliott's stationery is in the bottom drawer. Is there anything else you'll need?"

"No. Thank you, Milton."

"I'll send up his appointments as they arrive, and you can escort them into his office. Do you have any questions?"

"No. You've been very helpful." She smiled gratefully, and he returned a shy nod.

After he was gone, she looked around as she removed her cloak. She found the coat tree beside the door and hung her cloak on the brass hook, then moved to the narrow windows that overlooked the shipyard. The great hulking skeleton of a schooner was being constructed with many workers scurrying up and down a giant wooden scaffolding. She could see the giant rollers that would enable the craftsmen to slide the ship into the harbor when it was made seaworthy.

Another smaller building was near where the rollers ended at the waterfront, and she peered intently at the platforms built against the second-floor doorway as an overlook of the work going on below. She caught sight of Gabriel there, speaking to a man dressed in a long brown leather apron. She gauged the distance between him and the building in which she stood. This would be the time to search his desk, she realized, but even as the thought swept through her mind, fear pinched her heart with giant talons.

Was her freedom worth this dishonorable work? she asked herself, and she thought of Annie, her entire childhood spent in virtual slavery to the dictates of others. Belinda, at least, had had her youthful years, free of worry, enriched with lessons in art and music, and leisurely picnics in the park. Poor Annie would never experience any of that. It was so unfair!

Running her tongue over lips that suddenly went dry, she glanced again to where Gabriel stood with his foreman. She hesitated for one terrifying moment, then acted before she could change her mind, her chest heaving desperately as she hurried outside and alongside the glass partitions to the door to his office.

Once inside the forbidden area, she ran again to the windows, startled to find him no longer on the platform. Horrified, she searched frantically among the men in the yards and found him again, just below where he had stood before in the shadow of the enormous rudder. She wasted no more time, turning to his desk and jerking out the drawers one by one. Mostly she found neat piles of stationery, sharpened quills, ledgers, ink, business files, but the last drawer, the deep one at the bottom, was securely locked. There she would find the proof she needed against him, she felt sure of it.

Glancing outside, she found him now strolling along the edge of the great vessel, but when he stopped to confer with a different worker, she ran to the table and quickly sorted through the papers scattered there. There were maps and charts of the Atlantic Ocean, and several side-view engravings of the ship under construction, but though she shuffled frantically through most of the stacks, she found nothing that did not pertain to shipbuilding.

"What are you doing?"

Every muscle in Belinda's body turned to

granite. She had to physically force herself to turn around. Her mind went blank, then whirled for any acceptable answer. She turned and found Gabriel standing in the threshold. His expression was anything but pleased.

"I . . . I saw the clutter on the table, and I just thought I would straighten your papers before you returned. Did I do something wrong?"

Her voice did not quiver, surprisingly, for her insides tossed like a typhoon at sea. The way he stared at her made her knees turn to water. She put her hand on the table to steady herself.

"Did Milton not tell you that I allow no one in this office while I'm gone?"

"Yes, sir, he did. I thought he meant to work. I am very sorry."

Even in her own ears the excuse was pitiful. No, even worse than that, it was lame and made her sound like a moron. He would probably fire her on the spot. Yes, she wished he would, that's what she wanted, to go back to the house so she wouldn't find out anything about him.

By the annoyed look on his face she decided he had decided to send her packing, but she was saved, or condemned, when Milton appeared on the landing with Gabriel's first appointment of the afternoon.

"Mr. Daffron is here to see you, Mr. Elliott."

Gabriel turned at once. "Thank you. Adam, good to see you. Please come in."

As the tall, elderly gentleman walked toward them. Gabriel turned back to Belinda. "That will be all. Return to your desk and we'll discuss this later."

"Yes, sir."

Relieved, Belinda beat a hasty retreat to her desk and immediately drew a piece of parchment before her, picked up a quill pen, and dipped it into the open inkwell. She began to copy the order forms while unobtrusively spying on the two men talking together on the other side of the glass partition. Not for long, however. Gabriel pulled the curtains together, blocking off her view. Surely, he suspected her now. Or was he innocent of everything of which Bart accused him? That's what she wanted to believe. She wanted him to be a loyalist so she would never have to turn him in.

For several moments she carefully set down the copious figures, checking sums as she went. After a time she realized she could hear the murmur of the men's voices, and she strained her ears to hear what they were saying. The words remained indistinguishable, and she hazarded a peek toward the stairs to see if Milton was about.

Heart thumping, she stood, then inched slowly to her side of the draped window. She leaned close. Although she could not pick up every word they said, she did hear the name of a ship. *H.M.S. Halifax*, a British ship.

"What time will they strike?" The question came from Gabriel's visitor.

Gabriel lowered his voice, but she was able to

make out the words. "Eleven o'clock. Whitehall Slip. Don't let us down."

When a chair scraped as if someone had stood up, Belinda fled like a felon back to the table, trying to look hard at work when Gabriel and the man stepped into view. Her hands were shaking when Gabriel appeared at the threshold of her office.

"I'm going to have to leave for a while, Belinda. When you finish those reports, you may return home. Do you think you can find your way back to the house?"

"Yes, sir."

"Tell Dulcimer that I won't be home in time for dinner. In fact, tell her I've need to go out to Long Island so I'll be very late. There's no need for any of you to wait up. I may even wait until tomorrow to return."

"Yes, sir."

He smiled at her then, and she visibly relaxed, afraid he had been ready to give her a tongue-lashing for being inside his office. "Why don't you take Annie to the park after you're finished here? You've been working hard and could use some fresh air. Tell Dulcimer I gave you permission."

"You're too kind, sir."

He was kind, and the more she learned about him, the more she felt that Bart's suspicious were off the mark. Every indication thus far branded him as a loyal subject of King George. But now she had information for Bartholomew that might be important. She wanted to see Bart in person so she would extricate herself from this bargain with the devil.

"Why do we have to go back to the mean man's house, Bee? I don't like him."

"I know, darling, but we have to. This may be our only chance to get out of the house by ourselves."

"I'm scared."

Belinda looked down at the frightened little girl. She knelt and put her arms around her. "I know. Me, too. But I'll be there with you the whole time, I promise."

"I want to stay with Dulcimer and Lizzie. I like them. They play with me and sing me funny songs."

"We're going back soon. I just have to talk to Mr. Smythe for a few minutes, then we can go home."

Once they reached Water Street, it only took a short walk to reach the front door of Bartholomew Smythe's clapboard house. If the information proved not to be incriminating to Gabriel, maybe Bart would let her quit, even send her back to Canada. Not only had she grown to admire Gabriel as a person, she hated having Annie involved in such a mess. She had been a fool to agree to become a spy.

To her shock, Bartholomew himself thrust open the door. "What the hell are you doing here?" he growled furiously, looking up and

down the street to see if she had been followed.
"I told you never to come here."

Annie hid behind Belinda's skirts, and Belinda
raised her chin, tired of being bullied about by
first one man then another. "I've heard something that I felt you must know at once."

"Get inside," he said harshly. "You better
hope you weren't followed."

"Mr. Elliott has gone away on business—with
a man named Adam Daffron."

"Daffron?" He shut the door and took hold
of her arm. "I don't know that name."

"Come along, Annie," she began as Bartholomew pulled her down the hall. He stopped and
shook his head.

"No, leave her here. I don't want the child
around while we talk."

"Annie, why don't you wait for me in the
kitchen? Maybe Betsy's there."

"Betsy's gone and good riddance," Bart
growled. "Just sit here in the hall, girl, and don't
touch anything."

Annie obeyed at once, wide-eyed and silent,
and Belinda smiled reassuringly at her before
she followed Bartholomew inside the drawing
room. As always, he made her feel uncomfortable and wary that his explosive anger would
erupt at any moment, but she struggled to hide
her dislike of him. He had called Gabriel Elliott
a dangerous man, but he was the one whose
eyes looked like frozen chips of ice.

"Has Elliott begun to suspect you?" he asked,

lighting a taper from the hearth blaze and puffing a cheroot to flame.

"I don't think so. I've been cautious around him. Actually, he's been most kind to us."

Bartholomew's lips compressed in a tight seam that passed as an ugly smile. "How very like him. Where did he go with this man named Daffron? Did he tell you?"

"He said he was going somewhere called Long Island."

"Good girl," he muttered, but he still did not look pleased. "I have people there who can apprise me of his destination if I get word to them in time."

Belinda nodded but volunteered nothing else. Now that she was there, she was suddenly reluctant to give over the information she had gathered.

"Well, don't just stand there staring at me. You said you had information. What is it?" He looked like a hawk, looming over her, his eyes piercing and unblinking. "Well, out with it, chit. I'm a busy man."

"When he learned that I was skilled with letters and numbers, he put me to work at the shipping office."

She had surprised him with that. Bartholomew's elbow left the mantel where he had propped it. He straightened, a different kind of smile spreading across his face.

"Indeed. So dear old Gabe has taken a liking

to you, after all. I knew he would. I take it he noticed your resemblance to Patsy?"

Belinda tried not to show her contempt for his underhanded tactic to rattle Gabriel. "Why didn't you tell me I looked like his wife? I saw a miniature of her. I felt terrible dredging up such painful memories for him."

Bart's interested look faded, and his dark brows formed into a straight, angry slash. "Well, that's goddamn touching, wench. But don't be taken in by him. He's the one who took his family up the Bronx River into the wilds. My cousin and her daughter would still be alive if he had left them here on Manhattan where they'd have been safe."

When Belinda remained silent, he prodded her. "All right, what else? Surely, you didn't come here to tell me he took you down to his office. What kind of tasks is he giving you?"

"I've been copying order forms and repair reports for his shipyard business."

"*My* shipyard, you mean. That was part of my cousin's inheritance that rightfully should have come to me."

Belinda said nothing, aware by his tone of voice just how deep his hatred for Gabriel ran. This was a personal vendetta, she realized, and not just a loyalist wishing to uncover a traitor.

"Have you seen anything that could brand him a rebel yet? Any kind of orders or letters from other patriots?"

Belinda wished she had not heard anything,

wished she had never come here. "No, sir. Only accounts and interactions at the shipyards."

He frowned. "Is that it then? You said you had something important for me."

"I've got a list of the people with whom he had appointments this afternoon, but he left with Daffron before he could see most of them." She took it from the pocket of her skirt and handed it over to him. "Actually, other than the soiree that you attended, he's only entertained close friends, such as Mistress Annabelle and Monsieur LeClerc—"

"That Frenchman is just as much a traitor as Gabe is. I'd wager my life on it. We've just got to catch them in something that would prove it." Suddenly, he grew angry, flicked his cigar into the flames, then slammed his balled fist down upon the mantelpiece. "I want results, do you hear me, Belinda? You find me enough ammunition to have him arrested, or forget about keeping your sister with you. By God, I'll separate you and send her back to Quebec for good."

Belinda stood very still, shocked by his sudden, vituperative burst of rage. He got angry so quickly that he seemed mentally unstable. Was he? If so, he was certainly capable of taking Annie away from her.

"I'll try my best, I swear."

"You'll do better than that. Have you searched his desk? His bedchamber at home?"

She shook her head. "No. I've been afraid his housekeeper would catch me."

"Then do it late at night after she's abed. Use your wits, girl, and don't come back here again without something I can use against him."

He began to stalk to and fro in extreme agitation. "Maybe I should keep the brat here now. Maybe that would give you some incentive."

A shiver ran up her arms, and she hugged her shoulders. She was more afraid of him than she was of Gabriel. Bart would not hesitate to imprison Annie in his house if he felt such a whim. She waited a moment longer, fighting her reluctance, then willfully gathered her ragged nerves.

"There is something else. I don't know if it's important."

Bartholomew stopped his pacing and turned to her. He waited, still scowling. "Tell me. I'll decide if it is or not."

"I overheard something this afternoon—when he was closeted with Daffron. They closed the doors and shut the draperies, but I listened through the glass."

"Now you're beginning to show some ingenuity, girl."

Belinda screwed up her nerve. "If I tell you what I heard, will you let me leave his house? I don't like spying on him. I'm not good at it, and I'm afraid he's going to catch me."

"You knew that when you went there."

"It's not as easy as I thought it would be."

Bartholomew's eyes had gotten that dead look in them again. Belinda took a step backward.

"You'll do as I say, do you understand? And for as long as I want."

"Send us both back to the Greenleighs, I beg you. I've changed my mind."

"Then you'll have to change it back." He stopped, eyes narrowing to slits. "Or perhaps you'll do better if I keep your sister here with me now, starting today. Just to keep you honest."

"You promised we could stay together!"

"And you shall, as long as you do what I say." He paused. "Now, what did you overhear?"

"He mentioned something about a ship, a British one called the *Halifax*. I got the feeling they were planning something."

Bartholomew's face changed, rigid with intensity as he came forth quickly and grabbed her by both arms. "When is it to happen? Did you hear when?"

Belinda bit her lip. If she told him, if Gabriel was involved in some kind of espionage, they would catch him, hang him.

"Tell me, dammit, or you can kiss that sister of yours good-bye."

"Tonight," she said thickly. "At eleven o'clock."

"What else? Tell me everything you heard!"

"That's all. It might be nothing at all."

Bartholomew stared into her eyes for one long minute, then he let go of her arms. She shrank away and clutched her trembling fingers together as he left the room, called for his horse, then was gone. Was Gabriel really a rebel? Had she repaid his kindness to Annie and her with a trip to the gallows? Oh God, how could she live with herself if that happened?

Seven

So it was Bartholomew Smythe she worked for, Gabriel thought with a sinking heart as Belinda and Annie disappeared into Bart's house. Just as he had suspected, Belinda was a Tory spy. He chastised himself now for the guilt he had felt when he followed her home from the office. At first he thought she was merely taking Annie to the park as he suggested, but quickly knew she was up to no good when she headed straight for Water Street.

Good God, he wouldn't have thought Bart clever enough to pull off such a complicated hoax. The man was usually drunk, or at the very least carousing with his unsavory British friends. Gabriel had long known the man hated his guts, but enough to want to stretch his neck in the hangman's noose?

Disappointment attacked him as well, deeper, in a place he didn't want to analyze. He liked Belinda, and though he had caught her going through his office, he still hadn't wanted to believe she was out to destroy him. Now he had no choice but accept it. He and Daffron had spoken loud enough for her to hear their conversation through the partition, and now she had come to Bart to tell him about the attack on the *Halifax*. Well, good, that's exactly what they had wanted her to do.

A sense of regret came swiftly on the heels of his anger. He truly liked the girl: even now, he felt a kind of protectiveness concerning her. What he wanted to know was how she had gotten involved with a man like Bart. Gabriel could not believe she was a spy, trained by the British to infiltrate his house. For one thing she was terrible at it. Every move she made, every expression on her face, was as transparent as washed glass.

More than that, he found it impossible to believe her mission against him was sanctioned by Major John Andre, the head of British intelligence. In the last few months he had heard many tales about Andre's cleverness at planting his agents. Andre was deemed to be an honorable man as well, a gentleman, and a gentleman would not place some innocent young woman in this kind of danger. And what about Annie? Why would Belinda want to drag a four-year-old child into a mess like this?

It had to be a personal grudge on Bart's part. Bart made no bones about resenting Gabriel's ownership of the shipyards, but going to this extreme on a personal matter? It seemed ridiculous. But then Bart had few scruples about anything. Gabe didn't like him, had never trusted him, not even when Patsy was alive.

He kept himself hidden behind a bricked garden wall a few doors down from Bart's house, but his eyes never wavered from the front door. He had trailed Belinda and Annie on foot, keeping well back from them, but Belinda had not even had sense enough to make sure she wasn't being followed. She had walked swiftly, determinedly, holding Annie's hand, though she had hesitated on the street outside Bart's place.

Was she really an indentured servant? Or had that identity been fabricated? And if not, who the hell was she? What was her name? He shook his head. A stinging reproach assaulted him, for he could not deny that he had fallen into the trap. He did feel an attraction for her, and it wasn't just because she looked like Patsy. The more he had been around her, the more differences he saw between them, both in looks and mannerisms. But there was no doubt that was the reason she had been chosen. In addition to being young and looking as innocent as an angel. Plenty enough to suck him straight down into Bartholomew Smythe's damnable plot.

Still, he longed to find another answer, one that would prove Belinda innocent on all charges. He would know for sure that night. If she did pass along the false information he had fed to her, the British would show up at precisely eleven o'clock. If that happened, there could be no doubt that she was an acting British agent. She would have to be dealt with, and he would have to be the one to do it. He frowned, thinking how dire was her fate. Enemy agents were hanged every day, or imprisoned in patriot jails. Lord help him, even if she was guilty, he hated the thought of seeing her languish in some dank cell.

Continuing his vigil, he tried to relax his tense muscles. He would have to wait until she left and follow her again. She could very well lead him to a second accomplice, perhaps even a secret Tory leading the life of a patriot. For the first time real anger assailed him, a deep-rooted disgust that brought a heated flush up his neck. How had a reprobate like Bartholomew gotten a young woman like Belinda into his clutches? Had they been lovers? Were they still? Bart had always liked women and was certainly not above using them to his own ends, but usually his needs were met by the loose tarts in whose company he ran, actresses whose reputations were widely known.

Even though his mind turned over the possibility that they were lovers, he couldn't quite believe it. The expression on Belinda's face when Bart had approached her that night in the kitchen had not been faked, he would stake his life on it. She had been frightened, yet here she was seeking Bart out in his own home. He was honest enough to admit that he was trying to rationalize her behavior, to make excuses for her running straight to Bart. Down deep in his heart he knew why. Belinda Scott had gotten to him in other, more disturbing ways. Frowning in self-reproach, he clenched his jaw in an effort to strengthen his resolve. She was undoubtedly a spy; it was his duty to reveal her as one and take her out of commission.

Now he was faced with the decision whether to continue to use her against herself. As inept as she appeared to be, he could feed her reams of false information to disrupt the British intelligence service. That would justify keeping her in his house for a time, as if nothing had happened. Or, he thought with some interest, perhaps they could turn her somehow, convince, or coerce her to join their side. If she could identify some of the hidden Tory traitors lurking in their own ranks, she could be invaluable to the patriot cause.

He pulled back when he saw Bart rush from the house and mount his horse. Moments later, he was cantering down the street in the direction of the river. On his way to report in to Andre?

A few minutes later, Belinda and Annie stepped outside. He hardened his heart. She was full of lies. She had proven it. Disgusted, he waited until they were well down the block, then trailed them as far as Broad Street before he knew for sure that they were returning to his own house. He veered left and headed for his meeting with Namasset and Henri. He could waste no more time feeling sorry Belinda: she

was a traitor, the enemy. He had to concentrate
on the patriots' real mission that night, one that
Belinda had guaranteed success by alerting the
lobsterbacks to converge on the *Halifax*.

The same night, just after the hour of eleven,
Gabriel lay on his stomach on the shore of the
East River, watching the wharves south of his
position. Namasset lay close beside him, five
loyal patriot friends flanking them. All was quiet
on the waterfront. The mast lanterns of British
vessels anchored in the dark harbor set forth
pinpoints of yellow light in the inky night.

Perhaps he had been wrong about Belinda,
after all, he thought, chagrined by the pleasure
that thought brought him. Perhaps she had not
given over the information about the *Halifax* to
Bart. Perhaps there was a legitimate cause for
her visit that afternoon. Might she know someone there, on Bart's staff perhaps, a maid or
serving girl who had come with her from
Quebec?

He hadn't considered that explanation until
that very moment. His spirit lifted, appalling
him, for the knowledge told him much more
about his own feelings than he wanted to admit.
Such hopes plunged at once, however, as the
tramp of foot soldiers drifted in a harsh cadence
over the still calm of the water. He clamped his
teeth, rage returning as a platoon of musket-
carrying, red-coated soldiers arrived at quick-
step from either direction in front of the *Halifax*'s

berth. An order brought them up, and the sounds of bayonets being affixed to muskets filtered to them. Belinda had betrayed him to them, damn her.

He raised his hand in signal to his waiting companions, and they began to disperse toward the water. He moved out behind them, now determined to carry out the real mission of the evening. Out in the water lay the frigate *Ramona*, which had only recently left the log rollers as the most recently launched ship from his own master carpenters. She was being used for the moment as an armory with dozens of stacked crates in her hold, brand-new muskets, lead balls, and most important to the patriot forces, barrels of the gunpowder General Washington needed so desperately for his army.

As several of his men entered the bobbing rowboat hidden in the bushes, he looked back across the water. The diversion he had planned to help them get onto the *Ramona* undetected had now begun in earnest. He could hear sporadic gunshots erupt from the spots where he had positioned his own agents, well hidden on warehouse roofs overlooking the slip. An answering spattering of fire from the British sounded, and he smiled grimly. The English fools had been manipulated to fire upon their own ship. And its crew, as loyal to the Crown as any, would no doubt answer in kind. He hoped the redcoats would go so far in their diligent suppression of the rebellion to torch the innocent vessel, giving the patriots one less warship to worry about.

In front of him Namasset moved soundlessly, wading waist deep into the river to hold the skiff steady for the rest of them to board. Not even a ripple sounded in the quiet night, and Gabriel's confidence soared as he took his spot in the bow. The men bent silently to their oars, and within minutes they reached the towering hulk of the *Ramona*.

The firing continued across the shore, and he followed Namasset out, swiftly mounting the rope handholds he had ordered affixed to the hull during construction for this very purpose. The starboard sentry was already unconscious by the time he scaled the deck rail, lying flat on his back with the Oneida squatting beside him. The port sentry would be downed by the men scaling the ladders on the far side.

They hadn't much time left now, but he could hear some commotion on some of the other ships anchored nearby and the running footsteps of sailors alerted to the fracas. The subterfuge was working, and Belinda's treachery was making it possible. It wouldn't be long until he could thank her personally for the desperately needed munitions they would obtain for the patriots within the next hour. He quickly set up a human cordon, then forced the iron padlock on the hatch. Moments later, the latest English muskets were being passed, man to man, over the side and down into the boat bobbing in the water below.

He continually prodded the men to hurry, for he knew they had little time. Within ten minutes the cargo was stowed away, but he sat tense and wary as they dipped the oars again and glided silently toward the opposite shore. They would escape without detection now, hidden by the moonless night, underneath the very nose of a dozen armed warships, whose decks loomed far too high over the river surface to notice the smaller craft.

Once across the North River on the New Jersey side waiting patriot soldiers would transport the cargo by wagon to the encampment of the Continental Army. Highly pleased by the success of the operation, he barely glanced at the shooting battle still going on at the *Halifax* as he jumped into the water and helped drag the boat into the shallows. By tomorrow he would be back in New York as if nothing had happened.

Eight

The following afternoon Belinda strolled east along the planked sidewalk edging the Exchange Market on Broad Street, feeling better than she had in some time. Gabriel had not returned yet from Long Island, and she had spent the morning quietly at home with Annie helping Dulcimer with her kitchen chores. When her little sister had skipped away to help Lizzie polish silver at the dining room table, she had offered to walk to the market for Dulcimer. She was returning home now, Dulcimer's roomy wicker basket hooked over her arm.

Inside its depths lay a tiny nosegay of violets for Annie and a large bouquet of yellow chrysanthemums for Dulcimer's kitchen window. Belinda increased her step, eager to present her small gifts. She loved to give things to people, but rarely had the opportunity.

The sun was shining brightly in a bright blue sky. A pair of robins in a tree branch overhanging the road flitted happily from twig to twig, and she forced herself not to think of unhappy things, especially not yesterday's meeting with Bart Smythe. She didn't want to know what he had done with the information she had passed on: she never wanted to know what damage she had caused.

As she reached the corner of Broad and Stone, she paused at the curb to allow a horseman to trot past on the wide dirt avenue. In the opposite direction a well-polished black coach jingled its way along. She waited patiently for it to pass by, smiling as she thought of the delicious two-crusted pie Dulcimer would make with the huge red apples she had purchased at the market stalls. If they hurried through their chores, they might have time to go down to the Battery park to stroll along the waterfront before darkness fell over the North River.

When the driver suddenly swerved his horses to a skidding stop in front of her, Belinda stepped back, startled. The door swung open and revealed Bartholomew Smythe's furious face, and she struggled to hide her dismay at encountering him again. His frowning visage darkened into a thunderous black scowl as he motioned impatiently for her enter the coach. Afraid, she glanced around uncertainly. It was foolish for Bart to approach her on a public thoroughfare in such a way. What if someone saw them together and told Gabriel?

"Damnation, get in," Bart ground out through tightly clenched teeth, slamming down the iron mounting step with a metallic clang.

His show of rage propelled Belinda hastily up into the interior, fearing he would jerk her up beside him if she hesitated longer. Warily, she sat down on the opposite seat, as far away from him as she could get. His clothing was rumpled, and his long hair straggled in unkempt fashion around his shoulders. She grew more alarmed when she picked up the overpowering smell of brandy. He had been drinking, she realized as he slammed the door, snapped a curt command to his driver, then jerked down both shades so that no one could see them.

"Isn't it unwise to be seen together like this, Mr. Smythe?" she said timidly. "What if we're seen—"

Her query ended abruptly when he brought up a gloved hand, and his open palm connected against her cheek with a sharp, forceful crack. Belinda cried out, cupping her stinging face with her palm and backing away from him. Shocked to the quick, she couldn't believe he had physically assaulted her. She had never been struck, never, not by anyone, and she fought the tears welling in her eyes.

"You little bitch, you're working for them, aren't you?"

"No," she cried in confusion. His furious accusation terrified her. What did he intend to do with her? He was half-drunk, and red-faced with rage. He could take her anywhere, do anything, and no one would ever know. "I don't understand. I've done everything you've told me to! What's happened to make you so angry?"

Bart's mouth formed an ugly, tight-stitched seam. "Let me tell you what's happened, you stupid girl. The message you gave me about the *Halifax* was a damnable trick that made me look like the biggest fool in town. No patriot was within miles of that ship last night." He leaned toward her, and she cowered, but he remained close, his words coarse, grinding out through clenched jaws. "They boarded the *Ramona* instead, as if you didn't know, and escaped with hundreds of newly arrived muskets and an entire hold of gunpowder."

"But I *didn't* know! I told you exactly what I overheard! I'm quite positive they mentioned the *Halifax!* More than once! They were speaking together in low tones, but I heard them mention that ship. I swear it!"

She winced when he suddenly reached out and grabbed her hand. He twisted her wrist until she had to bite her lip to keep from crying out.

"Tell me the truth, Belinda. I'm too angry to put up with any more of your lies."

"I'm not lying! Why would I? I don't know why the *Halifax* wasn't involved. Maybe they saw your men there and changed their plans at the last minute. Please, you're hurting me!"

The awful grip did not lessen, but intensified until she groaned out loud. "Perhaps they did, but you listen to me well, you little twit. The next time you make a laughingstock out of me, you'll pay the price. Do you understand me, Belinda? When you pass along information to me, you best make damn sure it's accurate!"

He released her wrist, but shoved her back against the seat to punctuate his warning.

"Remember I can snatch Annie any time I want. I can sell her onto any ship leaving port, and you'd never lay eyes on her again."

"You wouldn't do that! She's just a baby!"

Bartholomew gave a laugh that was so ugly, so mean-spirited, a shudder crept up Belinda's back and lifted up the hairs on her nape. She stared silently at him as he banged the head of his cane on the ceiling. Belinda did not move, did not speak as the driver brought the horses to a lurching stop.

"Now get the hell out of here and find me something that'll make Elliott dangle from a noose."

Within moments Belinda stood at the side of the road again, every limb trembling as Bart hurled the basket onto the street beside her. She watched the coach drive off, swirling the dead leaves in the gutter into a dusty dance. Cold fear took hold of her as she bent to retrieve the basket and quickly gathered up the scattered flowers, fruits, and vegetables. Her dread intensified when she thought of his threats against her little sister. He'd do it, too. He was cruel enough to take Annie away from her. She had to do exactly what he said; she had no choice.

She rubbed her aching wrist as she swiftly walked along. His harsh grip had already begun to bruise her tender skin, and the swelling was detectable. When she entered the kitchen, she tried to smile at Dulcimer where she sat at the kitchen table, busily peeling potatoes for the evening repast.

"You're a quick one, Belinda. Did you fetch fresh scallions for my broth?"

"Aye, Dulcimer. And firm red apples for your pie."

"Good girl. Master Gabriel loves my apple pie with honey in the crust," Dulcimer answered, removing the vegetables to the pump for a through dousing.

"Any word from the master?" Belinda asked, trying to sound casual when she felt the need to burst into tears and cry like a baby. The side of her face still hurt from where Bart had hit her, and she averted her cheek from Dulcimer as she removed her woolen cloak and bonnet and hung them beside the door.

"No. I daresay he'll be back before the dinner hour."

"Is Annie still in the dining room?"

"The little ducky's eyes were droppin' so I told her to go upstairs and take a nap. She's as sweet as pie, she is." Dulcimer smiled fondly.

"Then I suppose this will be a good time for me to finish cleaning the bedchambers. Annie helped me change the linens earlier, but I need to oil the furniture before the master returns."

"Sit down and rest a spell, dearie. You had a long walk down to the marketplace. No need to tucker yerself out with the master gone and all."

"Thank you, Dulcimer, but I wouldn't feel right until my chores are done." She hesitated, then told a lie, hoping Dulcimer wouldn't see through it. "The master asked me to finish my work on his accounts at the desk in his bed-chamber if I found an extra minute this day. So I will do that after I finish polishing the furniture."

"I can't fathom you bein' learned in figures," Dulcimer declared with obvious admiration. "I ain't heard of any other chambermaids bein' as schooled as a gent."

Belinda smiled, but she was eager to be away, and very glad Dulcimer would be distracted with preparing dinner. She was desperate now to find something for Bart, and she intended to go through Gabriel's desk in the sitting room adjoining his bedchamber. He was an intelligent man. He would hide incriminating documents, if he had them, not scatter them around for her to find.

Even though she knew Gabriel was not in the house and the other servants were busy on the first floor, she still hesitated when she reached the closed door of his private chambers. She tapped lightly, just to make sure, but found no one around. She stepped inside and shut the door behind her.

Breathing hard, she looked around the room.

Her nerves were jumping, but somehow she felt sure he kept his private papers somewhere inside this very room. She knew she would be severely reprimanded if he caught her snooping again, perhaps even dismissed. She nearly succumbed to the compelling urge to flee, until she remembered the vindictive glare on Bart Smythe's face.

Swallowing her fears, she forced herself to move across the carpet, absently swiping her dust cloth over the table beside Gabriel's reading chair. Where would he keep secret documents? Where would he hide a safe? Behind the bookcase as her father had done in their London home, perhaps?

She rounded the desk and performed a hasty but thorough search through its drawers, looking for a hidden clasp or hinge of some sort, but found nothing but stacks of expensive white bonded stationery and a few files about his family holdings, all extremely neat and orderly, like everything else about Gabriel. Nothing seemed improper, or out of place, at least not that she could tell. She sat down in the leather chair and tried to think with the craftiness of a spy. There were several bookcases in the room, and that, of course, was the best place to hide a cache of traitorous documents.

She rose and began to pull out one volume after another, fanning through the pages one book at a time, careful to place them all back into their place, then halted when she hoisted a

Greek history in her hand. The tome seemed less weighty than the others, and she quickly opened the cover and found inside a secret compartment, one that held a tiny ivory key. A key to what? Her gaze swept the room again and fell on an ornate black-and-crimson Chinese cabinet positioned against the far wall. It did not appear to have any drawers, but her mother had once owned a black lacquered desk from China that had contained many hidden compartments within its design.

Excited at the prospect of finding something there, she rushed across the room and knelt at the cabinet's base. She felt with her fingers along the front panel. About two feet long, it was intricately painted with a mountain scene populated by Chinese peasants pulling a wagon alongside a mist-shrouded lake. She searched diligently for the same kind of indentations her mother's desk had had.

Finally, she found one and, exultant, she pressed it down then turned the latch a fraction before she found the keyhole. She inserted the key, turned it, and heard a tiny click as the lock gave way. A drawer, invisible a moment before, slid open for her examination. She reached inside and triumphantly brought out a bottle of liquid and a sheaf of white papers.

Disappointed to find them blank, she unstoppered the lid of the bottle and sniffed the contents, recognizing it at once as a form of disappearing ink that her father had once experimented with in their own shop. Did the papers have invisible writing on them? Information that Bart could turn over to the British? That would be all he needed to have Gabriel arrested. Could she do that? Bring harm to him? Yes, she thought, if it meant saving Annie from Bart.

Nine

Gabriel sat completely still in the deep wing chair across the room. He had been watching Belinda for the last ten minutes as she methodically searched his bedchamber, absolutely astounded at how inept a secret agent she was. Anyone should know to make a thorough search for occupants before proceeding with her furtive agenda. His chair was angled away from her, and she probably couldn't see him from her vantage point; all that was true, but had Bart given her no training whatsoever before sending her into such a dangerous assignment?

She had managed to open the hidden compartment in his Chinese bureau, no easy feat; he would give her that much for her ingenuity, and now she had even found the disappearing ink and some secret missives he could not let her turn over to Bart. The time had come to make himself known. Scourging himself for still feeling disappointed by her treachery, he rose to confront her with her crime.

"Very clever, Belinda."

His utterance was low, completely calm, but so jolted Belinda that she nearly jumped out of her mobcap and sent the papers she held flying up in the air like a flock of fluttering birds. Whirling around, she stared at him, still on her knees, her mouth hanging ajar, her big azure eyes so full of horror at being caught red-handed, that he might have smiled if he hadn't felt so sick inside.

"So you *are* spying on me," he remarked with a nonchalance he didn't quite feel. She had betrayed him, and he was irked at himself at how rotten that made him feel. He had grown to like her, because she was beautiful and smart and shy. He wondered if he really knew her at all, or if everything she had revealed about herself had been designed to bring on the very feelings he now fought? The time was at hand to find out.

Absolute terror still held her face in its grip, all the natural pink flushing out of her cheeks until she looked like a milk white porcelain figure. It was then he saw the ugly mark marring the elegant high curve of her cheekbone. The bruise was beginning to turn purple and hadn't been there yesterday at his office. Someone had hit her. Today. Not long before this moment. Bart?

The idea sent a flash of anger scorching through his veins, a protective fury as unwanted as it was ridiculous. Why should he care if there was trouble between two enemies working together to get him hanged? But he did care, and the idea of the man slapping Belinda in the face twisted around inside him, as if a razor blade lacerated his gut.

Frowning at his own overreaction, he strode to the hall door and turned the key. He stood still for a moment before facing her, hardening a heart that had grown too soft where she was concerned. From the very beginning she had gotten to him, eliciting deep protective instincts. He had not welcomed them then, and even less now that he had seen what she was capable of. The young woman standing before him was a British spy, plotting his downfall with a man who would like nothing better than to see him dancing on the wind. He had caught her in the act, more than once. He could not let himself show pity. Would she weep now, he wondered sardonically, and beg prettily for mercy? Or would she try to lie her way out of it? He found out quickly enough as she struggled to her feet, still clutching the ink bottle in one hand.

"Please forgive me, sir, but I was examining your Chinese chest, because, you see, my mother had one quite similar in design back in London. I was always fascinated by all the hidden drawers."

A fairly good explanation, under the circumstances, and especially one concocted on the spur of the moment under duress, but unfortunately not good enough. "Shall I assume then that she had a desk like mine, with the same sort of drawers? And bookshelves with books that needed to be searched? I realize this might come as a great shock to you, dear Belinda, but I've been sitting right there by the window since you walked into this room."

"Oh, do forgive me, sir," she said in a husky voice that sounded forced over a huge knot in her throat. "Dulcimer told me you were still away. I meant only to clean the books, sir, so as not to bother you after you returned . . ."

"Shut up, Belinda," he ordered harshly, his patience at an end. "Don't think me a fool. I am not one, nor am I gullible enough to believe any lies you might manufacture at the moment."

His words ended her bravado. Her narrow shoulders drooped with resignation. Her eyes filled up, and one tear overflowed her thick bottom lashes and rolled down over the darkening bruise. She began to tremble, all over, until she was forced to hug herself to stop shaking. He remained coldly unaffected, wondering if they were tears of remorse or tears of dismay at getting caught.

"Sit down while I decide what the devil to do with you."

Shakily, she retreated until the backs of her knees hit the crimson wing chair behind her, then sank down into the cushion as if her legs wouldn't hold her any longer. He kept an eye on her as he poured himself a glass of port, but she wasn't going anywhere. She was caught like a rat in a wooden bucket. Henri had insisted that they should force her to turncoat and spy on her Tory masters, but Gabriel wasn't sure he wanted to trust her that far. She was an Englishwoman. She had no reason to put her life on the line for the newly forming United States.

"I suppose we should begin with how Smythe managed to recruit you?"

Again, openmouthed astonishment, no doubt because he already knew whom she was working for, followed by a hastily concocted string of outright lies. "Sir, please, I don't know what you mean, I truly don't. I don't know anyone named Smythe—"

"Listen to me, Belinda, before you say another word. I don't want to hear any more lies. It'll go worse for you if you continue to deny the truth. Now tell me what I want to know, or I'll be forced to hand you over to the patriots and let them hang you for the English-loving spy you are."

She stiffened, and before his cynical gaze, seemed to cover herself with a cape of pride. "I bear no love for the English."

"Your accent tells me a different story about your allegiance."

" 'Tis true I was born in England with its high and mighty lords, but since my family's misfortune, the nobility has never shown me any favor."

Another tactic meant to disarm? he wondered, but found her remark intriguing, which could be the reason why she tossed it out with her chin lifted so high. That he didn't want to believe she was a cold-hearted villainess no doubt helped his willingness to sit still for whatever tale she was getting ready to spin for him.

"Are you ready to tell me the truth now? Is that what you're saying?"

She fidgeted nervously, and he noticed how she kept rubbing her right wrist, as if it pained her. He said nothing, but pinned her with an expectant stare.

"I will talk, but only if you will grant me a condition."

At first he was too shocked by her gall to answer, then his gaze grew frigid. "Believe me, wench, you are in no position to make demands. One word from me and you'll be hauled to the gallows."

His threat got to her. She forced down a very hard swallow. She raised tearful eyes to his face. He braced himself against feeling sorry for her.

"I beg you then to listen to what I have to say. I did not wish any part in these secret Tory affairs. I have no interest in your war. If I must choose, however, I support the colonials right to self-govern. That's one reason I agreed to come to Manhattan with Mr. Smythe, in order to make a new start for Annie and me."

"Your first mistake," he said coldly, mentally debating his options concerning her. Even if she cooperated, told him everything she knew, he wasn't sure just what he should do with her. Perhaps he should leave it up to General Washington. As a woman she would most likely be imprisoned, then transferred in a British prisoner exchange, but Belinda would have no way of knowing that.

Now she sat silently, gazing steadily at him, only her shallow breathing alerting him that she was still upset. Slowly, however, he saw her begin to pull herself together and consider what she should do. She lifted her left hand and twisted her finger around a tendril of black hair that had escaped the mobcap. His eyes went again to the bruise on her cheek, but now she was speaking, still cradling her right wrist in her lap.

"I had no desire to come here, or to enter your house in order to betray you. When Bartholomew approached me, Annie was sick, and he told me she wouldn't have to work anymore if I did what he wanted." She heaved in a trembling breath. "But by the time we arrived in New York, I knew I'd made a terrible mistake." Her eyes looked darker now, like smoke trapped inside a pale blue bottle, huge, imploring him to understand. Any other time he might have softened considerably under the extreme vulnerability she was displaying, but not now.

"I'm losing patience, Belinda."

"I'm telling the truth!" Forcibly, she controlled her agitation and spoke more quietly. "I swear I am. I came into your office to search because he threatened me today. He said he'd take Annie and send her far away where I'd never find her."

For the first time Gabriel tended to believe her. Such gutless coercion sounded like something Bart would stoop to. He knew firsthand how much she cared about her little sister. Another tear rolled down her face, and she would have to be one hell of a fine actress to fabricate the fear and misery she was displaying.

"Don't you see, Mr. Elliott, she's all I have left. If Bart takes her away from me, I'll be alone. She'll be alone. Please, I beg you to help me. He's already furious with me because I gave him wrong information yesterday."

"You've seen him today?" Gabriel asked, watching her rub her wrist. When she removed her fingers, he saw the bracelet of dark bruises she had been hiding. His eyes narrowed as she continued in a subdued voice.

"Aye, he took me into his carriage when I was returning home from the market. He thought I was working for you and had told him the wrong ship on purpose." She gazed remorsefully down at her hands. "You see, I listened at your office window yesterday when you were closeted with your friend Daffron."

She wouldn't look at him, and she absently reached up to touch the bruise on her cheek.

"Is that where Bart struck you?"

She nodded, but her small chin went up a bare notch. "Yes, and he twisted my wrist. That's why I felt desperate enough to search your chambers. He told me I'd better find something else, or he'd come for Annie. I know I don't deserve any pity from you, but please help me protect my sister from him. I'll do anything you say, anything at all, both of us will, if you'll just help me get her away from him."

"You agreed to infiltrate my house for the sake of your sister's health, and for no other reason?"

When she hesitated, his suspicions prickled again.

"That wasn't the main reason," she admitted uncomfortably. "He offered us our freedom." Her voice hoarsened slightly on the last words. She repeated them as if she savored the sound. "Our *freedom*. That's what I wanted, to be free again as we were before my father went into debt. I wanted to live here in America where we could be a family and not be looked down on and ordered around."

Gabriel understood her desire for freedom, only too well. Did he not fight and put his life and worldly possessions in jeopardy every day for that very privilege? Did that not motivate all the loyal patriots?

"Bart won't get his hands on Annie, rest assured on that. I'm going to lock you inside your room until I decide what to do with you. But if you try to escape or communicate with Smythe, the consequences will be dire, do you understand, Belinda?"

She nodded and looked mightily relieved, and

without speaking again he escorted her to the bedchamber where Annie lay asleep and locked the door behind her. He needed to get word to General Washington for orders on how to proceed with her capture. Perhaps the Americans would want to use her for a double agent, but he certainly wouldn't trust her again. All Bart and the Tories would have to do was get their hands on Annie, and she would turn back to their side. Whatever was to be done with her, he needed to find out, and soon, but it would have to wait until tomorrow. Tonight he was due at a rendezvous on the Jersey shore to set up an ambush on a British patrol due to leave the city within the next twenty-four hours.

Ten

"Bee? Is he gonna take us off to jail?" Belinda stopped folding Annie's soft white nightgown and looked at her sister where she perched at the foot of the bed, her arm around the bedpost. Annie's eyes were wide upon her, full of dread and uncertainty.

Belinda put the garment in their battered valise, then moved quickly to draw the little girl onto her lap. Annie hid her face in her shoulder as Belinda rocked her gently, hugging her tight and murmuring comforting words against her soft, dark curls.

"Sweetheart, don't you worry about such things. No one's going to hurt you."

"What about you, Bee? Are the redcoats gonna get you?"

Patting Annie's back reassuringly, Belinda wasn't sure how she should answer the questions. Her fate was completely in Gabriel Elliott's hands. Would he be merciful? Again she saw the cold contempt in his eyes when he had listened to her excuses, and she knew she could not tell Annie that everything would be all right.

"Bee, you won't leave me, will you?" Annie pushed herself away from Belinda and looked up into her face with brimming, sorrowful eyes. Belinda smiled and dabbed at the child's tears with her handkerchief.

"Darling, please don't cry. I might have to go away for a little while, but perhaps not for so very long."

Her voice thickened, then caught tightly in her throat. The truth was it could be a very long time, indeed. Forever, if Gabriel found no compassion in his heart. She was guilty. He knew it; she knew it. She had deceived him—entered his home expressly to destroy him. Why should he show leniency to her?

"But if you go away, where will I go? Who will take care of me?"

Annie moaned out her fears, her childish voice so full of anxiety that Belinda's heart twisted with regret. Why had she been so foolish? Why, in God's name had she let Bart Smythe talk her into doing his dirty work?

Forcing her voice to remain light, she said brightly, "Now don't you worry about that. You like Master Gabriel, don't you? He'll find someone to take care of you if I must go away. Maybe he'll even let you stay here with Dulcimer and Lizzie."

"But I don't want to; I only want to be with

you. Don't go off and leave me. Take me with you, promise me, Bee, promise me you will."

Annie grabbed her around the neck and held on as if she would never let go. Belinda bit her lip, fighting her own tears. How could she ever leave Annie? She was all Belinda had left in the world. Oh, why had she ever left Quebec. They would have been safe there, and together.

She stiffened, trying not to panic as footsteps sounded in the hall, then stopped just outside the door. A key scraped inside the lock. Annie's thin arms tightened into a stranglehold as the door swung open.

"No, no, no!" Annie's cries turned to shrieks when she saw Gabriel standing on the threshold.

"Hush, Annie, shhh," Belinda whispered, but her own gaze riveted on Gabriel's attire. Dark traveling clothes—a heavy black wool cloak over a dark surtout and a black tricorne shielded his face.

"What's the matter with Annie?" He took a step toward them, but was stopped by Annie's terrified wail.

"She's scared that you're here to take me away from her."

Gabriel showed little reaction. "Well, I'm not. Come on, it's time to go. I've brought you both warm clothes to wear. It's cold out on the water."

"What water? Where are you taking us?" she asked cautiously, her initial relief about keeping

Annie with her beginning to fade. Was he sending them back to England? Or to some other faraway shore?

"A place where your Tory friends can't find you."

As he crossed the floor and thrust a couple of warm fur-lined cloaks into her hands, she didn't question him further, but helped Annie off the bed and quickly wrapped her up snugly for their journey. The child continued to sob until Gabriel knelt on one knee and spoke directly to her. "Stop your weeping, girl. I'm not going to hurt you or Belinda. I'm just taking you on a boatride."

Annie apparently believed him because she calmed down considerably. Belinda wished she could be as trusting. He could be taking them anywhere, even to a prison. Again they were pawns with no choice but to go with him.

"Be quick now, gather up your belongings. We have no time to waste."

His tone was uncompromising, so she hastily closed the tattered, tapestry-covered satchel that held their meager possessions. Little left, indeed, from the comfortable life they had enjoyed in London.

"Is that all you have?" Gabriel frowned down at the pitiably small collection of their worldly goods, then at Annie, who clutched the new rag doll with button eyes that Dulcimer had made for her.

Dulcimer and the other servants had been so

kind to them, never suspecting that Belinda harbored secrets against their master. Annie had suffered so much since they had left England. Sometimes Belinda hoped she would not remember these awful years of her childhood. She wished she could forget.

"Fetch a couple of quilts from the blanket chest. You're going to need them."

A sense of helplessness, dread over what faced them now that she had been caught as a spy, assailed her as she took a tight hold on Annie's hand and followed him through the dark house.

On the rear driveway a wagon waited. To her surprise the Indian named Namasset sat high on the driver's perch. A bay mare was tied to the rear wheel, and the horse sidestepped skittishly when she heard their feet crunching on the gravel.

Annie made no protest when Gabriel lifted her lightly into the bed of the wagon. He took Belinda's arm and led her a few steps away. He kept his voice low, but his grip tightened around her arm.

"I give you fair warning, Belinda. If you try to escape, I'll wash my hands of you. I owe you no favors. God knows you're getting better than you deserve."

Belinda nodded without speaking, not daring to annoy him, and very grateful when she was allowed to scramble under the canvas tarpaulin tied over the wagon where Annie was waiting for her. She covered herself and Annie in the soft patchwork quilts from their beds, shivering from the frosty air. Winter was fast approaching. Where would they spend it?

Hidden beneath the cover, she strained her ears for what transpired between the two men, able to ascertain that Gabriel had mounted the mare. Seconds later, Namasset slapped the reins and the wagon began to roll toward their unknown destination.

"Master Gabriel won't let anyone hurt us, will he, Bee? He's a nice man, isn't he?"

"No, sweetheart, we're going to be all right. You'll see."

Annie cuddled herself closer, and Belinda stroked her silky curls. Poor little thing was emotionally exhausted. She would sleep soon. But Annie was right about Gabriel Elliott. He was a good man. Belinda'd seen subtle glimpses of his true character every day they'd lived in his house. He was not unfair, and certainly harbored no cruel streak like Bartholomew Smythe. Forever, to the end of her days, she would be grateful that Gabriel had been the man whom Bart had forced her to betray. There were some, no, many, who would have handed her over to the patriot executioner without a backward glance.

She managed to sleep a portion of the trip, despite her unease and the rumbling and creaking of the old wagon. Her rest was fitful, filled with hideous dreams full of dark, hulking shapes and endless gloomy corridors. Once, Bart Smythe's snarling image and hard fists came at her, frightening her awake.

Annie awoke from time to time, but was too drowsy to stay awake for long. She curled up again, this time with her head in Belinda's lap. Belinda tucked the coverlet around her shoulders, then leaned back against the grain sacks stacked behind them. She wondered what fate Gabriel had in store for them. They had ridden a long way. They must be heading north toward the upper end of Manhattan Island. She knew very little about the geography of the American colonies, only that Quebec and all of Canada lay quite far to the north.

Bartholomew had brought them to New York by ship because the overland route was perilous, both in terrain and danger from the wild red savages. Surely, Gabriel did not mean to take them into that hostile territory. She thought of his wife and daughter, and shivered to think of their fate.

After a time, her mind pricked by every kind of frightening possibility, she dozed again, until the wheels finally rolled to a stop.

Her eyes snapped open as the canvas was jerked off. A rush of crisp, moist air hit her in the face. She lunged up, slightly disoriented, and Annie complained sleepily at being disturbed. It was still dark outside.

Gabriel's voice came out of the night, ordering them out of the wagon. She obeyed, grabbing their bag and throwing it over the side before she climbed down and helped Annie do the same. They were near a river. She could hear the swift gushing of the current, and the rank fishy odor of the harbor filled her nostrils.

She jumped when Gabriel suddenly materialized at their side, scooping Annie up and carrying her off in his arms. Belinda reached for the valise and gathered up the quilts as she stumbled after him down a steep muddy embankment. She slipped once, and Gabriel caught her before she could fall. He held onto her arm firmly the rest of the way down to the riverbank.

There was no moon and no sign of the gray light of dawn, but she could make out the shape of a long, narrow canoe. Namasset already awaited them in the bow, and Gabriel lifted Annie into the middle, then picked up Belinda and swung her in behind her sister. He pushed off from the bank, then agilely leapt into the stern.

All had transpired in eerie silence, without even a splash of water to give their presence away. Both men dipped long paddles deep into the black water, joining together in an easy stroking rhythm that indicated they had worked in tandem many times before. The lightweight craft glided smoothly across the surface with hardly a ripple to mark its passing, and the soft rushing of the current was the only sound to be heard, whispering, rustling, haunting, like unhappy ghosts hovering over the cold black water.

Eleven

They were making extremely good time, much better than Gabriel had expected. In time his vision had adapted to a night so dark that it felt as if a black velvet blindfold pressed against his eyes. Over and over, he plunged his paddle deep into the water at the side of the canoe, creating swirling eddies that gurgled until they disappeared into the current.

Surprisingly, he was not particularly tired. Although he had been awake now for nearly thirty-six hours, he was used to this trip north to the mill farm that lay on the bank of the Bronx River. He had made the journey often throughout his lifetime, first as a young lad with his father, then with his faithful friend, Namasset. Since the war had commenced, at least once every week, he had secretly navigated up the East River until he eventually reached the mouth of the Bronx.

Usually, however, he traveled alone in the swift birchbark canoe. Never before had he thought to bring anyone else, not since Patsy and Jessie had died. He quickly locked that thought away. The truth was he probably shouldn't have this time, either. In front of him he could see the two Scott girls curled together in the bottom of the canoe. Poor little Annie had slept like the baby she was, as if being smuggled out of the city in the dead of night was a common occurrence for her. Who could say? With an enterprising spy like Belinda for a sister, maybe it was.

On the other hand, both she and Belinda had been through a great deal of tragedy in their young lives, more than either deserved. He shook his head and dug his paddle deeper. Once again he was letting his sympathy for their misfortunes color his good sense. Belinda had gotten to him. He couldn't stop thinking about her, which was not a good sign. There hadn't been a woman in years who had plagued his every waking moment, and he sure as hell didn't like it. He could be wrong about her. Maybe she wasn't such a greenhorn at spying; maybe she was good enough to worm herself into his affections the way she had. *Affections?* The realization hit him like a shock wave because for the first time he admitted his true feelings to himself.

Scowling fiercely, he paddled harder, inwardly cursing himself for a fool. He had thought her beautiful from the beginning, but had quickly explained that away to himself because of her resemblance to Patsy. But it was more than that. He wanted her, desired her in his bed, possibly in his life, and he'd known it from the first moment he had looked into her azure eyes. But he had ignored it because he knew better than to trust a woman like her. He still knew he should not.

Despite that distrust, he had gone against his own better judgment, and Namasset's, gone against Henri's advice concerning her, and brought her with him to a secret patriot safe house. He hoped to God he didn't live to regret that decision.

The sky was finally beginning to lighten, first in a dim, pearly glow above the treetops to the east, the faint early rays revealing the mist rolling in wispy shreds over the surface of the river.

Belinda had extricated herself from underneath the warm quilts where she had slept with Annie, and now sat silently staring at the foggy shoreline. He wondered if she was attempting to identify landmarks to lead Bart and his Tory regiment back to him. Deep in his gut, with the intuition he had grown to trust, he didn't think she'd do that. God help him if he was wrong.

In any case, there was little chance she could actually figure out where they had been or where they were going. She was English, new to the wilds north of New York, and his place on the Bronx River was almost as remote as the banks of the Ohio farther to the west. The majority of the British troops were garrisoned in New York and would remain there. Only roaming bands of Indians and loyal patriot militiamen with homesteads along the river would have reason to seek out his isolated mill farm. The march was too far, through hostile, tangled terrain impossible for an army on foot, and wildly surging river currents if they attacked by boat. The British would not stray so far without good cause and someone familiar with the area to guide them.

For almost an hour the light craft sped along, the rising sun beginning to burn off the river mists. He tried to harness any further thoughts about Belinda, rest his own mind when she burrowed under the patchwork quilts again and slept with her sister, warm and secure. So, if she was noting landmarks, she wasn't very diligent. The chirping of birds awakening and beginning to feed, began to filter out of the dense forest, trills and whistles that were loud and clear in the crisp, cold air.

They were well up the Bronx River now, and paddling was easier in the slower-flowing current than in the turmoil and crosscurrents in the East River and in and around New York harbor. They were getting close now. Anticipation began to blossom inside his breast, and he kept his eyes peeled on the river ahead, searching for the wide, angling bend that would take him into sight of his grandfather's log cabin and water-driven gristmill.

Much of his boyhood had been spent inside those sturdy log walls, the best days of his

youth. He had not taken easily to his father's
life of ship captains, bankers, and business asso-
ciates. Although he had learned the shipping in-
dustry well at his father's side, he had loved
this wilderness best, the stalking of deer with
Namasset and his tribesmen, the silent starry
firmament stretching out to infinity high above
softly whispering pine boughs. He had wanted
to share those same joys with Patsy and Jessie.

Raw unbridled pain caught him in the stomach as if he'd been clubbed there, and for one
awful instant, a moment in time burst like a
rocket in his conscience and revealed his family
the way the Mohawks had left them. His throat
lurched in a gag reflex, and he squeezed his eyes
shut, clenching his jaw until the dreadful images
of death dissolved. Sometimes it happened this
way, out of the blue, and he was hit by the horror until his hands shook. He had thought of it
even more often since Belinda had come into
his life. He brought out the paddle and held it
dripping across his knees. He pulled off his tricorne, shoved it into the river, then dumped the
frigid water over his head.

He welcomed the shock; it felt good and sent
the horrible memories slithering back into the
past where they belonged. He dragged both
palms down over his face, calming himself. It
wasn't unusual, this flashing glimpse of the
worst day of his life. Usually when it happened,
he was mentally and physically exhausted, as he
was now. Namasset never intruded, which was

one reason why Gabriel valued the man so much.

Feeling better, he wielded the paddle again, watching again for the mill house. The farm would come into sight any time now. His heart lifted when he saw the log structures in their clearing on the far bank of the river.

Bending to his task, thrusting with deeper strokes, he grinned at the new enthusiasm with which Namasset paddled. The Oneida was eager to see his wife and children. Namasset disliked Manhattan, and nearly everyone on it, and would be pleased indeed to learn Gabriel wanted him to stay at the mill farm to guard Belinda and her sister.

A wafting plume of blue hickory smoke rose from the massive stone chimney hugging the far end of the main cabin where Namasset's gentle wife would be preparing breakfast for their three strapping sons. They lived on the place now, in their own cabin just behind the mainhouse, having left the village of their tribe upriver. With Namasset often gone now on patriot errands, Willamette and her boys kept the mill house running smoothly and the cornfields tilled and harvested.

As they approached, Namasset's oldest son, Wynett, a lad of twelve years, appeared on the wide front veranda. Dressed in a fringed hunting shirt of tanned moose skin, and leather leggings and moccasins, he lazily stretched his arms high above his head, then turned and looked out over the river. When he saw them approaching, he gave a joyful shout that echoed far out over the water.

Namasset stopped his steady strokes and lifted his arm in a wide arc of greeting, then increased his effort tenfold as his boy ran down the steps and raced toward the log pilings at the landing. The shout roused Belinda, and she sat upright, rubbing her eyes with her fists like a small child.

Against his will, Gabriel watched her stretch, watched the white mobcap slide off, releasing long curling tresses that fell like black shiny silk over her shoulders, swinging down almost to her waist. When she used her outstretched fingers to comb through the tangles, he found himself wanting to grab the soft raven hair up in both his fists and bring it against his face. He averted his eyes and forced the idea out of his mind.

To his relief, Belinda tucked her hair back into her cap as she studied the log buildings they were rapidly approaching. He matched his paddle strokes to Namasset's and watched the two younger boys, Konoc and Timon, burst out the front door, followed by Willamette, who wiped her hands on her apron as she hurried after her excited children. Gabriel's attention drifted back to Belinda as she splashed water over her face and rolled her neck from side to side as if it hurt her. He winced inwardly at the bruise on the side of her face, now a dark purple, when she turned around to look at him.

Their gazes connected as if fused by lightning, and the corners of her mouth curved uncertainly. He turned away, keeping his expression cold and unresponsive, berating himself for finding her desirable even now, when she was swollen-eyed and bruised, her hair and clothes disheveled by a night spent cramped in the bottom of his canoe. His less than friendly attitude did not discourage her from asking a question, but her voice was tentative.

"Are you going to leave us here with these people?" She shielded her eyes against the bright sunlight that had finally burst over the horizon, nearly blinding them.

"Aye, you'll stay here under Namasset's guard until the war ends. You should thank me for the favor. Most men in my position would have had you thrown into irons."

Belinda stared hard at him, her chin rising a bare notch in a way he had seen of late, indicating a streak of stubbornness and pride she had not revealed often.

"I am grateful to you, Mr. Elliott, for all your kindnesses. I know full well that I do not deserve them."

Gabriel concentrated on angling the canoe alongside the rough log planks of the mill house landing. Namasset leapt lightly from the bow, embracing all his boys in a giant bear hug, then released them in order to enfold his beloved wife. He smiled and patted the roundness of her abdomen, for Willamette was to bear him another child in the spring. They spoke together rapidly in their own tongue, and Gabriel heard her asking about the two white girls as he climbed out, secured the canoe, then stretched out his hand to assist first Annie then Belinda onto the dock.

"I didn't know Namasset had a family," Belinda said, smiling at the happy reunion.

"We don't tell much to people we can't trust," he said sharply, in a tone more cutting than he had intended. She looked at him in surprise, and though he should have been embarrassed by his churlish remark, he could not seem to block his anger. He was furious with her for betraying him, and with himself for desiring her anyway.

"They're good people, so don't make trouble for them, understand me, Belinda?"

Again she showed a proud reaction to his scorn. Her spine stiffened visibly. "I know I am a prisoner here. I will cause your friends no hardship."

"Just do exactly what you're told."

Belinda nodded and put a protective arm around a sleepy, silent Annie, who, Namasset's youngest boy, a child of seven, eyed with not a little curiosity.

"Good day, Willamette." Gabriel greeted the Indian woman in her own language, one he had become proficient at many years ago. She smiled happily, no doubt more than pleased that she was to have her husband home full-time, as he had been before the war.

"It is good you come, Gabe," she answered in her soft voice. "All is well here. Monsieur Henri come at nightfall two suns ago. Others come from north to meet with him."

As she spoke, she scrutinized the newcomers, Belinda, in particular, but without comment, for he knew Willamette would not question his reasons for bringing them to his home.

"They are to stay here with you for a while," he explained in Oneida. "The oldest one is a British spy who came into my house to betray me. She cannot be trusted."

His revelations shocked Willamette—he could see that by the quick intake of her breath and the change in her usual placid expression. She stared fearfully at Belinda.

"Don't worry. She's not dangerous," he reassured her, though he wondered if that was completely true. "I brought her here so the British couldn't use her against us again. The little girl is her sister. Her name's Annie."

"Annie is sick?"

"She has been. She's better now." Gabriel wasn't surprised Willamette noticed signs of the child's ill health. She was known all along the river for her skills as a healing woman.

"Perhaps you can help her with your medicines."

"I will try, Gabe. And the bad one, she has been beaten?"

Gabriel nodded without explaining, glancing at Belinda, who had been listening intently to their rapid discourse as if trying to understand the guttural language.

"Go with Willamette, Belinda. She'll show you where you're to sleep."

"Does she speak the King's English at all?"

Her reference to George and the English Crown annoyed him. "Aye, well enough. You are not to leave the house without my permission. Obey me in that regard, and I won't have you locked inside your room."

"I give you my word that I will not."

He wanted to tell her how little that meant to him, but instead said nothing. When Belinda realized he was not going to reply, she took Annie's hand and followed Willamette up the grassy incline to the wide veranda of the main log cabin. Namasset and the boys followed.

Gabriel stayed on the dock and watched them go, feeling the guilt of robbing his blood brother of so many days and nights with his loved ones. Namasset had never complained; he hated the British even more than Gabriel did. Relieved to have Belinda out of his sight for a while, he headed toward the mill house.

The old mill wheel turned, creaking and lumbering, as it had since it had been constructed in 1760 by his grandfather as an supply outpost for the king's rural militia. Now it served as a sanctuary for subversive patriot activity against that same army. Today he was slated to meet with couriers down from Canada. He sometimes met the courier riders here with intelligence he had garnered from his network of agents, often receiving his own orders from General Washington.

The mill rose two stories, the main level reached by a flight of stairs leading into a large open room where the gigantic wheel revolved slowly with loud, laborious squeaking. Upstairs were storage rooms with burlap bags full of maize and wheat. The patriots used a secret room built at the surface of the river, reached only by a hidden trapdoor.

His grandfather had built it in case of Indian attack, with access to the water for hasty escapes. The safeguard had not been good enough to save Gabriel's own family. The thought came, hurt him, and was banished as he stepped down the ladder into the midst of his fellow American spies.

"Gabe, *mon Dieu*, I fear for you when you do not come on time."

Henri stood beside an old wooden table with a scarred top, one which had been there for as long as Gabriel could remember. Across the room a small printing press lay idle, but was often clacking off underground pamphlets with tidings of patriot victories.

Gabriel clasped his friend's hand and greeted the other conspirators with a nod. They were good men, one and all, had fought together since the beginning of the war. Both were of

French-Canadian descent, and distant cousins of Henri.

Erique, short, square-built with a swarthy skin, was as tough as nails, and looked it, with his matted black beard that hung nearly to his waist. He lived among the Indians inhabiting the banks of the St. Lawrence River and kept a close watch on British naval excursions between Quebec to Montreal. The other man was known to him only as Louis, and was an innkeeper in the lower city of Quebec, where British soldiers nightly toasted their king. It was Louis who began their discourse.

"I searched out the Greenleigh mansion as you requested, Monsieur Gabriel. The girl with black hair and the small child were maidservants in the kitchen. They came south several months ago with a man named Smythe."

"I found that out the hard way. He set them on me in my own house."

The Canadians looked concerned.

"I brought them here with me."

"Here?" Henri echoed quickly. "Do you think that wise?"

"I didn't know what else to do with them."

Henri searched Gabriel's face with the wisdom of an old and trusted friend, and Gabriel knew full well that Henri could probably guess the real reason he dragged them all the way up here. He had rarely been able to fool his friend, especially when it came to women, and he doubted if he would now.

Frowning, he sat down, not wanting to discuss Belinda.

"All right, men, let's get down to business. I have to return to Manhattan as soon as possible."

Within moments, he was engrossed in the task of poring over the hand-drawn maps showing the location of the British troop transports in the north. He memorized each detail so that he would be able to transfer it verbatim to the agents he was to meet two nights from now on Long Island. The information would then be carried to Philadelphia and southward, from one agent to the next, until it reached Charleston and all the loyal patriots fighting the war against the British.

Twelve

The stars glittered with spangled glory over the river as Belinda sat in the ancient cane-bottomed rocking chair she had found on the spacious, timbered veranda. This is a beautiful place to which Gabriel had brought them, she thought with an absurd rush of gratitude. Fighting her own overwhelming emotions, she gazed out over the darkness of the water, which seemed peaceful and serene, here so far away from the city.

Though she knew full well that she was his captive, guarded as a prisoner, an enemy, in this peaceful enclave she felt better than she had in a long time, relaxed, and even harder for her to understand, happy. In the hours since they had arrived, she had found the Indian family quite strange in appearance and manner. All spoke in broken English, but with more expertise than she had expected. They had been more than kind, under the circumstances.

The woman, Willamette, had served them baked wheat bread and thick slices of smoked turkey breast, then offered them the opportunity to bathe away the grit and grime of their all-night journey. Belinda had accepted with great pleasure, luxuriating in the deep wooden barrel that acted as a hip bath, hidden in a warm nook behind the chimney and shielded with hanging blankets for privacy. She had washed her hair and then scrubbed Annie from head to toe.

Her little sister had already won the hearts of all Namasset's sons, so much so in fact, that Willamette had graciously allowed Annie outside to spend most of the afternoon on the landing with the boys, learning how to hook perch from the swift stream.

Appreciative of the woman's kindness and aware that Namasset's wife was pregnant with another child, Belinda had immediately offered to help Willamette prepare supper. Although the Indian had nodded and handed her a clean linen apron, she had made no attempt to converse while they stood side by side, chopping turnips and yams for the pot of venison stew simmering on a tripod over the fire.

So as Belinda worked, she conjectured endlessly about this settlement so far up the river with the primeval forest encroaching on all sides to hide it from civilization—especially about what was going on inside the mill house. She knew Gabriel had gone there directly from the boat landing when they had arrived at dawn. Now the hour was late, shrouding the river with an inky curtain, and he had still not reappeared.

Had he already shoved off in the canoe again, without so much as a farewell?

She almost laughed at herself, so ridiculous was her wish to have him bid her a warm good-bye. Gabriel had made it clear, in no uncertain terms, that everything about her sickened him. He was contemptuous of her, and he had every reason to be. But still it hurt. She didn't want him to hate her. She found herself longing to see him again, frantic to explain to him why she had betrayed him.

Painful though it was, she admitted to herself that she didn't want him to think ill of her. She didn't want him to go away. She didn't want him to look at her with disgust in his dark blue eyes. And that was the reason she was still up so late, she admitted at last. She was waiting for him to appear, though now her eyes were red-rimmed with fatigue and her muscles aching to stretch out for sleep.

Annie was fast asleep, snuggled deep in the soft feather mattress in her own bedchamber on the second story. Belinda had been given her own small room as well, cozy and comfortable under the eaves, for the first time since they had lost their house in London. Willamette had long since herded her family into the cabin they occupied behind the main house. They had all been so happy to see Namasset. They had gathered around him and hung onto his arms as she and Annie had done years ago when their father had come home from his printer's shop.

Sighing, gripped by weepy nostalgia that knifed deep into her heart, she leaned her head against the back of the chair. How strange life had turned out for them. Two years ago when she was secure and happy in a fine house in London, how could she have predicted all these terrible and bizarre things that had happened to them?

Life was so uncertain, like some mysterious chess game that moved people here and there like pawns, tossing Annie and her onto a different continent, into the midst of a bloody war. In a short space of time she had gone from respectable apprentice to serving wench to unwilling spy to captive enemy.

When she heard footsteps approaching the house, crackling through the layers of fallen leaves, she sat up. Tense and alert, her eyes scanned the pitch blackness. The mill farm lay so far out in the wilderness. Red savages could be lurking anywhere, not peaceable ones like Namasset and Willamette, but the others, the murderers who carried sharp hatchets and knives, the ones who had killed Gabriel's wife and child.

To her relief, followed swiftly by a warm flood of pleasure, it was Gabriel who stepped into view on the footpath leading to the mill. A candle lantern swung from his hand, throwing erratic shadows across the lean planes and contours of his handsome face. When he saw her on the veranda, he stopped at the bottom of the steps. He did not look pleased to see her.

"Why aren't you in bed?" His voice was curt.

"I tried, but I couldn't sleep." She wondered if he knew she was lying. He usually did somehow, and his keen eyes always seemed able to pierce through her. They stared at each other for a moment until the silence felt heavy and hard around them as if four walls were pressing in on them. She felt an overwhelming desire to say something, anything, for fear that he would move past her, into the house, out of her life forever.

"Willamette left food for you warming on the hearth. Are you hungry enough to eat?"

She sounded so hopeful that he was hungry, she knew she did, and so eager to please him that she felt hot embarrassment rising into her face. Even she could hear the almost desperate appeal in her voice.

"I guess so."

"I'll fetch it for you," she offered, rising quickly and hurrying inside before he could deny her that privilege.

The house was cloaked in dark shadows, for Willamette had left only a single tin lantern burning in the front hall. She stopped at the door leading into the big kitchen to make sure he was following. He stopped, too, looking quizzically at her.

Pleased, she rushed on, eager to do something good for him, anything to make up for her many crimes against him. She set about ladling the thick, flavorful deer meat and vegetables into a wooden trencher, then poured a good portion of ale into one of the pewter mugs she found hanging over the fireplace. While he pulled out a chair and sat down at the long harvest table, she sliced a large chunk of Willamette's bread and placed the bread board on the table beside his plate.

He said not a word to her, spooning up the stew as if she were not there. He didn't look at her either, and she perched on a backless bench directly across from him and rehearsed in her mind all the things she had waited up to tell him. After some time had passed while she struggled to work up the courage to begin, she finally blurted out her apology in one long, breathless stream.

"I'm so sorry, Gabriel, please believe me. I never wanted to tell you lies, or hurt you in any way. All I wanted was to be free again." She stopped, flushing scarlet when he stopped eating and stared across the table at her. She rushed on, desperate to make him understand. "You don't know how it feels to lose your freedom and have to do whatever you are told, to have to work until you're exhausted, until your fingers are raw and your back aches until you can't straighten up, and to have to obey masters, men you detest, terrible men who want to, who try to take . . ."

She heard her voice fail, but fought against

the closing sensation as a huge lump knotted at the base of her throat. He had already freed her from those indignities, and she had been the one who had nearly destroyed him. She jumped up and turned her face away so he wouldn't see the tears filling her eyes. She stared down into the banked logs, then buried her face inside her cupped palms, trying to get a grip on herself.

Silent sobs shook through her, but she would not let them escape for him to hear. She clutched her arms tightly around herself, fighting to contain the flood of grief she had held so tightly within since her father had died in her arms aboard that filthy, horrible ship, penniless, his body broken and full of agony.

Every day since, every minute, she had kept her emotions reined with rigid control, while everything else in her life spun totally out of control. But this night she was tired beyond belief, upset, her feelings in a turmoil and stifled. Buried emotions gushed up like a burning geyser and came out in a rush of tears that appalled her. She turned to flee the room, unwilling to make such a humiliating spectacle of herself in front of a man who hated her.

She ran squarely into the solid wall of Gabriel's chest. Shocked that he had come up behind her without her knowing, she started to back away, but his arms encircled her, immobilizing her. She did not fight, had no desire to struggle when he enveloped her in a firm embrace. She could not speak, but she clung to him, leaned against him, and tried to absorb some of his immense strength.

It had been so long since she had been comforted or touched kindly by another adult. No one but Annie had shared her grief, her pain, and fears. She buried her face against the soft leather fabric of his vest and gripped her arms tightly around his waist. She never wanted to let go.

"Don't cry, Belinda." His whispered entreaty fanned the top of her hair. "You're safe here."

"I'm so sorry to weep like this, truly I am," she blubbered out through her streaming tears, her words nearly inaudible. "Don't you see? I don't care a whit about your war. I never wanted to work for Bart, especially after we came to your house and I saw how kind you were. You were so nice to us, and now you've brought us here to live in this beautiful place, instead of throwing us in prison as you should have."

She felt his hand leave her shoulder and tangle in her hair. He forced her face up, wet now with distressed tears, and she bit off another sob as their eyes met and connected in the way that always sent a jolt surging through her, for it seemed he looked so deeply into her soul, where all her secrets lay bare, that he knew everything about her.

Then his mouth was on hers, and her eyes closed of their own accord, her lips softening instinctively against his kiss. As if from somewhere far outside her body, she felt his hands holding her upper arms, his fingers gripping her hard. His mouth was ravaging over hers now— insistently, hungrily, desperately—trapping her breath in her throat.

His eagerness was astonishing to her, and his left arm came up around her waist and held her tightly as he bent her backward, forcing her lips open. His tongue plunged into the depths of her mouth, shocking her, numbing her until her own heartbeat tripled to thunder and her inexperienced body flamed up with searing, unbridled response.

She pressed herself against him, wanting desperately for his kisses to continue. She put her hands around his neck to keep his mouth upon hers and heard his muffled groan before he lifted her feet clear off the floor, her body pressed flat against his chest, his fingers pulling off her mobcap, then twisting through the softness of her hair. She gasped weakly for breath when his mouth finally left hers, moaning when hot male lips found the cording at the side of her throat, then the sensitive hollow beneath her ear, eliciting shivers that raced through her core and down her arms and legs.

His mouth found hers again, and she was lost, unable to think of anything, unable to fathom the consequences of what was happening between them, and so innocent of a man's needs that the hot and cold sensations pebbling her flesh seemed unreal, as if she were in some lovely, incomprehensible dream.

Then he was no longer there, his warmth and passion gone in the wink of an eye. She blinked, then tottered on her feet, not understanding what had happened until she opened her eyes and saw him standing away from her. He was tunneling his fingers through his blond hair, muttering something low and indistinguishable under his breath. She reached out and put her hand against the warm stones of the fireplace, so shaky she felt she might fall. Devastated by her internal longings, her mouth swollen by his hard, demanding kisses, her lips still throbbing and warm, her eyes dreamy and heavy-lidded from her first experience with passion, she could only stare up at him in confusion.

"I can't do this," he muttered, more to himself than to her, but his words were hoarse, tortured, and she saw how the muscles of his cheek flexed and jumped as he clenched his jaw.

Belinda tried to think straight, tried to comprehend what she had done to make him pull away in anger.

"Get the hell away from me," he said then, low, his tone harsh and threatening. "Do you hear me, Belinda, leave me alone. I want nothing to do with you."

Belinda waited no longer, but fled up the steps and away from him, feeling humiliated, degraded, but still trembling all over, her body on fire from the intimate touch of his hands and mouth.

Thirteen

Gabriel had left the mill farm early the morning after he had grabbed Belinda like some adolescent swain and had stayed away from the Bronx River for well over a month. Now he was on his way back there, and as he allowed his mount free rein to pick a path down the icy, rock-strewn incline that led through the woods to the back of the cabin, he already regretted his decision to return. Early the day before he had ridden north for a rendezvous near the Harlem River, and since he was so close to the farm had decided to ride on and make sure all was well.

The truth was he should have continued his weekly visits as before, and could have easily enough if he hadn't been so eager to avoid contact with Belinda Scott. He'd sent Henri in his stead, who had reported all was in order, but Gabriel's suspicions had risen again when Henri told him that Belinda had offered her printing and engraving skills to the patriots. A legitimate offer to help? he wondered, or was it just another tactic to garner information? He grimaced and jerked up his collar to ward off the frigid wind invading the back of his neck.

The low-hanging, leaden clouds humped together overhead like a herd of cowering bison. Snow had been threatening since early afternoon, and now it had begun to flurry, with hard gusts blowing straight into his face. He hoped to God the snow wouldn't be heavy. He had not planned to stay but overnight. He flushed, thinking about the way he had manhandled Belinda that night by the fire.

A fire had been inside him, that was for damned sure, and it still was. He grimaced, ruing the day he had ever laid eyes on her. She had cost him time and trouble he didn't need and didn't want, and still, though it chagrined him no end, he was looking forward to seeing her again. What a fool he was where she was concerned.

The snow began to fall harder, in huge, spinning flakes that had already blanketed the ground with a thin layer of white. The temperature had plummeted in the last hour. Winter had arrived, and snow would probably cover the ground until the spring thaw. A harsh winter was predicted and such a prospect did not bode well for the under-equipped, Continental army suffering in their ragged uniforms and worn-out leather boots.

Gabriel ducked his head away from the biting wind and pressed on, thinking he was lucky to have gotten this far before the weather had turned so bad. As he descended the hill edging Beaver Pond, he saw a thin crust of ice had begun to form across its surface. Before long Namasset's boys would be eagerly strapping on their skates, but Willamette would have to give up that wintry sport she enjoyed so thoroughly until after the baby was born, perhaps a girl-child this time. An image of his daughter rose, wavery and wraithlike in the misty fringes of his memory. He jutted his jaw and forced Jessie's image away. Snow and ice always brought the tragedy back. Gabriel had hated winter since that long-ago day when he had found his massacred family.

Stinging bits of sleet hit him in the face, reddening his cheeks. His breath condensed in the air, hanging in a frosty cloud with each exhalation. Namasset would have built up the fire to a roaring blaze, and Willamette would have something hot and tasty boiling in her cook pot. He urged his horse onward, feeling frozen to the bone and ready to reach a warm haven, even if Belinda was there. Or was it *because* she was there? he asked himself with a disgusted frown.

As he reached the cleared cornfields forming the back perimeter of the farm, Namasset stepped out from behind the barn. Gabriel was not surprised the Oneida had known he was coming. Namasset was always vigilant, protecting his family at the mill.

Gabriel walked his horse to the barn, smiling

at his friend as he dismounted and stretched his stiff body.

"Welcome, Gabe."

"Good to be back."

They clasped right wrists as they had greeted each another since they had become blood brothers as boys.

"Any trouble since Henri left?" Gabriel asked, pulling his horse by the reins into the sheltering warmth of the barn. The familiar scent of the interior assailed him—hay, manure, horseflesh, leather. He unbuckled the girth and pulled off the saddle, then slung it over the rail of the nearest stall.

Namasset grasped a handful of straw and wiped the ice and snow off the horse's wet hide. "Your woman gave us no trouble."

"Henri said she was behaving herself."

Namasset nodded. "She work hard. Do much to help Willamette."

Belinda's industriousness did not surprise Gabe. She had never been lazy, nor one to shirk her duties, but, unfortunately, that included spying.

The Indian shook his head. "She cook, talk to boys. They like the little one. Annie."

Gabriel was secretly pleased to hear they had settled in as well as they had, but niggling doubts about Belinda's trustworthiness still ate at him as he followed Namasset the short distance to the main cabin.

Inside the kitchen they found the women and

children gathered around the warmth of the
hearth fire. Belinda sat in the cane rocker that
was usually kept outside on the veranda, with
all the children on the floor around her. It appeared she had been reading a story, for she
held a book in her lap.

When she saw him with Namasset, however,
she jumped to her feet, the forgotten book dropping to the floor with a thud. Everyone else
turned to see what had disturbed her, and when
the boys saw Gabriel, they came running with
glad greetings and huge grins.

Willamette smiled from where she sat at the
long, planked table, her hands covered with
flour as she kneaded a crock of bread dough.

Gabriel said hello to her, then glanced back at
Belinda. Her face was frozen in an expression
that looked more scared than anything else. That
bothered him. Why should she be afraid of him?
He hadn't hurt her, had he?

Taking off his hat, he knocked the snow from
it, then nodded a polite greeting to Belinda. Her
reaction was immediate. Pure relief, easy for
him to read, smoothed away the wariness on
her face, and she flashed him one of the most
dazzling smiles he had ever seen. It left him
staring at her for several seconds before he
forced his gaze away, distinctly embarrassed.
Even more humiliating, he felt his loins reacting,
found himself hardening with desire to pull her
slender warm body against him again. Good
God, he had been celibate too long this time.

"Are you here for long, Gabe?" Wynett asked eagerly as Gabe took off his heavy fur-lined cloak. "Will you stay for a deer hunt?"

"Depends on the weather, I reckon."

Gabriel pulled off his deer hide gloves and hung his tricorne up beside the door as the younger boys gathered around, regaling him with tales of the giant buck Wynett had bagged with his bow several days before.

A sidelong glance told him that Belinda had moved now and was seated on the overstuffed horsehair sofa facing the fire, one covered with the hide of a bear Gabe had shot and skinned out when he was eleven. She had picked up a stack of papers and had begun to draw. Gabriel watched for a moment, wondering what she was doing.

Namasset called for his boys to bundle up and help him round up the cattle to bring into the barn, and Willamette offered Gabriel a piece of fresh-baked apple cobbler, which he declined. He took instead the mug of steaming mulled cider she brought to him, but Annie ran over and asked for a piece of the fruit pastry. He carried his drink across the room and sat down in an armchair directly across from Belinda. Annie stayed with Willamette at the table, digging with relish into a plate of the cobbler.

Though they sat within feet of each other now, Belinda did not initiate conversation, in fact would not even look at him. She seemed calm enough, however, her face serene. Then his gaze fell upon her hands, which trembled noticeably as she shaded her picture with a small lump of charcoal.

Seeking to alleviate her uneasiness, though he had sworn to himself all the way there that he would show her no attention whatsoever, Gabriel asked, "What are you drawing, Belinda?"

"Nothing, really. Just a picture."

"Did your father teach you to draw?"

He wanted to know more about her past, true, but this polite chitchat seemed absurd when all he could think about was the way he'd held her and kissed her the last time they were together. By the high spots of scarlet color on her cheeks, he had a feeling she was thinking about the same thing.

Her long curls were bound at her nape with a red ribbon, no mobcap in sight, but as she shook her head, one strand escaped its anchor and lay in a tendril across her forehead.

"Not really. Drawing's just a hobby."

Her last remark was followed by an incredibly awkward silence while he considered the appropriateness of formally apologizing to her for grabbing her like some pillaging Viking beast. He had planned to do so, but he found himself reluctant, embarrassed that he, at his age and place in life, had lost control enough to allow something like that to happen. Instead, he remained with the more innocuous subject they were already pursuing.

"May I see them?"

She seemed mightily startled by his request. She colored slightly. "I'd rather you didn't. They're not very good. I really haven't had time to finish them to my liking."

"I don't mind. I'd like to look at them."

Her obvious reluctance began to make him suspicious, as did the way she put one sheet of parchment aside before handing him the rest of her work. Wondering what she was trying to hide, and why, he glanced down at the picture on top and saw it was an etching of the river flowing alongside the mill wheel. He found her work surprisingly good. He slid it underneath the stack and stared down at the second, a beautifully executed drawing of the big barn cat that lived in the loft. She was surrounded by her new litter of six kittens.

"You're very talented," he observed when he found the next picture was a lifelike portrait of Willamette sitting outside on the veranda steps.

Belinda blushed, but looked immensely pleased with his compliment, though he realized she was trying to hide her reaction. Gabriel glanced pointedly at the one she had placed aside.

"What about that one?"

She registered guilt, so openly that he marveled at how transparent her face could be. She had never learned to mask her emotions. That's why she was such a godawful liar. And she was lying when she answered, her voice too nervous and quick.

"I'd rather you didn't. It's not finished." She snatched it up and actually hid it behind her back.

"I really want to see it," he insisted firmly, glancing back at Willamette, who had looked up when his tone had become harder. After another moment's hesitation, Belinda acquiesced and handed it to him, albeit reluctantly.

The moment he saw the highly intricate drawing he knew exactly why she had not wanted to show it to him. The scene depicted the mill farm, in precise detail, every building, every window. She had even drawn his own likeness on the face of the man sitting in a canoe alongside the boat landing. Anger ripped through him, for there was only one reason to make such a drawing then hide it from him.

"I suppose this is for your friend, Bart?" Tight-jawed and narrow-eyed, he leveled an accusing gaze upon her. "To show him exactly which farm along the river is used by the patriots? How do you intend to get it to him, Belinda? Have you already bribed one of my couriers to take it downriver?"

Her face blanched, slowly assuming the gray color of cold ashes. While he watched, furious over what he believed to be another betrayal, he could see her own anger reveal itself in a crimson tide that rose slowly up her neck to darken her face.

"Is that what you think?" she demanded

tightly, bridling with what appeared to be righteous indignation.

"Why the hell else would you make a detailed sketch of this place, then hide it from me?"

She had come to her feet now, trembling, her fists balled at her sides.

"Aye, why else would I? There is no other reason, is there?"

Before he knew what she was about, she snatched the paper from his hand and flung it onto the flaming logs. "There," she cried contemptuously, "and we had better burn the rest of my drawings as well. Bart might recognize your cat, too, you know, and have you arrested!"

She sent all her sketches hurling into the fireplace, then glared fiercely at him before she turned and stalked stiffly from the room, her head held high.

Gabriel stood still, stunned by the audacity of her outrage, and thinking she had certainly shed any shyness she used to show around him. Irked that he was the one feeling a streak of guilt, he scowled and braced his fists on his hips. He stared down at the grate and watched the flames eat through the fragile paper until it all curled and blackened.

"Mistress Bee work many suns on those pictures," Willamette informed him quietly. But he heard the uncharacteristic disapproval in her voice, loud and clear.

"Aye, I daresay she did. The Tories would pay well for finding our safe houses."

Namasset's wife shook her head, making her long braids swing. "She make pictures for Annie and boys for Christmas present. The one she hide, she do for you, Gabe."

Gabriel stared at her for a long moment, having forgotten all about Christmas. Other than attending a ball or two, he hadn't celebrated the holiday for years, not since Patsy had died. He looked back at the blazing logs, but Belinda's fine drawings had long since turned to ash.

Fourteen

The snowstorm continued unabated throughout the night, with howling winds and raging sleet, transforming itself into a full-fledged blizzard before roaring off northward toward the next valley. In its wake was left a sparkling landscape shrouded with hump-backed mountains of snow and great sloping drifts mounding magnificently against the cabins and barn like rolling ocean waves. Gigantic icicles hung from the eaves, and the paddle wheel at the mill stood still in a frozen tableau, icy spouts of water spilling onto each descending rung like a milliner's display of white lace jabots.

Belinda awakened to behold a winter wonderland the likes of which she had never seen before, the great forest tracts unblemished by ugly soot from coal-fed fires that dirtied the narrow, crowded streets of London with unsightly grime. No horse-drawn sleighs or sliding carriages turned the pristine snow to slushy black mire, and Belinda felt she must be witnessing the most beautiful vision on earth.

Wrapping herself in a heavy quilted robe, she tiptoed next door to her sister's room. Annie awoke with a start when Belinda crept into her bed, but soon caught sight of the snow on the windowpanes. She ran to the window and pressed her small nose against cold glass frosted with wonderfully intricate designs made by ice crystals. She squealed with delight when she saw the glittering white ground.

Belinda shivered from the chill, but was glad she had none of the chores to perform for the master of the house, which had been expected of her every other morning before Gabriel had brought her here. She snuggled deeper into the soft feather ticking, not prepared to leave her snug nest quite yet. She had suffered a restless night, lying awake well into the early morning hours and trying to come to terms with her anger over Gabriel's unfair accusations.

On the other hand, she knew full well that she had no right whatsoever to harbor such self-righteous outrage. Why should Gabe ever trust her again? She had injured him in the most underhanded fashion. But she had taken encouragement when he had decided not to jail her, instead transporting her to a place that clearly held a special meaning in his life. She had been desperately trying to make things up to him by making herself useful to his friends.

And then there was the incident in the kitchen. Never in her life had she felt the way she had when Gabriel held her. His mouth had been so hot and forceful, his body so hard and strong. A fluttering quiver of desire gripped her belly and spiraled lower into the core of her womanhood.

It wasn't as if she had not been courted by gentlemen callers in London when she had come of marriageable age. Several suitors had even stolen chaste kisses underneath the garden trellis, but none had clutched her with such urgency, with the male passion that Gabriel had exhibited and that she found so exciting and frightening. She wanted to experience it again. She wanted him to kiss her and teach her all the secrets she longed to know. She wanted him to love her, she admitted sadly, but now he was so full of scorn and resentment she wasn't sure he ever could.

"Take me outside, Bee," Annie was begging from where she perched on the frosty windowsill. "Please, please, Bee? Come and look, Konoc and Timon are making balls of snow and throwing them at Wynett!"

"Oh no, Annie, it's much too early, and too cold to go out," she resisted, just now growing warm again. "Besides, the boys must do their morning chores before they can play with you. Come back to bed and snuggle up with me."

Annie came dancing back across the cold, carpetless wood floor, and Belinda lifted the edge of the downy coverlet to welcome her, then gathered her warm little body in tightly against her. She groaned, however, when Annie thrust ice-cold feet against her bare calves.

"Oh, Annie, quit! Your toes feel like icicles! Let's stay in today and read by the fire."

"No, no, please, Bee, we can put on lots of clothes and wear those long brown leggings with beads on the fringe like Willamette's. I wanna go out 'cuz Timon told me he'd teach me to skate on the pond. You skate real good, too, and can turn around on your toes, 'member?" She sobered and captured Belinda's eyes. " 'Member when Papa used to take us out to the park after the lake got ice on it?"

"Yes, darling, I remember it well." Too well, she decided, nostalgic for those more happy times when she'd glided and weaved on her curved blades, in and out among other velvet-caped ladies and gentlemen, her hands warmed in a furry white muff. She had loved it, had gone skating at every opportunity. The cold air and scrape and swoosh of flying blades had made her feel free and exhilarated.

"Please, Bee, pretty please. I wanna go so much!"

Belinda had to smile when her baby sister held her lips in a childish pout, but Annie looked so healthy and happy now with flushed cheeks and bright eyes. The purple half-moon smudges underneath her eyes had disappeared, and her chest had long been completely clear of congestion. The quiet weeks they'd spent here on the river, deep in the wild American forest, in the clean healthy air, had been good for both of them. No doubt the bizarre-tasting remedies Willamette fed to Annie each night before bed—peculiar concoctions made from all sorts of dried roots and crushed flowers petals—certainly appeared to help Annie regain her energy and high spirits.

"Timon told me they have lots of skates and snowshoes hangin' up in the barn loft. He wants me to go 'cuz he likes me."

Belinda laughed and lightly tapped Annie's turned-up nose with her forefinger. "Everybody loves you 'cuz you're as sweet as honey and molasses."

"I'm hungry," was Annie's immediate response, one quite wonderful to Belinda's ears when she remembered how she used to have to coax the little girl to eat anything at all.

"I want to eat a hundred of Willamette's skinny griddle cakes!"

"A hundred? That's an awful lot."

"Then you can have one," Annie offered generously.

"All right, sweetheart, but we'll wait until the sun is fully up before we go to the pond."

"Hurry, hurry, let's get on those leggings!"

Belinda reluctantly followed the boisterous child out from under the piles of thick quilts and handwoven red-and-black plaid wool blankets, shivering from head to toe as she hurriedly broke the ice in the pitcher and washed her face. She would bathe better downstairs in warm water, she thought as she rapidly donned her shift and pantalettes. As she buttoned up her heaviest wool gown, she envied Willamette her warm rawhide tunic and long skirt with rows of fringe, and especially the tight leggings that covered her legs.

Perhaps Annie's idea about borrowing the warm Indian garments wasn't such a bad idea, especially if they went skating. And she hoped they did before she met up with Gabe again. Though her own anger was thoroughly spent, she did not look forward to facing him. His resentment and suspicion still burned strong. He had made that clear enough.

As it turned out, she had no opportunity to run into Gabriel that morning, for he had left before dawn with Namasset to run the trapline along the creek above the farm. She and Annie breakfasted with Willamette and her brood by the warmth of the huge fireplace. Griddlecakes were indeed their fare, and Annie did manage six, an unbelievable number for such a small child, though Belinda heartily enjoyed four of them herself.

The boys did not finish their barnyard duties until early afternoon when the sun shone with unrivaled brilliance, transforming the snow into a vast carpet of sparkling diamond dust.

Once outside the cabin she was glad she had agreed to go with the children, even more pleased that Willamette had found Oneida attire that fit both of them. She laughed softly at her own clumsiness as she clomped along, trying to manipulate the gigantic snowshoes woven from river reeds and which the Indians used to walk atop the deep snow drifts.

Willamette was relegated to remain home and tend the fire, but her children knew the trail to the pond very well. For a quarter of an hour they tramped along, leaving a wide swath of peculiar tracks on the glittering mantle of snow beneath huge bare-branched oaks and syca- mores. In time a small L-shaped pond appeared before them, the icy surface shining like a pol- ished white-blue mirror.

"Be sure to test the ice before you go out too far, Wynett," she called to the oldest boy as he ran out onto the pond. As she sat down on a log and helped strap onto Annie's moccasins the blades that she had borrowed from eight-year- old Konoc, Wynett yelled ecstatically that the pond was frozen solid.

Belinda didn't doubt it, shivering under the cold wind against her cheeks as she put on the skates lent to her by the middle boy, Timon, who at ten was more her size. She hardly felt the cold elsewhere, however, genuinely amazed at how warm she remained in Willamette's deer hide garments—certainly more so than in her own drafty skirts and bodice. And the knee-high leggings and moccasins kept her feet dryer than her leather slippers ever could.

She wondered if Gabe had worn Indian attire that morning to keep him warm. She day- dreamed momentarily about how rugged and handsome he would look in them, then shook the images of him out of her mind. Any personal relationship between them was impossible. He had made that decision. She didn't want to think about it. She would concentrate on having fun with the children and recall better times and better places, though she had to admit she could think of few more lovely places than this beautiful wooded sanctuary far up the Bronx River.

"Don't forget, Annie, you have to hold your ankles stiff and straight."

She couldn't help but chuckle as the little girl struggled across the ice on ankles that wobbled like wet noodles. Stepping onto the ice herself, a few smooth strokes took her sliding up to Annie's side. She held her sister's arm and supported her as best she could as they clomped jerkily onward. The three boys whooped and hooted with fierce war cries as they spun and cavorted and knocked each other down with their exuberant, freewheeling maneuvers.

The physical exertion was good for Belinda, too, despite the freezing wind that invaded her lungs and made her chest burn. Before long, Annie, doing considerably well for her first time, was trudging along stiff-legged, her cold-reddened face set in severe concentration.

Belinda let Annie practice on her own and took a few turns around the ice herself. She twirled and spun with the familiar shushing sound of blades cutting through ice each time she brought herself to an abrupt standstill. With all her travails in the past few years, she had almost forgotten how much she loved to skate. Actually, she loved winter, everything about it, especially the crisp, cold air and crystal-clear blue sky.

"Bee," Wynett shouted from far across the pond where the ice curved around a small snow-covered rise. "We brought hooks so we could fish through the ice. Down there, by the stump!" He stretched out his arm and pointed his forefinger at a huge stump protruding from the ice, not too far from a thicket of sycamores lining the shore.

She nodded, grabbing both Annie's hands in hers, as the three boys skated away to catch their supper. She skated backward, weaving her skates back and forth to propel her along, occasionally glancing over her shoulder to watch the boys. They were on their knees, using a hatchet to chop a hole near the base of the stump. Did they plan to sit on it while they fished? she wondered, returning her attention to her sister when Annie slipped and landed hard on her padded bottom.

Time flew by as she and Annie laughed and played in a way they hadn't done in a very long time. Wynett and his brothers had long since created a hole in the ice and sat like a trio of motionless statues on their knees around it, patiently holding the end of strings while their baited hooks enticed fish swimming below the surface.

She had never seen anyone catch fish in such a way and watched with interest, though she wondered if they ever caught anything sprawled so long atop ice, other than nasty head colds.

After a time Annie grew tired, and Belinda was helping her off with her skates when an awful yell split the quiet afternoon. She jerked around, shocked when she saw only two boys standing beside the hole. Appalled, she knew at once what had happened, and horror filled her so fast she could barely breathe.

"Stay here, Annie, do you hear? Don't you dare move! And don't get on the ice until I come back!"

Annie nodded, her cinnamon brown eyes wide with fright, as Belinda left her and flew across the ice. She found with sinking heart that it was Konoc, the little one, who had slid off into the frigid water. He was flailing his arms helplessly at the edge of the hole, causing the ice to crack more and break off in short, jagged chunks in his hands each time he grabbed hold. She slid to a stop a short distance away, alarmed at how close the other two boys were to the breaking ice. She could hear it crackling and snapping with Konoc's frantic fight to stay afloat.

"Get back, Wynett!" she cried harshly. "The ice is splitting under your feet! Go get your father, quick, quick! Go, Wynett, run as fast as you can!"

The boy hesitated, looking back at his little brother, then skated for the far side with all his strength, his arms pumping hard to gain momentum. Timon began to wail loudly in his own tongue when Konoc's splashing stopped. "Get back, Timon!" she cried, looking around desperately. "Konoc, Konoc, don't give up! Here—" She jerked off the heavy wool coat she had on over her clothes and flung one end out over the ice toward the boy. "Catch hold . . . try to catch the end, Konoc!"

The child tried desperately to reach it, but it was too far out of his grasp. To Belinda's horror, he began to slip back away from her and slowly sank beneath the surface. She did not hesitate, but leapt in feet first. The sudden plunge into the icy water shocked her system to a standstill and nearly stopped her heart.

She gasped for breath and struggled toward where the child had been thrashing. Frantically, she groped beneath the dark water until her fingers touched something solid. She grasped his coat and jerked him up with all her strength. Then he was out, coughing and sputtering, and spitting up water. Somehow she managed to get under him with her arms and made a desperate attempt to boost him atop the frozen tree stump. She finally managed it, and as he lay there motionlessly on his belly, Belinda stretched her arms around his legs, clutching her fingers together to hold him in place.

"Don't move, Konoc. Just lie still. Wynett's gone for your father and Gabe. They'll get us out." She turned to Timon and found him kneeling on the ice a few yards away, his eyes huge and round. When another crack sounded, she clung tighter to Konoc, her legs already so numb with cold she could barely feel them.

"Take Annie home, Timon, and get your mother and tell her to bring a rope. I'll hold on to Konoc until you get back! But hurry, you must hurry!"

The boy obeyed without delay, and Belinda tried to reassure Konoc, who hung precariously across the trunk. He was whimpering and shivering so hard she almost lost her grip. She locked her fingers tighter, praying the men would get there soon.

Fifteen

Gabriel was about a mile up the winding creek bed when he first heard a sound over the loud gurgling of the swift-running water. He straightened from where he had gone down on one knee to reset a sprung trap at the edge of the stream. Namasset stopped skinning the beaver he had just retrieved from the basket, long knife poised in his hand.

At first neither man could pinpoint exactly from where the shouts were coming. Gabriel scanned the terrain between the creek and the mill and saw only black tree trunks in stark silhouette against white snow. A second later he caught a movement out of the corners of his eyes and swiveled quickly to gaze downstream. Wynett was running full speed up the shallows toward them, his feet flying, his face contorted with effort. Gabriel dropped the reed-woven trap, but Namasset was already splashing down the creek to meet his son.

By the age of twelve a young Oneida brave like Wynett did not easily show fear, but at the moment the look on his face was frozen terror. Something extremely bad had happened. Gabriel wasn't prepared for just how awful it was.

"Konoc went through the ice!" Wynett was using his own language, yelling at the top of his lungs. "We can't get to him! The ice is broken all around him."

Namasset grabbed the boy's shoulders to calm him. "Where is he?"

"The pond," Wynett panted out in hard rasping breaths. He bent over and held his stomach while trying to catch his breath. "We . . . were ice fishing . . . by the old stump . . . and he fell in . . ."

Namasset wasted no more time on words, taking only an instant to strap on his snowshoes before taking off at a run through the woods in the direction of the pond. Gabriel snatched up his musket and thrust his hatchet into its leather sheath at his waist. Then he was loping along in Namasset's wake, both moving as fast as they could on their unwieldly snowshoes. But without them they would sink to their waists in the deep drifts before managing to travel even three feet.

The shortest path to the pond lay along the crest of a hill that eventually sloped down to the water. They fought their way up the incline, struggling for stability on the slippery, ice-glazed snow. Once atop the ridge, Namasset slipped and nearly fell, but managed to right himself and take off down the other side.

Gabriel kept pace, but a quick backward glance told him Wynett had fallen far behind. Without warning Jessie's little face welled up in his mind, and he saw her eyes, frozen, wide open, staring at him as if asking why. His gut tightened, and he prayed to God Namasset wouldn't have to see Konoc look that way.

After what seemed a year of running as fast as they could along the high point of the hill, they burst out onto a rock bluff overlooking the pond. A great silence lay over the scene, no movement, no screams for help piercing the air. He found the broken part of the ice immediately, and his heart came up into his throat.

Little Konoc was out of immediate danger, his small body stretched out over a narrow stump rising from the water about twenty feet off the bank. But, oh God, Belinda was the one in the water, holding on to the stump for dear life with only her head showing among bobbing chunks of ice. How long had she been submerged like that? She could hold on only so long in such frigid water.

Then he was half sliding, half falling down the snow to the edge of the pond. He stepped out onto the ice, heard it crackle, and saw a fissure run like a jagged bolt of lightning out toward the middle. Another step, and he would go in with them. Namasset was calling his son's name, and then Gabriel heard Konoc's frightened sobs. But Belinda was silent. Fear gripped him and revealed itself in the shrillness of his cry.

"Belinda! Can you hear me?"

Relief hit him when she lifted her head, but his urgency accelerated when he saw that her skin was turning blue. She stared across the ice at him, but he wasn't sure she knew he was there. Trying not to panic, he stopped Namasset from crawling out onto the ice on his hands and knees.

"We can't get to them that way," he told him, his eyes latching onto a sturdy sapling on the bank directly in line with the stump. "But we can fell a tree and use its branches to get out to them! Hurry, quick, let's get it down!"

Jerking out the hatchet, he swung hard, notching the tree so that it would fall out over the ice. Chips of bark flew as Namasset joined in, both of them hacking with all their might until the trunk gave a loud snap, then began to fall over. Gabriel pushed against it as hard as he could, trying to get it to land close to the stump.

Namasset helped him, throwing his shoulder against the wood, then stood back as it fell with a loud crash and crackling and breaking of ice. Both men scrambled across the fallen tree, heading out over the trunk, using the limbs for handholds to keep them out of the water. Gabriel knew now that they could reach Belinda and Konoc, but he breathed easier nonetheless when his fingers closed over the child's ice-stiff coat. He tried to pull him off his perch but could not.

Then he realized that Belinda clutched one of the boy's legs in a death grip.

"Belinda, listen to me! Let him go! I've got him! Do you hear me? I've got him!" His entreaties made no impact; she held him tightly, her fingers locked around his ankle. Gabriel inched out farther, holding onto the limbs, the front of his legs going into the water, but he was finally close enough to touch her. He forced calmness into his voice and kept his words low.

"Look at me, Belinda. I'm right here. I've got hold of Konoc's coat. Let him go so that I can get you out of the water."

"I can't." Her lips barely moved they were so stiff and blue.

He kept his tight grip on Konoc, then reached out with his other hand and covered her locked fingers. Her skin felt like frozen meat. He tried to pry her hand loose, and finally she let go. When she did, he caught her arm with one hand as he pulled Konoc's limp body to where Namasset could reach him, too.

As soon as Namasset got his hands on his son, he began to drag him backward toward the bank. Gabriel concentrated on Belinda, who now babbled incoherently as he struggled to pull her out of the icy water. Shifting his weight, he managed to heave her bodily across the log in front of him, despite the weight of her waterlogged clothing. She groaned softly, then lapsed into unconsciousness.

At that point his fear built so hard and fast it

nearly overwhelmed him. She was so unbelievably cold, so rigid and blue, that she already
seemed dead. She looked like Patsy and Jessie
when he had found them. Oh, God, she was
going to die, too. The thought redoubled his
strength, and he pulled and dragged until he
somehow got her inert body over his shoulder,
then slowly began to inch backward down the
log to safety.

Namasset was halfway around the lake now,
his son lying lifeless in his arms, and he could
see Willamette on the far shore, struggling
through the snow to meet them.

When Gabriel's feet finally hit solid ground,
he stood up, hoisted Belinda over his shoulder
again, and began to run for the cabin.

Sixteen

Belinda could hear a voice. From somewhere far away. Weak and indistinct, as if she lay miles underground, trapped in some dark, dank cave. *Gabriel? Yes, it was him.* He was calling her name. Even through the dense cloud that obscured her thoughts, she felt his intensity, sensed his worry. She struggled to open her eyes, but could not lift lids that seemed weighted down by heavy gold coins. She felt oddly disembodied, as if she danced like a wisp of thistledown before the wind—light, airy, free as a spirit.

"Belinda! Dammit, open your eyes and look at me!"

Why was Gabriel so upset? She tried to think about that, to capture thoughts as slippery as eels, but the effort was too much and she let herself sink again into that warm distant cavern of forgetfulness, wrapping the darkness around her like a black velvet shawl. Such peace proved to be fleeting, however, because Gabriel's voice became too insistent, too loud and angry, forcing her up, up through the murky stone corridors to the dim light gleaming faintly in the distance.

She opened her eyes to a bright red-orange glow. Flames. She blinked and watched them leap and dart and spit sparks up the chimney. She lay on the hearthstone, she realized, and much too close to the fire, but why couldn't she feel the heat? Confused, she tried to think about that, but was too weary to fret overly much. Her eyes drifted closed once more.

After a moment she realized someone was undressing her, roughly jerking off the Indian leggings, then the leather skirt, then her bodice and stays; even her shift was torn from her. She felt hands upon her, on her arms and legs, rubbing vigorously, relentlessly massaging her skin. Then suddenly, for the first time, she felt the heat of the fire burning her bare flesh. She groaned and tried to move away.

"Gabe! Look, she's tryin' to get up!"

"Annie?"

Belinda thought she heard her sister's voice, but she couldn't quite get her lips to move the way she wanted them to. Had that awful, hoarse grunt really come from her? When she tried to focus her gaze, she found Annie's pixie face hovering just above her, searching her face with huge, worried brown eyes.

"Bee, I was so scared for you! You turned blue all over! Did you know that?" Annie's whisper was full of amazed relief. "Are you all right now that you're all dry again, Bee?"

"I think so," Belinda managed gruffly, thinking she probably was if she could only remember exactly what had happened to her. She concentrated hard and the image of Konoc flailing in the icy pond came barging back like a wide-awake nightmare.

"Where's Konoc? Did you get him out?" she asked in a stronger voice, almost afraid to hear of the boy's fate.

"He's with his mama," Annie told her happily. "Don't you 'member, Bee? You jumped in and saved him!"

Thankful to learn the boy was all right, she wanted to ask more, but was completely distracted when she realized the firm hands were back, moving over every inch of her body. She knew the hands belonged to Gabe.

"Wait . . . stop . . ." she croaked out like a startled bullfrog, but he continued to chafe her bare calves without pause. Belinda realized then with some alarm that she was completely naked except for a patchwork quilt lying over her. The coverlet provided little obstacle to him, however, because his hands burrowed under it at every turn, warming cold skin wherever he found it. He was working on her feet now, gently kneading his way up her legs, and when he reached her thighs, a weak, horrified moan of protest was forced from her.

"Run along and let Wynett tuck you in,

Annie." Gabriel was telling her sister while he blithely continued his intimate exploration. "I'll get Belinda nice and warm again, then I'm going to put her to bed. You can see her again in the morning when she feels better."

Belinda felt Annie's mouth on her cheek in a wet, smacking kiss. " 'Nite, Bee."

She couldn't answer, so tired was she, and despite wanting to wake up, wanting to know why Gabriel was doing these things to her, she could not resist the sleep that wrapped around her like long, sticky tentacles and dragged her deeply into the bowels of the silent subterranean world. When she came to once more, she wore a nightdress and was tightly wrapped inside a fluffy quilt. She was being carried in Gabriel's arms.

"Where are you taking me?"

"Shh, everything's fine. You're going to sleep in my room tonight by the fireplace. You'll be warmer there."

"I'm so cold, freezing . . ." she muttered, her limbs beginning to shake of their own accord. She tried, but could not make them stop.

By the time they climbed the steps and entered his bedroom where the fire was blazing high and throwing elongated shadows over the walls and ceiling, her entire body was shuddering uncontrollably. He put her down gently, immediately covering her with more blankets topped off by a heavy coverlet made of soft rabbit fur.

"I've got a couple of stones heating to put against your feet," he whispered close beside her ear, but then he was gone.

For some reason she felt afraid when she was left alone, but as she lay shivering, her skin began to hurt. She was finally regaining feeling, she realized, but it was so painful, as if her flesh was being eaten by a million hungry ants. Most of her numbness was gone, and though she still felt cold, she burned all over. Worst of all, she could not control her muscles, which trembled so hard her teeth chattered.

Gabriel was back within minutes, sliding several blanket-wrapped hot stones in around her bare feet.

"How do you feel now, sweetheart? Can you move your fingers and toes?"

Belinda nodded, but couldn't harness her voice any better than her quaking body. *Wait, did Gabriel say "sweetheart"?* The chills racking her made her forget about that and seemed to get worse instead of better as the stones unthawed her frozen toes. She groaned as the tingling agony moved upward and invaded her legs and back.

Gabriel knelt beside her, tucking the covers closer around her and tenderly brushing damp hair off her flushed forehead.

"Your color's coming back. You're going to be all right, but it's going to hurt for a while."

Belinda didn't feel all right, her quivering so

intense that she hugged her arms around herself in order to stop it.

"I . . . can't stop shaking . . . it hurts so much . . ." she got out through clamped teeth.

She shut her eyes to stop the tears that were threatening, but only forced them to spill over her lashes and roll down her cheeks. She started in shock when the covers were thrown back and Gabriel slid into the bed beside her. He drew her in bodily against his chest, and his tunic of tanned leather actually felt good against her tortured skin. He wrapped his arms tightly around her, holding her full-length, stilling her trembling in a way she could not do.

"Forgive me for taking this liberty, Belinda," he murmured softly against her temple, "but I can't bear to see you suffer without doing anything to help you. My body heat will warm you far quicker than anything else."

Forgive him? she thought, so utterly grateful to be enclosed in his strong arms that more tears sprang up and burned behind her eyes. She had longed for him to embrace her in such a way, to hold her and comfort her. She felt safe and secure in his embrace, and snuggled even closer, burying her face in the warm hollow of his shoulder. He stroked her back, murmuring soothing reassurances, and she clung to him, wishing they could always share this warmth and intimacy.

Had he let go of his angry feelings about her betrayal? Could he forgive her? He had to care something about her, or he wouldn't be holding her so tenderly and comforting her in a voice so full of concern. Her throat thickened, her emotions overwhelming, and she pressed her body as close to him as she could in an attempt to absorb his heat, his strength, his gentleness.

He held her that way for a long time, and she gradually stopped quaking as her blood flow became normal and her body regained its natural temperature.

The warmth was accompanied by an ache that invaded every joint and muscle, but in time she was able to drift into a more peaceful sleep, pressed tightly against him, his arms still wrapped possessively around her.

Hours passed before Gabriel turned from his side to his back, carefully taking Belinda with him. Nestled close underneath his arm, she had finally fallen asleep, and, thank God, her skin was warm again. Immensely relieved that she would recover, he tried in vain to relax his own muscles that were wound as tight as a watch spring.

Everyone else in the house was asleep now, but he could not rid his mind of the events of the afternoon. He had been absolutely terrified when he had seen how blue Belinda's skin was—and gripped with horror at the fear that she would freeze to death like Patsy and Jessie. Jessie's skin had been blue, her eyes frozen open. He forced down rising bile, swallowing the bitter taste of grief, but the vision left him agitated, upset, gripped by emotions long suppressed. He eased his left arm out from underneath Belinda's slender shoulders, then raised himself on an elbow and looked down at her.

Extreme tenderness flooded through him, and he caressed her cheek, pink and flushed now at last, thank God, and as soft as a silk scarf. She could have lost her life saving Namasset's son. She had not hesitated when she went in after Konoc, but he knew full well that if she'd lost her grip on that stump, if she'd gone under the ice, they never would have found her alive. She would be dead, out of his life forever. The idea rocked him, and that awareness sent him scrambling out of the bed.

He had not planned to become involved with her this way. He had sworn not to be that foolish. He had fought his feelings night and day, first of all, because he distrusted her, but now, God help him, he didn't care what she had done to him. From the beginning he had felt protective of Belinda and Annie, but he had initially attributed those feelings to their resemblance to Patsy and Jessie. But his feelings had gradually become more. He feared he was falling in love with her, and if nothing else, his reaction to her near drowning proved it.

"Gabe?"

He turned slowly and found her sitting up. He had not bothered to tie the ribbon when he had slipped the nightgown over her head, and the open neckline had slipped off her shoulders, baring her slender collarbone. Her curly black hair fell around her shoulders, making her look even younger, even more vulnerable.

"I love you, Gabe," she murmured so low that he could barely hear her. "I have to tell you that, even if you don't feel the same about me." She stopped, then dropped her long black eyelashes when he did not respond.

Gabriel moved back to her, and she stretched out her arms to welcome him. He sat down and pulled her against him. "I thought I was going to lose you today."

She turned her face up to him, a look of love shining from her eyes. He bent his head, touching her lips with his, gently at first, but as soon as she leaned backward, pulling him down with her, his blood began to burn, and he attacked her mouth with all the passion he had denied for so long.

Belinda closed her eyes and held her breath, and with a gentleness that belied his great strength, one powerful arm folded around her back, bringing her tight against his hard chest. His hand was anchored firmly in her hair as he forced her to look at him. Then his lips were upon hers again, sweetly, softly, persuasively, until waves of desire pulsated through her blood, making her heart thunder. Her will began to crumble as his lips continued to devour hers, ravaging her with a demanding hunger he could no longer withhold.

Belinda could not think, could only feel that this moment between them was meant to be. Gabriel was her destiny as sure as the stars and moon revolved through the night skies. She surrendered with a muffled moan, willingly offering to him the honeyed nectar of her mouth. Flaming currents brought wild desires racing through her veins, and she slid her arms around his neck, pulling him to her, wanting to touch him, wanting him to touch her.

Gabriel groaned, one hand in the long silken curls, the other sliding slowly down a curved hip that felt like warm satin against his fingertips. Belinda gasped as his weight left the bed, watching out of desire-darkened eyes as he undressed, his broad chest emerging from the Indian tunic, his long, muscular legs from the deer hide breeches. Then he was beside her again, his lips tasting her mouth, her cheeks, her closed eyes. His arm came up beneath her back, lifting her, flattening her breasts against his bare chest, and Belinda's world began to dip and whirl as his hands explored her trembling flesh in a slow, erotic search.

Her lashes fluttered and closed, and she groaned helplessly as his mouth skirted the satiny angle of her jaw, dipping to the indentation of her fragile collarbone. His lips sought and found the hammering pulse in her throat, and Belinda lay in the mists of rapture as his fingers slid down the hollow of her belly and lower, probing, arousing her with slow, tender expertise. She sighed softly, involuntarily arching up against his hand, feeling as if she'd come home, as if they fit together, her softness now a part of his hard strength, as if they'd both been created to join together in this moment.

Each soft stroke of his fingertips ignited her already burning nerve endings, and Belinda moaned as his tongue swirled a molten path from one nipple to the other, bringing them erect with sensations of exquisite pleasure. All inhibitions evaporated, all rational thoughts, and she responded to him, her fingers kneading the sinewy muscles of his back, moving over the lean, hard flesh at his narrow waist.

Nothing mattered to her any longer. There was no anger, no distrust, no reason, as the fierce, never-before-understood needs of her body took over until she wanted him so desperately that her mouth found his, opening for his tongue in greedy, hungry abandon. Her hands glided over the hard muscles of his hips until he rose above her, the heat of his body welcoming her embrace. She tensed when he entered her, slowly, carefully, and she felt the stabbing pain as he pierced the proof of her maidenhood, but she did not mourn the loss long because his whispered reassurances against her ear were so soft and gentle and loving. They moved together as one, limbs entwined, muscles flexed, breaths mingled, ragged and hoarse, and she let him take her with him to exquisite heights where love and pleasure and need were soldered into one.

"Gabriel . . ." she breathed out, not aware that she had spoken at all, and Gabriel groaned as he reached his climax, the explosion of their union bursting between them as all the love Gabriel had suppressed and all the love Belinda had longed for came forth in a white-hot shower of pure sensation.

In the aftermath of their passion, both lay limp and sated, realizing only love could create such a joyous union; then with their breathing calm and content, their bodies tightly entwined, they slept, Gabriel's fingers still tangled in her hair.

Seventeen

Belinda came awake the moment Gabriel eased his arm out from under her shoulders and inched quietly out of the bed. She opened sleepy eyes and turned onto her side to watch him. He strode across the room and went down on one knee to stoke the dwindling fire. He was completely naked, the first time she had seen him so, and she admired the way his muscles moved, with slow masculine grace.

Instead of embarrassment, which she might have expected from herself under the circumstances, his magnificent body, so big and strong, the immense shoulders and narrow hips, the long muscular limbs, shamelessly aroused her. She was filled with hitherto unknown longing. Her initiation into lovemaking had been swift and complete, as had been the deepening of her feelings for him.

Gabriel had held her tightly against his chest, his touch so unbelievably tender as he whispered words of love that the mere memory sent waves of warm affection through her body. But, she thought, catching her bottom lip between her teeth, now that his arms were no longer around her, doubts began to nibble at her happiness. Would he regret the intimacy they had shared as man and woman? It had been so magical, such a gift to her, but had it been the same for him? A man who had no doubt lain with many other women?

She grappled with such fears as Gabriel threw a log on the dwindling embers. A burst of glowing sparks flew up the chimney like a bevy of startled red quail. What was he thinking? Was he sorry for what had happened? Surely, he had only meant to warm her frozen flesh. Did he blame her for clutching him the way she had and pressing herself against him so brazenly?

For the first time, a flush of shame rose to her face and caused her eyes to slide away from Gabriel as he headed back to the bed. She took heart, however, when he smiled and quickly gathered her back into his embrace. His mouth nuzzled the top of her head, his whisper husky in her unbound hair.

"How are you feeling, sweet? Are you warm now?"

Belinda nodded, hiding her blush of pleasure at his endearment against the hollow of his shoulder, loving the smell of him, the masculine mingling of shaving soap and leather and pipe tobacco. She touched the mat of dark blond hair that edged along the hard plane of his breastbone, sliding her fingertips slowly across the molded contours of his well-defined chest muscles. His body fascinated her, so hard and strong, so different and exciting.

Gabriel shifted and turned slightly so they were face-to-face. "Is anything wrong?"

Reluctant to ask him the questions that battled inside her mind, Belinda said nothing. Gabriel raised her chin with a forefinger and forced her to gaze into his eyes. Still, she was gripped by a deep-rooted shyness now that their passion had cooled, and she didn't know what to say to him. She wanted to tell him again that she loved him, but it was different now that he had made love to her, and she could not bring herself to be so vulnerable.

When Gabriel took a deep inhalation, hard enough to cause his chest to heave beneath her palm, her heart sank at the implication of what such a sigh of resignation might mean. A rush of emotion rose like air bubbles to the surface because she was afraid she knew exactly what it meant.

"I'm sorry, Belinda. I should never have compromised you this way. It was completely inexcusable of me."

Her words were nearly inaudible. "I'm glad it happened. I thought it was wonderful."

Gabriel searched her eyes, picking up a strand of her hair and caressing it between his thumb and forefinger. "As did I. But you are an innocent, and I shouldn't have taken advantage of your inexperience."

Belinda shook her head. "Please don't feel guilty. I put my arms around you and enticed you to me. You saved my life, Gabe, how can I ever forget that?"

"Thank God, we got there in time." He smiled again, bringing her fingers up against his mouth. He kissed them one at a time. "But there are other considerations now that I've taken you into my bed and made love to you."

He meant he could not offer her marriage, she realized at once, saddened that it had to be so, but not surprised. She had known all along they could never be husband and wife, but she didn't really care. Here, now, at this moment, being with him was enough, basking under his exquisite tenderness and sharing such moments of close intimacy. Suddenly, she wanted him to know that, know how she felt.

"I love you, Gabe, and I hope that someday you'll love me as much, but don't think I expect you to want me as your wife. I know I'm not the kind of woman you would wish to wed. I was a born lady but now am merely a servant in your household . . ."

She got no further, a gasp of surprise torn from her when he grabbed her face and held it between his palms.

"Good God, Belinda, is that the kind of man you think I am? One who would bed you one minute then shun you the next as beneath my station?"

He was angry, she could see how his eyes had

darkened to indigo, for once his emotions openly revealed. Miserable, because she could not deny his accusations, she was appalled when she felt a sting of tears behind her eyes. She forcibly contained them, refusing to weep again.

"Belinda, you're a beautiful woman, good and kind and brave. Do you truly think me so shallow that I would not find you a suitable wife?"

Pleasure came swiftly, bringing her tremulous smile back. "But I thought . . . you just said that there were other considerations now that you've bedded me."

"Aye, that's true, but not the ones you think. I walk a dangerous path, Belinda, and I will have to continue to do so until this war is over. I could be taken by the British and branded a traitor at any time. I swore never to leave a widow and family to fend for themselves like so many men have been forced to do in the last five years. You're already known to them, and things would go hard for you if they knew you were my wife. I can't put you into that kind of danger."

Belinda didn't care a whit about any kind of danger. "Are you saying that you *do* wish to marry me?"

Her eyes were so full of amazed disbelief that Gabriel's serious face lightened to a more tender expression. He gave a low laugh. "Is that so hard to believe?"

She nodded. "I only harbored the hope that

you would someday love me." She searched his face, determined now to know. "Do you, Gabe? Do you love me?"

"I'm afraid I do, though heaven knows I fought it every step of the way."

Joy so filled Belinda that she couldn't speak for a moment. Her eyes brimmed with happy tears this time, but Gabriel kissed them away.

"But even loving you doesn't excuse my actions this night. I had no right to take you into my bed without the saying of our vows."

"But I wanted you to. I want you to again."

Gabriel smiled at her eager innocence. "You did little to seduce me. You were pure of a man's touch until I came to you. I'm the one who should have shown gentlemanly restraint." A wry smile tugged at his lips. "Though the truth is that I have shown little restraint in any circumstances where you're concerned since I made your acquaintance."

His eyes grew tender as he drew his thumb down the soft curvature of her cheek.

"I suppose now all that is left to me is to do the honorable thing and marry you as soon as the war is over. And I pray to God that will be soon."

Belinda absorbed the shock of his proposal as best she could. *Could he truly mean that?* She had nothing, no property, no money to bring into the marriage.

"Even though I am alone except for my baby sister, and can give you no dowry?" she whispered, afraid to believe he could truly wish to wed her given those things.

"Belinda, Belinda, how can you talk like this? You're as fine as any woman in New York, or anywhere else for that matter. Better than any of the ladies I know." He propped his head on his palm and observed her with smiling eyes. "In any case, you are *my* lady now. My Lady Belinda."

Though joy blossomed like the swelling petals of a new-blown rose, she still doubted that it could be true, that he could want her for his bride.

"Dulcimer told me that you still mourned your wife and would never wed again." Her tone lowered out of respect for his loss, but there was one question she felt she had to ask. A secret question that had plagued her since the first time he had kissed her. "Do you want me for myself, Gabe, or do you want me because I remind you of your wife?"

As she had feared, Gabriel's soft, unguarded expression closed up as if he had thrown shutters over his face. He frowned and turned away from her until he lay on his back, his eyes on the ceiling.

Silence descended between them, dragging out for so long that Belinda deeply regretted bringing up the subject of his past. She had caused him pain, but she felt she had to know if he loved her, or if she was a substitute for the woman he had lost. She waited, with only the popping and crackling of logs shifting in the grate filling the quiet room.

"I don't like to talk about Patsy." He paused there, and Belinda dared not push him for more. "Or Jessie, either. I blame myself for . . . what happened to them."

Belinda could feel the tension riddling his muscles, and she turned and took his hand between hers. She said nothing, though she wanted to do something to erase the agony in his eyes. She watched the way the angle of his jaw worked as he clenched his teeth over and over, as if to bite back tears. His gaze was fixed on the timber beams in the ceiling where the flickering light of the fire played in shadow dances.

"I brought them up here in the dead of winter, when the snows were heavy, even heavier than they are now. God help me, every time it clouds up and snows I think about that day. About what they must have suffered."

Perhaps she had done the right thing to ask him, she thought, watching his features struggle for composure. Maybe he should talk about it, face the horror and absolve himself of the guilt he felt. He must have suffered terribly, living with such horrible recriminations.

She laced her fingers through his, and squeezed his hand encouragingly as she whispered, "Whatever happened, I know you would never have allowed harm to come to them if you could have prevented it."

Gabriel screwed his eyes shut. "I shouldn't have brought them up the river, not back then. I loved it here so much that I wanted to share it with them. Especially Jessie."

"How old was she?" Belinda asked gently.

"Almost five."

Like Annie, Belinda thought, recalling with a gush of anger what Bart had said about taking Annie into Gabriel's house with her. He'd said she'd be a nice touch. Now she understood what he'd meant. How cruel he was! And she had unwittingly been a part of his underhanded plot. She would regret that involvement for the rest of her life.

"It was nearly a decade ago," Gabriel was saying now. "The river was a lot more dangerous then, especially this far north. Mohawk war parties still came through on their way to Quebec. . . ." His face changed, his voice quivered with anger. "Along with the British butchers who paid them to rape and pillage. But I brought them anyway, and instead of staying here with them, instead of protecting them the way I should have, I went off upriver with Namasset to visit his village. I left half a dozen men here with them, and we weren't gone long, only for the space of a morning. Patsy didn't want me to go, but I did anyway. I told her she was perfectly safe, that we'd be back in time for lunch." He stopped and rubbed his eyes. "They must have attacked not long after we left. They killed the livestock, burned the cabins, and destroyed the mill. They murdered everyone except for Patsy and Jessie. They decided to take them with them."

Belinda felt nausea rise like a cobra and writhe across the floor of her belly, felt her throat tighten with dread at what Gabriel would tell her now. What horror had caused the terrible pain that was gripping his face, a full ten years after it had happened?

"They marched them north, in sub-zero weather, through snow and ice and wind." Now his words came so hard she could barely understand them. She lay within Gabriel's arms and rested her cheek against his chest. She felt the rush of his heartbeat, pounding fast, agitated. She suddenly wanted to stop him, put her fingers over his mouth so he wouldn't have to relive it.

"We found Patsy first. They had . . . used her vilely . . . then spilt her skull with a hatchet. The bastards left it embedded there for me to find."

"Oh, no, Gabe, no," she breathed out in absolute horror.

"It snowed all day while we searched for them, but we found her, because"—he swallowed convulsively—"her blood had turned the snow crimson, all around her in a big red circle." His jaw clamped down hard, his words forced and unnatural. "My baby was there, too. They just abandoned her there alone with her mother's body." His face went dead. "It looked like she just lay down close beside her mother and froze to death." He shook his head as if trying to force the images out of his mind. "Oh, God, when I turned her over, she was completely blue, and her eyes, oh, God, they were wide open, staring up at me."

Suddenly, he sat up and looked down at Belinda. His eyes were so full of horror that Belinda flinched, then put her arms around his head and pulled his face against her breast.

"That's what I thought about yesterday when I saw you and Konoc in the water. I thought you both were going to freeze to death."

"But you got us out, you saved us. And you would've saved Patsy and Jessie, too, if you could have reached them in time. You did nothing wrong, Gabe, nothing at all. Surely you know that?"

He did not know that. He blamed himself and probably always would; she could tell that by the haunted look in his eyes. She put her hand on the back of his neck and brought his mouth up to touch hers. They kissed slowly, tenderly, and then she held him, letting her closeness comfort him the way words could not. Finally, they both slept, while the fire slowly dwindled to a glow of spent embers.

Eighteen

Henri LeClerc grunted with effort as he dug the edge of his paddle into the slushy snow below Gabriel's Bronx River landing, propelling the bow of the birchbark canoe to a standstill alongside the bank. He had brought two men along with him this trip, Judson and Larrew, both patriot agents from Long Island. They had brought paper and ink for the press hidden in the mill house's secret room.

The underground newsletters printed there were invaluable in identifying uncovered Tory traitors to their patriot neighbors, as well as heralding American victories against the British. The redcoats confiscated and destroyed such papers at every turn and imprisoned those caught printing or reading subversive materials, but still the news came, giving hope to the war-weary populace.

While Judson and Larrew unloaded the pork barrels in which they had hidden their contraband, Henri stepped ashore and shielded his eyes from the bright morning sun slanting through bare-branched oaks like arrows of fire. Up at the main cabin, Namasset had come into view and was moving with his surefooted, silent tread down through melting patches of snow. The Indian wore his usual deerskin attire and smelled of woodsmoke and his wife's strong-brewed coffee when they clasped wrists. Henri placed his palm on Namasset's broad shoulder.

"*Mon ami*, you are well?"

The tall Oneida brave nodded, but did not answer Henri's broad smile, as was his way. He had known Namasset well for almost as long as he had known Gabriel. All three of their fathers had fought for survival along this river and become friends long before their sons had been born.

"I am well."

Henri glanced at the empty veranda, wondering where everyone was. "And the family? Is Willamette preparing one of her delicious breakfast feasts?"

Namasset nodded again. "She worry over Konoc. He and the English girl went through ice on pond. She saved Konoc."

"Belinda did? Are they all right?"

"We got them. Gabe make her warm in bed."

The laconic Oneida showed no suggestive intent at such a provocative revelation, but Henri grinned at the intriguing images that instantly formed inside his head. A chore most men would pay a ransom in gold to perform, even

Gabe, with his ingrained prejudice against the lady.

"I take it he's beginning to trust her?"

Namasset shrugged. "She saved Konoc. We do not forget."

As they walked together, Namasset filled him in on Belinda's valiant rescue of the boy, and when they entered the great room of the cabin, Henri welcomed the warm air that met his cold skin, that, and the mouth-watering smells of salt pork and hot coffee. Young Konoc sat at the table with his older brothers, looking hale and hearty despite his near escape, his round brown face sticky with maple syrup, his mouth full of his mother's hotcakes. Namasset's family was like Henri's own kin, and he tried not to think about what would have happened if not for Belinda's courage. He unbuttoned and struggled out of his heavy fur-lined surtout, which he draped on a wall peg, and stripped off his tricorne and gloves.

"*Bonjour*, my good friends," he called out, and there was a stir among the children as he strode forth.

Wynett jumped up, and he clasped wrists with the twelve-year-old, man to man, but he rubbed the top of Timon's hair with his left hand. Annie watched him shyly from her place at the table, but Willamette smiled in her tranquil way, hovering near to Konoc, as if she did not intend to let him out of her sight any time soon.

Henri took her hand, bowed gallantly, and pressed his mouth to the back of her brown, work-roughened fingers.

"Willamette, *cherie*, you are beautiful as you always are."

The woman blushed as she usually did when he complimented her, but her soft smile told him she was pleased to see him. She spoke to him in the fluent French she had learned from the Jesuit priest who lived in their village when she was a little girl.

"Welcome, Monsieur Henri. Do you wish breakfast after your long journey on the river?"

"That I do, Willamette. I've had nothing but hard tack and sour grog for a day and a half." He glanced around for Gabe, noticed his absence, and inquired of his hostess. "And where may my friend Gabriel be? And the brave mademoiselle who rescued young Konoc?"

He tickled the side of Annie's neck, and she gave a childish squeal before telling him amidst her giggles, "Wynett says they are still abed." Suddenly, her little face lost its smile, her eyes growing enormous. "Bee was in the ice a long time, Monsieur Henri, and she turned blue, all over, even her lips. I was scared when I saw what color she was." He could hear her fright, poor baby, and he squatted down beside her chair. He took her hand, found it sticky, and when he kissed her cheek he tasted maple syrup.

"She is fine, *ma petite*. Namasset said Gabe's taking good care of her."

Annie put her thin arms around his neck and had barely let up in her enthusiastic hug when footsteps sounded on the upstairs landing. Henri straightened and glanced toward the steps as Gabriel's voice murmured something too low for them to hear. Whatever he said brought a soft, private laugh from the woman he carried in his arms.

Henri knew instantly that things were indeed very different between his friend and the woman he had once caught spying on him. Gabriel was dressed in fringed Oneida garb, which he often wore when at the mill farm, but the lovely Belinda wore a billowing white nightdress and Gabe's thick navy robe. Gabriel carried her bundled inside one of Willamette's patchwork quilts, and he trod the steps with her carefully, as if she was indeed a treasured possession.

"Gabe, please, I'm perfectly able to walk," she protested with an embarrassed glance at the breakfast table, but just as crystal clear to Henri was the pleasure in her voice.

Gabriel ignored her complaint and carried her swiftly to a sofa drawn close to the hearth. He lowered her with supreme care, and Henri was not a little astonished by the look on Gabriel's face. Gabe was smiling indulgently at her pretty blush, and Henri shook his head, fearing his friend had utterly succumbed to the young Englishwoman, despite his hard-fought battle against her charm.

For a moment Henri thought he was going to have to wave his arms over his head to distract his friend from Belinda's loveliness, but Annie soon saved him the trouble. "Look, Bee!" she cried excitedly, sliding off her chair and heading toward her big sister. "Monsieur Henri's come today!"

Gabriel left Belinda's side as Annie reached her and gave her big sister a gigantic bear hug. He strode quickly toward the Frenchman. "When did you get here, Henri? I didn't know you were coming again so soon."

"I just arrived. Judson and Larrew are out at the mill."

"Did they get everything we need?" Gabe lowered his voice, but his eyes strayed back to Belinda, who was now accepting a mug of hot tea from Willamette.

"It seems you've made a truce of sorts with your little English spy."

Gabriel turned his attention back to him and completely astounded him with his next pronouncement. "Aye, and I've asked her to be my bride. After the war is over."

Henri stared unblinkingly at him and could think of nothing to say.

Gabriel grinned at his friend's bemusement. "I'll explain it all to you later," he said, but Henri knew him well enough to know he would not.

"But tell me what brings you here, Henri? You were not slated to make the journey with Judson." He lowered his voice. "Has something gone amiss in New York?"

They moved a few feet farther away from the fireplace, where Belinda was reassuring the chattering group around her that she was perfectly fine now, wonderful, in fact.

"General Washington ordered me to come to you," he told Gabriel, his manner now quite serious.

Gabriel's brows came together, and he searched Henri's face. "Why?"

"There's been a courier from the Carolinas. Word has it a British general in Savannah might be willing to turn."

"Is that right?" Gabriel's intent expression flickered with a hint of surprise. "Good tidings you bring, indeed, my friend. I'm sure the general is pleased, but why does he send you to me?"

"He wants you to sail there and see if you can make the man an offer, if the rumor turns out to be true."

"But I am needed here. It would be hard for me to leave my network to operate alone."

"Apparently the general who wants to turn-coat is an old friend of yours. General Phillip Laughton?"

"Good God, I've known Phillip for years. He's an honorable officer. I'm surprised he's willing to join us."

"It's reported that his mother was born in Savannah, a staunch patriot who shames his allegiance to the Crown."

"Abigail is strong-willed, I grant you, and heiress to one of the wealthiest shipping families in the south. That's how I made their acquaintance."

"General Washington believes he will come over if you're the one making the offer. Will Laughton have you arrested if you reveal your patriot leanings?"

"I'll have to be careful how I approach him. When am I to go?"

Henri noticed that his gaze again went to Belinda, and he realized by that revealing chink in his friend's well-disciplined emotional mask that Gabriel's feelings for the young woman who had duped him already ran deep. He hoped Gabe was not making a mistake trusting her. She had shown her deviousness on more than one occasion.

"Now," he answered. "Today, if you can arrange it."

Gabriel seemed surprised, but he contemplated the idea for a moment. "I had planned a trip to Philadelphia as soon as I left here. I suppose I could sail south instead."

"Good. We fear there's no time to lose."

Gabriel glanced across the room again, his manner troubled. "I'll have to leave Belinda and Annie up here alone."

Henri knew full well that Gabriel was reliving

that terrible day from a decade ago. He had not been there when Gabriel had found his family butchered in the snow, but he had borne witness to his grief in the months and years afterward. He laid a palm upon his friend's arm. "Namasset and I will keep watch over them, and Judson and Larrew will be here for a fortnight at least, working at the press. There's little danger of the British venturing this far in the middle of winter, and you'll be back long before spring."

Gabriel heard Henri's words, knew he was probably right, but he did not respond as Henri went on, filling him in on what had transpired in Manhattan during the last week or so.

A short time later, when Henri sought out Namasset and the others at the mill, Gabriel remained behind, realizing he would have to tell Belinda of his departure. It was a moment he did not savor. He had no desire to leave her here, especially after what had happened between them, but he had little choice. He couldn't take her with him, and Henri was probably right: She'd be safer here with loyal patriots than she'd be back in New York where Bart could get his hands on her again and punish her for skipping out on her indentured service.

The chance to speak privately with her did not come until Willamette had ushered her children out with her to their own cabin. Annie stayed behind, but was busy playing with a family of corncob dolls on the hearth.

Belinda's smile was almost shy once they

were alone. He sat down close beside her and put her palm against his. She entwined her fingers tightly, and he lifted the back of her hand to his lips.

"I missed you," she whispered, shivering as he turned over her hand and kissed the inside of her wrist.

The sweetness of her smile and the love revealed so openly in her eyes made it hard for him to find the right words. He found himself loathe to leave, and felt a spreading jolt of shock when he admitted to himself how important she had become to him. He did love her, and that made him vulnerable in a way he had sworn never to be again. How had he let this happen?

He looked into her gaze and felt momentarily lost in the pure azure depths, as warm and clear as a tranquil tropical sea. He pulled his eyes away and watched Annie by the fire. Her dark curls were silhouetted against the golden flames.

"Henri brought orders for me. I must leave at once for Savannah."

Her face fell, the happy smile melting away like warmed wax. Her eyes grew clouded, no longer turquoise but the color of smoke behind a blue windowpane.

"But Savannah is very far away, is it not?"

He nodded. "I'll go by sea, which is fastest. I can't tell you anything else, except that it's very important I leave at once."

She lowered her lashes and picked at a loose

red thread on the quilt, struggling openly for composure.

"How long must you be gone?"

"I'm not sure. A month perhaps, but it could be less if the seas are fair."

"Is it dangerous, this business you must do in Savannah?"

Gabriel could not bring himself to lie to her. There had been too many lies between them. "There are few places in this war that are not dangerous for loyal Americans, now that the British occupy our cities."

"You do plan to come back here, don't you?" she asked, searching his face.

"Nothing could keep me away from you, not anymore."

Belinda laid her cheek against his shoulder, and he put his arms around her, but his mind revisited another cold winter day when he had left behind a woman and child he loved. He saw billowing black smoke floating over his burning farm like the angel of death, smelled the acrid odor, and saw the snow turned crimson with blood.

Nineteen

Nearly a week had dragged past since Gabriel had taken leave of the farm. To Belinda it seemed he had been gone forever. The single night they had shared, snuggled together in the soft feather mattress, monopolized her every waking thought. And her nights were bittersweet, too, because when she awoke from dreams of him she was alone. He had touched her so gently and taught her the secrets of lovemaking with tenderness and patience.

Sometimes those hours spent in his arms seemed like misty illusions, but if she closed her eyes and let herself feel his fingers trailing over her naked flesh, let herself think about the heat of his tongue when his mouth closed over her nipple, the very real memory sent shivers up her spine.

Even now, sitting across from Willamette at the trestle table, her body burned helplessly with erotic longings she could not banish. Flustered, she shifted in her seat and bent her head so Willamette could not witness her breathlessness. She redoubled her concentration on the new portrait of Willamette that she was drawing. She had decided to redo all the drawings that she had impulsively hurled into the fire.

Christmas was only days from now, and though Gabriel was far away, she was determined that she would have a present for everyone. Her family had always celebrated with small gifts and candy, and she wanted Annie to follow those same traditions. Their past holidays had been safe and happy, and Belinda wanted to demonstrate to Annie the warmth provided by a loving close-knit family.

Though she had no money, and very few possessions of her own, she had made a wonderful discovery one day when she was cleaning the bedchambers. In a bureau drawer, beneath stacks of folded bed linen, she had found a hat box with half a dozen skeins of yarn. She had chosen the bright red for a shawl for Willamette, for she knew Namasset's gentle wife loved the bright scarlet of autumn leaves. She worked on it only in the privacy of her own room; she couldn't wait to see Willamette's surprise and delight on Christmas morning.

Not only that, but Belinda knew she'd also have enough yellow and blue yarn to knit warm mittens for Namasset, as well as Annie and the three boys. Though it seemed very little, she would give Gabriel drawings of his beloved farm, and perhaps others of his town house in

New York. This time he wouldn't suspect her. This time he would smile and kiss her.

Sighing deeply, she picked up her picture of the farm and shaded the roof of the mill house, then stopped, charcoal in hand, wondering where Gabriel was at that very moment. What he was doing? Who was he with? Did he ever long for her, as she did for him? Her brow furrowed to think he might be attending some fancy ball with his many friends as he so often did, mingling among the elite of society in elegant evening attire, hopelessly handsome as he was the night when she had served his guests at his own soiree.

Was he dancing with beautiful ladies in white-powdered wigs, diamonds and emeralds sparkling at their slender throats, and yards and yards of shiny satin and expensive lace swinging around them as they danced? Such possibilities made her almost physically ill, made her doubt his sweet promises.

How could he love her? She was his indentured servant. He practically owned her. She shook the doubts away, not wanting to believe them. Instead, she thought of the expression in his dark blue eyes when he had looked down into her face and lowered his mouth to her lips. His fair hair had shone like a golden halo around his head.

He had shared his past with her, a tragedy so painful that his voice had trembled in the telling. He had loved his wife and daughter so deeply, had lost them both at once in the most horrible way. And he blamed himself. Now that she knew the depths of his guilt, she detested Bart for bringing his suffering back, and she vowed that she would make amends to Gabriel for her part in the plot against him, even if it took her forever.

Belinda would stand by him, no matter what trouble they faced. And she would become his wife when the rebellion ended. She shook her head as she worked, still unable to believe he had proposed marriage, when any dowried lady in New York, in all the colonies, would want such a magnificent specimen of a man for her husband.

Her lovely daydreams disintegrated like smoke in a storm when Timon burst into the room. The look on his face brought Belinda's heart up and clogged the back of her throat.

"Mama, Mama, the redcoats come! In pirogues!"

Willamette dropped her rolling pin into a mound of biscuit dough. Her eyes locked with Belinda's. "Namasset runs his traps," she said, fear glowing in her dark eyes.

"Have they landed?" Belinda asked, her heartbeat tripling.

"They round bend. Wynett ran to the mill to warn the men. I come here."

"Annie! Konoc! Come here at once," Belinda ordered, trying to fight down panic, but it was rising too fast for her to stop it. She had seen what British soldiers did to the farms they raided. They dragged the men to prison or hanged them on the spot from the nearest tree without benefit of a trial. And she knew, too, what they did to the women.

Cold revulsion rushed forth. And if the patriots in the hidden room, with its printing press and enemy propaganda, were discovered, Gabriel would be destroyed. She could not let that happen.

"Timon, run quick and tell Mister Judson and Mister Larrew to secure the trapdoor and stay hidden. I will meet the soldiers and tell them that Willamette and I live here alone with the children. I am English; perhaps they will believe me."

Trembling, she grabbed up her cloak, not sure at all if such kinship to England would make any difference whatsoever to pillaging soldiers. She quickly walked outside onto the veranda, gasping when she saw that the boats had already nudged up against the landing platform.

There were only three of the flat-bottomed heavy pirogues used by the French-Canadians. Nearly a dozen redcoats manned the oars of each, however, and she struggled to remain calm as Annie ran out of the cabin and hid in the folds of her skirts.

The soldiers scrambled out of the boats, running down the planks of the landing. The clumping sounds of heavy jackboots and the metal clanking of sabers obliterated the rush of the river and startled sparrows from their roosts in the pines behind the cabins.

For the first time she realized that some of the men in the first canoe did not wear the scarlet coat and white trousers of the British uniform, but the kelly green jackets designating the Tory-manned brigades that Gabe and Henri despised so violently. Her heart stopped when she recognized the man at the forefront. God help them, it was Bartholomew Smythe. He had led the British here in a new attempt to destroy Gabriel. And he would succeed this time if he found the hidden patriots.

"It's the mean man, Bee." Annie's frightened words were muffled against Belinda's skirt.

Belinda's trepidation swelled in her breast like floodwater in a ravine, and she braced both hands on the rough-hewn banister to stop their shaking. As Bart came ever closer, her eyes never left his face. He grinned when he recognized her, a truly evil smirk. Her fingers tightened until her knuckles went white, and she swayed upon her feet. He was moving swiftly up to the cabin, apparently eager to get his hands on her, his breath smoking out in the cold air.

"I had a feeling I'd find you here" were his first words as he stopped on the step just below her. Then he grabbed her arm and squeezed down brutally enough to force a cry from her. "I suppose Elliott ran like a damnable coward when he saw us coming."

"Mr. Elliott's not here." She spoke softly so her voice wouldn't shake as much. "He sent Annie and me here to help the caretakers on his farm. I'm still his servant. He's done nothing improper, Bart, you're wrong about him."

"You lying little bitch," Bartholomew ground out, his face turning the mottled red of a side of beef. He lifted his arm as if to strike her, but before he could, an authoritative command stopped him. His hand stilled in the air.

"I warn you, Mr. Smythe, sir, if you strike a lady in my presence, you will pay severely."

Belinda froze where she stood. She knew the English-accented voice, knew it quite well. But it could not be! It would be inconceivable for John to be here in America, much less at the farm!

Then she saw him striding up behind Bart. He wore his British uniform and looked exactly as he had the last time she'd seen him at the counter of her father's print shop. Tall, handsome, charming. He did not wear the affectionate smile he had presented to her that day nearly three years before, but frowned furiously, his glare fixed unblinking on Bart's anger-flushed face.

"Major Andre?" she breathed without even realizing it. "Is that really you?"

Her father's friend whipped around to face her. He stared, his jaw going slack, all anger fading into a look of unadulterated shock.

"In God's name, Mistress Scott! What are you doing here?"

Then his wits returned, and he forgot about Bart and climbed the steps until he stood beside her. A delighted smile broke across his features as he took both her hands in his.

"I cannot believe this! Here you are standing before me in this godforsaken wasteland! How did you get here, Belinda? When did you leave London?"

Belinda glanced behind him at Bart, found his dark, suspicious eyes boring holes into her. She tried to compose herself, but she couldn't shake the sense of unreality. She had heard John Andre had left England to serve in the war, but here? And so far from the action?

She tried to think, to answer John's questions so as not to incriminate herself. "Annie and I are alone now, Major Andre. After you left London, I'm afraid our mother passed away, then soon after Father lost his business." The old humiliation darkened her face as she picked up Annie and held her in her arms. "We've both been indentured, for some time now. First in Canada, then in Mr. Elliott's house in the city, and now here on his farm."

Major John Andre looked as if she had taken a floor plank and slammed it down atop his head. He gave a peculiar-sounding laugh that stopped uncertainly when Belinda remained solemn. "Surely you jest, Belinda. You and Annie, indentured servants? Why, that's impossible."

"No. Father had no choice but to indenture us all when he was ruined. He died aboard ship on our voyage to Canada. We worked for a time in Quebec at Lord Greenleigh's estate." She looked coldly at Bartholomew. "Until Mr. Smythe brought me to New York and forced me to enter Mr. Elliott's house in order to spy on him."

"Forced you? To spy on your employer?" Major Andre repeated in an incredulous tone.

Belinda saw Bartholomew clench his fists, and she realized she had been given a perfect opportunity to vindicate Gabriel from Bart's accusations.

"Yes, Major, and when I could find nothing incriminating about this man, I felt so guilty that I confessed my treachery to Mr. Elliott. The truth is that he's a very kind-hearted and forgiving man, so he took pity on us and brought us here far away from the city where Mr. Smythe could not threaten us any longer."

John Andre's generous mouth turned into a tightly stitched seam. He gave Bart a contemptuous look. "Is that true, Smythe? Did you use this innocent young lady as a pawn in this personal vendetta of yours?"

"I bought her indenture, then sold it off to Elliott," Bart answered stiffly.

At the same time Belinda's eyes had found the squads of soldiers searching Namasset's cabin and the mill house. She held her breath as they thundered up the steps into the mill, her nerves standing on end as she waited for the eruption of gunfire or shouts of discovery when they found the hidden trapdoor. Then to her utter relief and disbelief, the soldiers were outside again, coming back toward their officers. They didn't find anything. Her knees began to shake, and she locked them, fearing she was close to collapse.

"We found nothing, Major," cried a young lieutenant who snapped to attention and saluted his commander.

"Then look again!" Bart ordered harshly. "I know Elliott is up to his neck with the rebel scum, and I intend to prove it!"

"I will remind you, sir, that you are not in charge of these men," Andre said, a hard edge to his words. "You've brought us on a long, cold, miserable wild-goose chase, Smythe, and all to no avail." He smiled kindly at Belinda and Annie. "And if it was not for finding these dear old friends of mine here, I would be damnably annoyed with you."

Bartholomew's face turned redder, and Belinda shifted her gaze away from the murderous look in his eyes.

Andre took her by the arm. "Come along, Belinda. I'm taking you and Annie back to New York where you'll be safe. This is no place for Englishwomen. The rebels would show no mercy if they found you living out here alone."

Returning to New York was the last thing Belinda wanted. "But we cannot, Major Andre. We are legally bound to Mr. Elliott. We must stay here."

"Nonsense, my dear. I will intervene in this shabby affair you've been caught up in. I'll buy your freedom myself from this Elliott chap if it becomes necessary. Despite Smythe's obvious obsession that he is a traitor, everyone else in the city seems to think the man a highly educated, honorable gentleman entirely faithful to the Crown."

Belinda turned to look at Willamette, who still stood ignored in the doorway, her arms around Konoc. Her face was impassive, but their eyes connected with mute understanding. In that shared moment they both knew Wynett and the hidden patriots could still be discovered in the mill. If Bart had his way, the place would be searched a second time. The sooner Andre and his men embarked, the safer it would be for all of them.

"I'm most grateful for your kindness, Major Andre." She smiled up at the English officer for the first time. "I had almost forgotten the civility and respect given to ladies by true English gentlemen."

Major Andre nodded with obvious pleasure. "You will have no need of worry from this moment on, Belinda, my dear. I will take good care of you and your sister. I give you my word on that."

Belinda thanked him and patted Annie's back reassuringly as she carried her past Bartholomew Smythe and his green-coated Tory friends. His glare told her that it was not over between them yet, but at least for now, he could use her no longer to get to Gabriel. Under Major John Andre's protection in New York, she and Annie would be safe from his revenge, and Gabriel would be safe from his constant harassment.

Twenty

Gabriel didn't bother to hide his annoyance, more than irritated that Annabelle Barton had insisted he be her escort to that evening's gala event. He had only just that afternoon arrived back in New York from a long, tedious, and eventually unproductive voyage to Savannah. He had never gotten to approach his friend, Phillip Laughton, who had been out in the field with his men the entire duration of Gabriel's stay in the southern city.

Gabriel had spent time with Phillip's mother and found her openly patriotic, but he did not endanger her by telling her his true reason for seeking out her son. Now that he was home, more than anything he wanted to get back to the mill farm and see Belinda. He had been gone for over a month, and he had missed her more than he thought possible. She had been on his mind constantly, was on his mind now.

"Darling, why are you so quiet? I would think you'd have something to say to me after being gone so long."

Gabriel glanced at his companion, who sat on the velvet seat across from him. The rocking of the coach caused the diamond drops hanging from her slender choker to swing and glitter fire in the lantern light. She was truly a beautiful woman, especially tonight, in black satin and sparkling jewels, warm, perfumed, willing to give herself to him if he gave the slightest hint of wanting her. But after the sweetness of Belinda's innocence, she no longer had any appeal for him. It was getting harder for him to play the game he was caught in, pandering to traitorous Tories who turned their backs on their own country to align with the Crown. He had no respect for her, and now had trouble hiding that fact, but still continued to use her to his own ends. That was the only reason he was with her now—because she had offered him an invitation he coveted, into the house of the new head of British intelligence in New York. Annabelle was still awaiting his answer, her annoyance visible.

Gabriel lifted a shoulder in a casual dismissal of her question. "I told you I was tired from the voyage. You should have invited someone else to escort you."

"Don't be cruel, Gabe." She turned her head to a different angle to observe him, but only because she knew it was her best side. "What's the matter with you? You've become so moody in the last few months."

Maybe because there was a bloody, godawful war waging, he thought contemptuously, with brave Americans dying on the battlefields and scaffolds every single day, while you dance and bat your damn eyelashes to charm the enemy.

His reply was much more bland. "I have more important things on my mind than dancing."

"Another woman, mayhap?" she asked, her ever-present jealousy seeping through, no matter how sugar-coated with flirtation. "Is that the real reason you've practically ignored me?"

Damn right, he thought, a real lady with raven curls that hang like black satin to her waist and eyes the color of the sky. And she would soon have jewels to rival the ones Annabelle wore with such careless pride, and drawing books and pencils, all of which he had bought in Savannah as Christmas presents for her. In fact, he had brought gifts back for everybody waiting for him up at the Bronx farm: tea and velvet and porcelain dolls, and all manner of goods difficult to obtain now that the war had waged on and limited supplies for so long.

"I haven't been ignoring you," he finally answered. "I've been away on business, as you well know."

Gabriel grimaced when Annabelle lifted her massive skirts and swept across the interior of the carriage in a great rustling of silk and satin. She pressed herself close against his side, snuggling in as if she belonged there, even pressing her breasts against his shoulder. She fiddled with the silver buttons at the front of his waistcoat, then slid her hand slowly downward to his lap, taking liberties with his person that would have shocked him if he didn't already know her lustful appetites so well.

The woman was determined to seduce him into her bed again, a fate he found particularly repugnant now that he had pledged himself to Belinda. He took her fingers from him, but she was not to be deterred, twisting and pressing her mouth against his in a long, heated kiss. He felt nothing except extreme impatience to get away from her. She moaned under his mouth, writhing her body against his arm as if caught in some sublime ecstasy. Thanks be to God, he thought, as her driver stopped the coach under a torch-lit portico. He pushed her off him.

"We've arrived, my dear."

Annabelle sat up breathlessly, chuckling softly as if they shared some delicious secret, patting her bodice and skirt into some semblance of order. He climbed out and waited impatiently, longing for the day when he could bring Belinda back to the city. He would dress her in silks and hand her down from coaches and give her everything within his power to attain. She would be beautiful beyond compare.

Possibly he might be able to journey up the Bronx River tonight, he thought as Annabelle alighted beside him, though he really should wait until he could brief Henri on his mission south. He had been disappointed to find Henri out of the city and not expected back for several days. He wasn't in the mood to tarry long, not with Belinda waiting in his bed at the farm.

In the last few days he had been considering the possibility of marrying her before the war ended. He had thought about that subject long and hard while he stared out over the white-capped waves. The war made their future together uncertain, their happiness elusive, but he wanted to give her his name. He had been the first man who had lain with her, and he wanted to make sure he was the last. And he wanted any child of their union to be blessed without question of legitimacy.

Inside the house, the party was in full swing, loud music filtering faintly into the courtyard, where many Tory carriages and horses sporting shiny British saddles were congregated. He would mingle freely among the revelers, especially in the smoking and gaming parlors set aside for the officers and gentlemen.

He felt Annabelle tuck her hand into the crook of his arm in a possessive show of affection. She was brazen tonight, no doubt because of his growing indifference to her charms. Annabelle loved manipulating men, and one who did not fall under her spell became the ultimate challenge. She was an interesting woman all right. Intelligent, generous in her own way, but he pitied her poor future husband and any other man stupid enough to linger long in her clutches.

A Negro butler in white livery and a gold turban bowed deeply as he swung open the front door. Inside, beautiful women glided past on the arms of gentlemen in satin knee breeches and silver-buckled shoes. Gabriel could hardly keep from registering his scorn because the house belonged to an old friend of his family, a patriot who had given his life at the Battle of Trenton. His property had been commandeered, his family thrown onto the street. It sickened Gabriel to see the scarlet coats milling about the marble hall as if they owned the place.

"There's our handsome host now," Annabelle was whispering to him. "Come, darling, let me introduce you to Major Andre. He's such a charming man."

Gabriel handed over his evening cloak and cane to a waiting servant and trailed Annabelle's wide rose-hued silk skirt to where the British officer stood, resplendent in his full-dress uniform. A woman wearing green satin stood nearby, but was turned away as she conversed with a small group of smiling British officers. Her hair was piled high upon her head in the elaborate ringlets that were so fashionable and powdered liberally with white, and she seemed to be charming her male admirers. But he was more interested in his prey, the notorious Major John Andre, who now greeted Annabelle with a gallant bow and effusive flattery. She twittered with pleasure as he pressed his mouth to the back of her hand.

"My dear Annabelle," Andre said while looking into her eyes. "You are absolutely radiant tonight."

Gabriel had never met Major Andre, but he had heard plenty about him. As he had been told the man was good-looking, even dashing in his immaculate, gold-epauletted uniform. But he was better known for his cunning against the enemy as well as his ruthlessness in ferreting out patriot agents.

"Major, please allow me to introduce my escort this evening," Annabelle was saying, drawing Gabriel up closer. Gabriel's eyes connected with Andre's keen, piercing regard as they shook hands, and Gabriel knew instantly that this Englishman was no fool. He would be a worthy adversary, and Gabe would do well to keep up his guard when dealing with him. "May I present Mister Gabriel Elliott."

Andre's face showed visible shock followed quickly by a wide grin that seemed almost excited. "I've been waiting to meet you, Mr. Elliott. I understand you've been in Savannah on business?"

Startled that Major Andre had been kept abreast of his movements, he hid his sudden wariness. "That's right. I arrived home only today."

"Well, I must tell you, sir, there's someone here tonight who is most anxious to see you."

"Indeed? And who might that be?"

Andre nodded toward the woman in green. "She's doing me the honor of acting as my host-

ess for tonight's festivities. If you'll excuse me.
I'll fetch her to you."

Gabriel watched Andre walk a few steps to
where the woman still stood in the midst of the
fascinated officers. Andre took hold of the woman's arm to catch her attention and bent to speak
a few words intimately into her ear.

Gabriel watched them curiously, wondering
who the woman was. A lover of Andre's, perhaps? Even more puzzling was why she might
want to see him. She held a goblet of cham-
pagne in one hand, but when she turned and
smiled up at Andre, every single muscle in Gabriel's body turned to granite. Completely
stunned, he watched Belinda approach them,
thinking, no, he had to be wrong. *It can't be her,
it can't be her.*

"What is it, my darling?" Annabelle was demanding, her eyes roaming over his face as he
tried in vain to hide his astonishment.

"I've a surprise for you, dear Belinda," Andre
was telling her as they drew near, and she was
smiling up at Andre. He could hardly recognize
her in the outlandish powdered coiffure and the
heart-shaped beauty patch pasted at the corner
of her mouth. She still had not seen Gabriel.

"Look who's here," Andre told her, gesturing
at Gabriel, and Belinda turned her smile on him,
froze, blinked, then blanched as white as her
hair. She almost dropped the glass from her
hand. "Gabe, Gabe . . . I . . ."

"I don't believe we've met. I am Annabelle

Barton. Mr. Elliott is my escort tonight," Annabelle told Belinda at once, obviously not recognizing her as the woman she had noticed at Gabriel's soiree. But why should she? Belinda looked like a completely different woman tonight.

Gabriel found himself immobile, his voice mute as he tried to absorb the impact of finding her in Andre's house. What was she doing there? How did she even get there from so far upriver? Then like a flash of lightning at midnight it all made a terrible kind of sense.

Oh, God, she was one of them after all, had been working for them from the beginning. He had been duped into being the worst kind of fool. Anger shot up like a fiery geyser, swelling in a great tidal wave that nearly staggered him.

Belinda's face was now devoid of shock, but drenched with fear, and he had to fight, had to physically stop himself from grabbing her by the throat and choking the life from her.

"I can see you're surprised, Mr. Elliott, but you cannot deny that Belinda looks beautiful now that I've gotten her a wardrobe of suitable clothes to wear. If you'll allow me, I'll explain how Belinda came to be staying at my house." Gabriel's eyes lowered to Andre's hands and the way he had taken up Belinda's gloved hand and was caressing her arm.

A red haze seemed to cloud his vision, but Gabriel locked his jaw and held himself strictly in check. He waited for Andre to finish. Was he about to order him seized for a traitor? Had this been Belinda's mission all along, to seduce him, then lead him like a sacrificial goat to Andre? How could he have been so blind, so stupid?

"You mustn't be upset with Belinda, Mr. Elliott," Andre was continuing blithely, ignorant of Gabe's inner turmoil. "I'm the one who insisted she and Annie come home with me."

Gabriel forced himself to remain impassive, forced his tongue to move. "I'm afraid I don't quite understand. Did you visit my mill farm, Major?"

Belinda now looked ill, as if she might swoon at any moment. What in God's name was going on? Apparently, she hadn't turned him in, not yet, anyway. What the devil were her intentions?

Major Andre's tone still waxed apologetic. "I am sorry to say, sir, that we went there with the expectations of finding a hotbed of rebel treason."

Gabriel forced a short laugh, as if he found the idea ridiculous. Belinda's blue eyes were huge now, terrified, never wavering an instant from Gabe's face. Beseeching him, begging him, while Andre held her elbow and stroked her arm as if he owned her. Were they lovers, too? Had she again exchanged her body for her freedom?

His back teeth ground together, working his jaw until he could feel the nerves jumping at the side of his face. But he smiled, stiffly, hu-

morlessly. "Dare I hope my farm and other servants survived your raid, Major Andre?"

"Of course, you have my reassurance on that
count, Mr. Elliott. We did search the premises,
but found nothing untoward." He eyed Gabe
soberly. "I suppose you already know, sir, that
one Bartholomew Smythe is no friend of yours.
Belinda explained to me, of course, how he
brought her here and placed her inside your
home as a spy. I will always be personally grateful that you realized Belinda's innocence in the
whole affair and did the right thing by her."

What the hell was going on? "I did little, Major,
except allow her and her sister to remain on my
staff. She seemed harmless enough at the time."
His eyes cut to Belinda, and she bit her lip.

"And I commend you for your generosity, sir.
But now, with the permission of these ladies, I
would enjoy the honor of toasting your health,
if you will join me for a drink."

"I would be delighted, Major."

Gabriel knew nothing else but to go along
with whatever scenario played out in this bizarre situation, and he inclined his head toward
Annabelle, who merely looked relieved that Belinda was no longer in his employ. He watched,
coldly revolted, as Andre pressed a brief kiss
against Belinda's temple.

"Don't worry, my dear, everything will be all
right, just as I've been telling you all these
weeks."

Weeks? Gabriel thought as Belinda met his

gaze, then avoided it as she hurried away and was lost in the milling throng. Was he to be apprehended now? Perhaps outside where there would not be a stir that would upset the other guests? He contemplated various escape routes as Andre led him down the hallway toward the back of the house. They ended up in the study, a small room filled with leather chairs and the smell of old books and beeswax polish. Gabriel looked at the polished desk where papers were stacked in neat piles. Orders for Andre's agents?

"I suppose you've guessed what I want to talk to you about?"

"Why don't you tell me?" Gabriel answered, taking the glass of cognac proffered him.

"I don't know if Belinda felt comfortable telling you about her past, but I can tell you that she deserves a far better life than one of thankless servitude."

"I suppose everyone deserves better than that."

Andre grinned. "She's a wonderful young lady, isn't she? I knew her family in London, you see. Our fathers were old friends. Therefore, I feel a certain responsibility for her now that she's alone in the world, and for little Annie, too, of course . . ."

"Does that mean Annie is here with her?"

"Yes, poor child. She's not known a normal childhood since her mother died. I'd like to restore them to the kind of life they should have had with their parents in London."

Gabriel waited. Could Belinda not have told Andre the truth about himself? Were they baiting him along in order to uncover his accomplices? He had trusted Belinda once; but now she was in the company of an old friend. Perhaps Andre had managed somehow to turn her loyalties back to the British side.

"I wish to buy their documents of indenture and give them the gift of their freedom. I'm quite well off financially, you understand. I can pay you whatever it costs. You have only to name it."

He must be in love with her, Gabriel realized; that was why he was going to all this trouble. A new kind of rage sloshed like acid through his stomach. His fingers tightened around the glass.

"I understand your eagerness. Belinda is a most beautiful young woman."

Andre assumed an offended expression with pursed lips and narrowed eyes. "I assure you, Mr. Elliott, my intentions concerning Belinda are completely honorable."

"I'm sure they are, Major." That was a damned lie, he thought, tossing back the remainder of the cognac and wanting more as it burned its way down his throat and into his stomach. "Actually, I have all the servants I need. I'll be happy to tear up their contracts myself. As you pointed out, Belinda and Annie deserve more out of life."

Andre stood and came forward, looking quite overwhelmed by Gabriel's immense generosity.

He extended his palm in a gesture of his friendship. "I am forever in your debt, sir."

They shook hands, then Andre refilled both their glasses.

"To freedom," Gabriel said sardonically, clinking his glass against that of the British head of intelligence in New York City, as if they were now the best of friends.

Later that evening Belinda entered her upstairs bedchamber in John Andre's house and leaned her back against the closed door. The ball was still going on downstairs, many couples still revolving around the dance floor, but she had excused herself to John, pleading fatigue so she could flee to the sanctuary of her private room where she could lose the facade she had frozen upon her face.

Finally, here alone, she could give vent to the awful pain that had been aching inside her breast since she had turned and seen Gabriel. She took a convulsive swallow and fought the nausea bubbling up into her throat.

Agitated, she threw her ivory fan onto the bed and buried her face in her open palms. Over and over she kept reliving the look on Gabriel's face when he first saw her there with Major Andre, until the old impassive mask had come down and turned his eyes into frozen sapphire chips. He had disappeared soon after, and she had not seen him again. Where had he gone? What must he be thinking about her?

Hooking a finger into her white evening gloves, she stripped them off and fumbled in the drawer of the dressing stand for a handkerchief. She pressed the soft linen to her wet eyes and stared helplessly at her pale face reflected in the mirror. She froze when she heard a click at the door latch. She spun around, startled, clutching both hands against her breast, as she saw Gabriel enter, shut the door behind him, then turn the key in the lock.

"Gabe," she breathed, joy rising, then falling just as quickly when she saw his face. She swallowed hard. "You shouldn't be here. They'll catch you."

"What, my love? Am I no longer welcome in your bedchamber? After I welcomed you so wholeheartedly into mine?"

Belinda stared at him, aghast at the empty, emotionless expression in his eyes, and felt a quivery chill of alarm undulate from the base of her spine. She had not seen him quite like this before, even in those first days in his house, when she had been petrified of him. Her voice wouldn't work, wedged tightly behind the huge lump in her throat.

"Did I serve my purpose, Belinda? Have you moved on now to your next lover? The next willing fool able to provide you with fancy satin gowns so you can pretend to be a lady."

"It's not what you think, Gabe," she forced out. "I swear it. Please, just listen to me for a moment. Let me explain what happened after you left for Savannah."

His laugh was totally devoid of humor, a chilling sound of cold, controlled rage. "I think I can figure it out on my own. Andre's the highest bidder, and you're the grand prize."

"Please, Gabe, don't—"

A soft tapping at the door interrupted her, and their eyes held.

"Belinda, my dear? May I come in?" It was Andre, his voice low, concerned.

Gabriel's gaze was so full of scorn that Belinda flinched. He withdrew a small silver pistol from somewhere underneath his dark blue frockcoat.

"I'm very tired, Major, and I'm suffering from a terrible headache. Could we speak in the morning, please?"

"Of course, my dear, forgive me for intruding. I'll look forward to seeing you at breakfast. Good night."

"Good night," she said, relieved he had not pressed her to allow him entry. She and Gabriel stood staring at each other as Andre's footsteps receded down the outside corridor.

"His concern is very touching, is it not?" Sarcasm dripped like acid from his words.

"He's an old friend of mine, Gabe," she whispered hoarsely, desperate to make him understand. "Nothing more. I swear it. He looks upon me as he would a little sister."

Gabe said nothing. Belinda tried again. "I missed you so much."

His face finally reacted, violently. "What happened to Namasset and his family? Were they taken by the British?"

"No, no one was. Bart ordered the place searched, but they didn't find Judson and Larrew in the hidden room. John arrested no one. He only took Annie and me because he felt responsible for us."

"You always manage to land on your feet, don't you, Belinda?"

"I haven't betrayed you, Gabe, please believe me. I never could, never."

"Not yet, you mean. Just out of a macabre sense of curiosity, why not?"

Her lower lip quivered, and she caught it between her teeth. "Because I believe in what you believe in."

"What do you think I am—a complete idiot?"

"I came with John because I wanted to get him off the mill farm before he found out what you were doing there. I was trying to protect you."

"Forgive me if I don't believe a word you say."

"I can be of value to you and the patriots here in John's house. He's the head of British intelligence in the city, did you know that? And he trusts me. I can gather information for you by living here."

"I'd rather trust a scorpion poised to strike."

She could not bear the way he looked at her, with utter disgust. She reached out and put her hand on his arm. He stepped back from her. "Then take me away from here. Take me back to the farm with you."

Gabriel's eyes were dark, emotionless ice. "I came up here to warn you, Belinda. If you betray me, betray any of my people, you'll pay the price. Do you understand me, Belinda? You will not be spared. As far as I'm concerned you're the enemy now, nothing more, nothing less."

Then he was gone, and Belinda was left to stare after him, her heart so twisted with pain that she could barely breathe.

Twenty-one

The weather had turned bad, lightning forking in currents that looked like a silver candelabra against the night sky. A torrent of rain pelted a road that was a winding ribbon of black mush. Gabriel slowed his mount and walked him through the raging tempest, cold water dripping off the shallow brim of his tricorne and soaking through his heavy woolen cloak. He plodded onward, the wind against his face, the air cool, smelling of wet pine needles and swamp marshes. He was getting close now to the encampment of the Continental Army, where Washington commanded the majority of his soldiers, and thank God, his hellish ride was about over.

Belinda's face welled up in his mind, the way she looked earlier that evening in her tight green bodice and full satin skirt, and he slammed the memory shut like a boring book.

Why was he such a fool where she was concerned? Why did he continue to want to believe her lies? Again and again and again. Was he so

blinded by love, or lust, or whatever the hell it
was he felt for her, that he could no longer trust
his own judgment? He didn't know what to
think. If she had lied about being a spy, if she
did work for the British, why hadn't she told
Andre the truth about Gabriel's patriot loyalties?

Her former relationship with Andre seemed
the contrived tale of a desperate woman, to say
the least. Yet Andre had verified they had been
old friends. It seemed so unlikely, and coinci-
dental as hell that Andre had come to the cabin
on a raid with no knowledge of her presence
there. Even more than the answers to these
questions, Gabriel wanted to know if Namasset
and his family were safe. Belinda had said they
were, but he needed better proof than that. He
had to find someone who had witnessed the
raid. Henri could tell him. He hoped he would
find the Frenchman at the encampment.

After another forty minutes of soaking rain
and rumbling thunder, dawn came slowly in an
ugly gray mantle of gloom. He finally reached
a rise that brought the outer perimeter of the
patriot camp into sight. A long valley stretched
out in front of him, with hundreds of campfires
beginning to glimmer as soldiers awoke and
dragged themselves out of their bedrolls. They
would be trying to keep warm and dry, an impossible feat, as they lived and fought together
for the first time as one army instead of individ-
ual state militias.

Pride filled him to think that they were all

one, at last, all Americans, and he wished to
God he could join them at their fires and fight
the war like a man instead of slinking around
spying in the midst of their enemies. The long
rows of tan canvas tents appeared as he moved
closer. He reined to a stop at a low warning
muttered by the first line of sentries. He
proffered the password to a man he had never
seen before and was allowed to proceed into
the camp.

Walking his horse, he passed one unit after
another; many identified by hand-lettered
boards stuck into the ground, and he read them
as he proceeded toward the center of the camp.
The *First Massachusetts*, the *Tenth Maine*, the
Twenty-second New York, on and on, all together
under one leadership.

The consolidation of colonies had not been an
easy feat, despite their common goal of independence from England. Many problems festered in
this camp where men from far-flung colonies
bickered among themselves and with each other,
but now they'd put their differences aside in
order to stand against the British tyranny.

Many of the men were hunkered down around
fires where cook pots hung suspended from tri-
pods. The soldiers he passed had suffered many
deprivations in the past few years of fighting.
Even now he could see how ragged and threadbare were their uniforms, and of many different
colors and designs, so shabby and unkempt
compared to the crisp scarlet jackets and spot-

less white trousers of the soldiers marching quick-step the length of Broad Street to hang more patriots at the Battery. Their leadership was often in the same turmoil, with many members of the newly formed Continental Congress blatantly critical of George Washington and the decisions he made as the commander-in-chief.

At the center of the valley floor near a sloppy, mud-clogged parade ground was the modest two-story farmhouse that Washington had made his headquarters. The structure bore little resemblance to the grandeur of Washington's own beautiful estate in Virginia. His wife, Martha, was at the camp as well, having given up the comforts of Mount Vernon to join her husband in his travails.

As early as it was, she would probably still be asleep upstairs, along with a few close female relatives who had made the journey with her, but the general had already risen for a sunrise meeting with his generals in the conference tent he had ordered constructed behind the house. Gabriel could see it now, and inside the sodden canvas walls, shadows moving about as some of the top-ranking officers took their places around the camp lantern lighting the interior.

Again Gabriel was stopped, checked thoroughly by a perimeter of posted guards. British assassins lurked everywhere, and others assigned to turn Washington's allegiance, or even kidnap him for ransom. Gabriel had heard the Crown was ready to offer Washington a duke-

dom to change his loyalties. It was a victory indeed for either side to woo enemy generals into
their own ranks. That was why Gabriel had been
sent south to approach Laughton in Savannah,
and rumors abounded constantly that American
generals were being enticed weekly with incred-
ible offers of money and English titles.

The tent was large, rectangular, its high ceiling supported by six sturdy poles. Washington
stood at the head of a camp table holding several glass-walled lanterns weighing down various maps of the colonies. He was a tall man,
one of the few Gabriel knew who met his gaze
at eye level. His face was craggy with lines of
worry and sun, his expression somber as he
stepped forth to meet Gabriel. He extended his
right hand and gave Gabriel's a quick firm
handshake.

"Good to see you, Gabe. How long have you
been back?"

"I landed on Manhattan yesterday morning. I
came here as soon as I could." Gabriel nodded
at Henri, glad to see his friend, who was grinning a broad welcome from a chair on the opposite side of the table. He sat beside his
countryman in the conflict, the courageous
French officer, the Marquis de Lafayette, who
had been instrumental in bringing the French
into the war a little over a year before.

Brigadier General Nathanael Greene, who
commanded the Rhode Island troops and was
also an old friend of Gabe's, nodded, as did the

officer beside him, General Horatio Gates who had forced Burgoyne's surrender at Freeman's Farm. The other officer present was a man Gabriel did not know. He rose as the commander-in-chief introduced him.

"Gabriel, I don't believe you've met General Arnold. Benedict's now in command at West Point."

Gabriel had heard of Benedict Arnold and knew him to be the American commander in Philadelphia earlier in the war who had stopped the advance of British forces under Carleton on Lake Champlain. He had not known he had been given the command of West Point. "It's an honor to meet you, sir."

As Gabriel took his seat beside Henri, General Arnold excused himself to return to his post, and while General Washington spoke privately with the departing officer just outside the tent flap, Henri slapped Gabe upon the back.

"Welcome home, my friend. I had begun to worry you were lost at sea."

"I'm glad to see you here in one piece," Gabe said, not sharing his friend's jovial mood. "Is everyone whole and well at the mill farm?"

Henri nodded. "I just came from there, and everything's in order, thanks to Belinda's friendship with Major Andre."

Gabriel's brows moved together, and he took a cup of coffee from the general's aide. "She's living with him in New York."

"He's a family friend, as I understand it."

Drinking the warm brew, Gabriel still scowled. "You don't mean you still trust her when she's living with the enemy?"

Henri appeared surprised by Gabe's remark. "Larrew said she was instrumental in getting the British off the farm. And Willamette said she staunchly defended you from Bart's accusations."

Had he been wrong? Jumped to the wrong conclusions? Gabriel wondered, but before he could question Henri further, Washington was back with his own inquiries for Gabriel.

"What news is there on the British girl Larrew was telling us about? The one staying at your Bronx farm."

Gabriel was surprised the general would be interested in discussing Belinda. He shrugged. "I know little, other than I saw her this past night at a ball given by Major John Andre. He seemed quite fond of her, but I'm not completely convinced we can trust her motives."

"Indeed?" Washington considered a moment. "Was I misinformed when told she kept Larrew and his team out of British hands?"

Gabriel glanced at Henri and knew his friend had related the incident at the mill. Gabriel still wasn't sure what to believe.

"I was able to spend a moment alone with her before I left the city." He hesitated, reluctant to pass along her suggestion. "She offered to work as our agent inside Andre's house. I did not agree because I wasn't sure she could be trusted."

"Andre often meets with his staff at his home," Henri interjected thoughtfully. "She might well be able to ferret out something important to us."

Washington's brows lifted, but he observed Gabriel in silence. "Yet you still harbor reservations, Gabe?"

Gabriel massaged the bridge of his nose with his thumb and forefinger, sighing, as he answered, "I'm not sure what to think, General. I trusted her until I found out she had such a close kinship with Andre. She's an Englishwoman after all, and his friend, and I fear he might be able to turn her to their side given the proper incentive."

Washington turned to Henri. "Henri, you've been in New York these last weeks. Have you heard rumors concerning the woman's allegiance?"

"I know her to have expressed a desire to help our cause," he said with a sidelong glance at Gabriel. "She was brought here as an indentured servant and has been working in Gabe's house. From what I understand she now wants to stay here. She has indicated to me and to others that she admires the Americans and supports our fight for independence. England was ultimately cruel to her and her family."

Washington rubbed his fingers against his clean-shaven jaw, considering everything he'd heard. "Then I will leave the decision as to her trustworthiness to your judgment, Gabe, since you seem to know her better than anyone else. Approach her again at the appropriate time and try to ascertain if she can be of value to us. Do you have any objections to that course of action?"

"No, sir."

"All right. Then let us talk about your trip to Savannah. Were you able to attain an audience with General Laughton?"

"I'm afraid the mission was a failure, sir. He was out in the field with his men. I never saw him. However, I did speak with his mother. She's a loyal patriot and is working to change his allegiance herself."

"Perhaps we'll leave the situation in her hands for the time being," Washington murmured then moved on to the next subject.

Gabriel listened attentively to the discussion as Greene spoke about the various officers involved in the British occupation of Philadelphia, but queasy misgivings squirmed through his gut. Somehow he knew it was a dangerous mistake to keep Belinda inside the enemy camp. Regardless of whether or not he was wrong about her, even if she was guiltless and completely on their side, she would be in terrible danger spying on a man like John Andre. No matter how hard he tried, he could not shake the feeling of doom that cinched his chest like a tight leather strap.

Well after dark, forty-eight hours later, Belinda led Annie by the hand up the steps and into the back door of Gabriel's Broad Street mansion. The moon was out, a silver of light turning the bare branches of the towering oak trees to silver. It was cold, but the January chill did not cause the strange sensations that overcame her as she raised the doorknocker and let it fall. She jumped at the loud clang it made, almost as nervous as she had been the first time she and Annie had come to Gabriel Elliott's house. It seemed so long ago now, but even then, when she was entering with the express intention to spy on him she was not as terrified as she was now.

"I wish we could come back here to live again, don't you, Bee?"

"Yes, I do, Annie."

Though Gabriel had sent word with Lizzie that he wanted to see her, she didn't know the reason why, but she had come as soon as she could get away. She smiled when Dulcimer opened the door for them.

"C'mon in out of the cold. It be good to see the both of you!" Dulcimer cried, grabbing up Annie and holding her tightly in her arms.

"Dulcimer! I'm so hungry!" Annie said, inhaling deeply. "And I smell some of that good punkin pie, don't I, Dulcimer?"

"You sure do, honey lamb, and you can have all you want, baby girl, and fresh cream on top, too!"

"I've missed you, Dulcimer," Belinda told her, realizing how true it was. She had missed Dulcimer and Lizzie both, and Paulie and Tommy, and Gabriel. She had missed Gabriel more than she could bear.

"I was pleased as I could be when the master say you was comin' back for a visit."

Belinda bent down to take off Annie's coat, then hung it up before she slipped out of her own cape. Lizzie was there as well, at the table now, cutting a huge piece of pie for Annie.

"Mr. Elliott be in his study." Dulcimer lowered her voice. "He say for me to keep Annie here in the kitchen while you go to him."

"Then I had better hurry. Annie, behave now, and don't make yourself sick on that pie."

Annie nodded, a smear of churned cream dripping down her chin.

Belinda moved through the downstairs, the dining room, the parlor, chastising herself because she felt as if she were coming home after a long absence. She rounded the newel post and found the door of his study wide open. Gabriel stood inside, one palm propped on the mantlepiece as he gazed down into the fire.

She could not stop the way her heartbeat quickened, the cadence growing until it slammed hard beneath her breastbone. She walked to the threshold, then stopped, trying to judge his mood, trying to stop the pulse jumping inside her wrists.

"Hello."

He looked up, straightened. He was dressed in evening attire, a well-tailored black frockcoat and silver waist coat, a snowy white stock. He looked wonderful. Was he escorting the beautiful Mistress Barton again? Hurt gripped her heart.

"Come in, Belinda."

He came toward her, and when he passed close enough, she could smell his shaving soap, the familiar spicy scent that reminded her of the pines along the Bronx River. Unlike the last time they met, he seemed relaxed, no anger on his face—in control, but not with the frigid, self-imposed iron will he displayed that night in her bedchamber at Andre's house.

"Please sit down."

She did so, in a wing chair at the right of the hearth. He resumed his post at the mantel. "Thank you for coming."

"I was very pleased to receive your summons," she said in all truthfulness, but she hated that her voice sounded so eager, even to her. "I've missed you, Gabe."

Her gaze met his, and she nearly recoiled with disappointment, for she could almost see the distrust lurking in the shadows of his dark blue eyes.

"Don't think I asked you here because I trust you," he told her in an even, unemotional voice. "I've been instructed to give you a second chance."

"Thank you. I know I can be of help. John often entertains British officers, sometimes in secret meetings late at night."

"How do you know that?"

"I've heard them arrive at the portico under my window long after everyone is asleep. They're heavily cloaked, and they closet themselves with Andre in his private study."

"Have you seen any of them well enough to identify them?"

"No, but I haven't gone downstairs and tried to see them. I'm willing to, if that's what you want me to do."

Gabriel turned away and moved to the window that overlooked the street. Belinda leaned back in her chair, pleased they were talking together without anger, that he was willing to give her a chance to prove herself.

"It could be dangerous if Andre catches you spying on him."

"John would never hurt me. I told you we were old friends. He feels responsible for me."

"Don't you mean he's in love with you?" Gabriel looked at her as he said it.

"No, you're wrong about that." She stood and walked toward him. "He thinks of me as a younger sister. Just as he does Annie."

"You're truly naive if you believe that. I saw the way he looked at you, the way he caressed your hand. And I was in your bedchamber when he meant to join you there."

Suddenly realizing that he was displaying signs of jealousy, which meant he still must care for her, she prayed she was right. She smiled a little. "I haven't noticed him looking at me. I think about you, Gabe, and the way you look at me. The way we were at the mill farm. I've done nothing to betray you, and I never would. I'd do anything for you."

"Yet you live in this man's house with no regard for propriety. Everyone in town assumes you to be lovers."

Belinda's heart lifted with hope. He was just hurt and upset that she was living with Andre.

She could not stop the gladness that curved her mouth into a smile. "I am not his lover. I have no wish to be." She stopped, wanting desperately for him to believe her. "I had no choice, you must know that. You have only to ask Willamette, or Timon, or anyone who was there the day Bart brought the British." She moved closer, every fiber of her body leaning out toward him, longing to feel his arms around her, strong, protecting her, loving her.

"I haven't stopped loving you, Gabe."

He seemed set in stone, his eyes tormented with conflicted emotions. He was fighting himself, she could see it so clearly. She could not stop herself, she had to touch him again, or die, if only for a brief moment. She pressed up against him, wrapping her arms around his waist. Her cheek lay against the soft folds of his linen neckcloth, and her voice came out low and husky.

"You can trust me, I swear it. I'd never do anything to hurt you."

For a moment he stood as still and hard as a

marble column, then she sighed with pleasure when his arms came around her. He said nothing, but as she looked up at him, she knew at once by the heat in his eyes that he wanted to kiss her. She raised her face eagerly, and his mouth touched hers, warm, firm, tentatively tasting her as if he did so against his will.

Then he seemed to give in to himself, and his arm came up behind her and brought her crushing against his chest. Her knees went weak, and she let him support her as he bent her over his arm, his mouth ravaging hers. She clutched him tighter, never wanting to let go, moaning from the sheer pleasure of his hands upon her, after so long apart. She was totally unprepared when his fingers closed tightly around her upper arms and thrust her back. An awful look was stamped on his face.

"You have learned the art of seduction well, Belinda. Did Andre succumb as easily as I?"

Shocked back to reality, all the pleasant sensations fled her, the insult all the more stinging in its impact from its sheer unexpectedness.

"No," she denied weakly, hurt, until her own pride rose like a vengeful viper to protect her. "You're the only man who has used me in his bed for his own ends—not Bart, not John Andre, only you."

The inscrutable mask he usually wore disintegrated under her attack. She saw guilt, clearly, before he hid it underneath a look of disdain.

When he spoke next, he was all business, as if they were total strangers.

"You're right, of course. Forgive me. It'll not happen again, I assure you. If you learn anything of value to us, come here or to my office on the docks. Now you'll have to excuse me. I'm due to escort Annabelle to the theater."

He left the room without another word, without a backward glance, leaving her trembling, nursing hurt feelings that quickly turned into anger. He had no right to treat her in such a way. She ought to go home and allow Andre to take care of her. She ought to forget Gabriel. She ought to hate him.

Later that night, however, snuggled up close with Annie in the big tester bed in John Andre's house, she lay awake and admitted the truth. She loved him. She had committed herself to him that snowy night in the cabin. She would have to find a way to make him trust her again. She would redouble her efforts to find out information that would prove herself a loyal patriot. With that resolution, she finally slept, her dreams turning to haunting nightmares in which Gabriel held Annabelle tightly, kissing her, caressing her, until Belinda woke, shivering and wondering if it were true.

Twenty-two

Nearly six weeks dragged by before Gabriel stood motionlessly at his office window, his hands clasped behind his back. His eyes were fixed on the choppy gray waters in the distance where ship masts rose like hundreds of up-ended spears against the brilliant blue sky. Mostly English frigates, transporters of the hundreds of lobster-backs who patrolled the streets of Manhattan, treating loyal Americans like the lowest slum vermin.

Disgust filled him at the sight of the English Union Jack everywhere he looked, snapping and waving in the early March wind. The war had dragged on so long. Would they never triumph against His Majesty's might?

Impatient to be off the confines of British-occupied Manhattan, he scanned the cobbled street below for Belinda. He had sent word for her to visit him at the docks because he now had a mission for her, one that she could perform better than anyone else.

Since they had given her permission to work

with them against her old friend, Major John Andre, she had become quite the social butterfly. He had heard much about her during the last weeks, from Tories, patriots, and British soldiers alike. Her soft beauty and innocent charm had turned the heads of gentlemen far and wide. He had seen her himself as the latest belle of New York balls, and hardly recognized her as the shy young servant who had first come into his house.

However, despite her celebrated socializing among Andre's Tory friends, she had yet to send him any information, had not even sent word that she wished to meet with him. Perhaps she liked her new status pretending to be an English lady. Lady Belinda, just as she'd always wanted. She had little to gain exposing Andre and his friends, he thought bitterly. Or perhaps she was merely waiting out the war to see which side would win before choosing the man she would marry. His face darkened at the thought, his mood growing even blacker than it already was.

A short time later, Major Andre's carriage—a well-polished rig Gabriel knew had been confiscated from a courageous American who died at Trenton early in the war—drew up before the planked sidewalk in front of Gabriel's building. The handsome British major stepped down, in full scarlet military regalia, no doubt on his way to preside over the afternoon's brutal hanging of patriot heroes.

Bile surged at the back of Gabriel's throat, sour and sickening. The dashing Englishman handed Belinda to the curb, gallant, poised, and Gabriel looked forward to the moment when he could meet the likes of Andre on a battleground, man to man, musket in hand.

Major John Andre was one of the worst of the British command, if only because of his affability and supposed honor. He was a dangerous opponent, not to be underestimated. He wielded a great deal of power over life and death to many an American, and Belinda held great sway over him.

Belinda had that power, to insinuate herself into a man's mind. She had done it with him. He had thought about little else since he had met her. He had tried to be objective, tried to forget his feelings about her living in Andre's house. No one else in his circle seemed to doubt her patriotic motives, but still he harbored misgivings. She seemed able to change sides as quickly as a spinning rooftop weather vane.

His jaw clamped when he saw Andre bend from the waist and press his mouth to the backs of her fingers. Not a brotherly gesture, as she would have Gabriel believe. Nor did he care for Belinda's beaming smile as the major climbed back inside. She waved a white lace hankie at the departing coach, and Gabriel sat down at his desk and waited for her to appear.

To his dismay he found anger rising like a wintry wind inside him, the same rage that had possessed him since he had returned from Savannah and found Belinda at the ball. Night and day he had wrestled with his frustration over Belinda, fought his shame at mingling daily with his Tory enemies, smiling and nodding at their stories of patriot buffoonery and American defeats.

Agitated, he sought to calm himself by watching the workman put the last touches on the *Pelican*, a newly constructed ship almost ready for commission into the British fleet. The deep-hulled brig was a troop transport, destined to bring even more of the bloody redcoats to American shores, or perhaps the dreaded German mercenaries called Hessians, who killed Continental soldiers for gold coin.

But this particular ship's usefulness would be limited, as would a good number of others he had watched launched from his shipyard in the past few years. He had ordered the most loyal of his crew to sabotage the construction. The *Pelican*'s rudder would weaken and break asunder the first time it experienced rough seas.

Sabotage was not the role he wished in this conflict, but he took pride in the number of naval vessels he had helped put out of commission. A grim smile curved his mouth as Belinda was announced. She appeared, looking lovely in a white dress striped with mint green and a beribboned velvet bonnet to match the sash at her waist.

"Mistress Belinda, how nice to see you. Please, sit down."

Belinda smiled so warmly, as if she was truly pleased to see him. She seated herself with a graceful sway of full skirts and rustling satin petticoats. He wondered what went on between Andre and her every night in that house. He remembered with all-too-vivid detail what had happened between Belinda and him when she had been in his house.

"What a lovely gown, Belinda."

"Major Andre has been most generous with Annie and me."

She had the grace to sound embarrassed, but he could not hide his sarcasm. "And how do you repay him for such generosity?"

Belinda stared at him a moment, then answered quietly without lowering her gaze. "As you well know, Gabriel, I repay him by betraying him to you."

Their eyes locked until he felt compelled to look away.

"I've done everything you've asked of me," she said softly a moment later. "I've tried to find out things for you, but he's very careful with his papers." She paused. "Why do you treat me like this? Can't you see how much it hurts me?"

Gabriel felt the sting of her accusation, then of his own conscience. "I don't trust his motives."

"Don't you mean you don't trust *my* motives?"

Twisting her gloved hands together as if

upset, she rose and stood at the windows. Without looking at him, she said, "He's a true gentleman. He would never take liberties with me. Nor would I let him. Can you say the same thing about yourself and Annabelle Barton?"

"I have no regard for Tories, especially Annabelle," he replied in a cold voice.

"Nor do I," she countered, swiveling back to look at him.

Her eyes implored his with such emotion that he almost rose and went to her. He forced himself to remain untouched.

"I'm leaving the city, Belinda. For good, this time."

She was stricken at the news and made no effort to hide it.

"We've learned that I'm soon to be arrested," he told her, pausing momentarily as Belinda gasped and steadied herself by grasping the back of her chair. Her face was so white, he could not help but believe her alarm was real.

"Oh, God help us," she muttered hoarsely. "Why do they suspect you?"

"Bart's behind their suspicions, which shouldn't surprise anybody. He couldn't persuade Andre, so he set forth his case before Sir Henry Clinton himself. They've set agents to watch me night and day. Two of them are on duty right now, down at the corner."

"What evidence do they have against you?"

Gabriel's smile was devoid of humor. "They manufacture evidence every day against the patriots they suspect. It will be no different in my case. They'll imprison me and worry about the cause later."

"Then of course you must flee!" she cried with feeling. "Before they can come for you! Please, Gabriel, they could hang you!"

Her concern was touching, he thought, *if it was real.* Yet somehow he knew it was. Despite his own accusations, his heart had begun to tell him she was genuine. She had been loyal, proven it by not turning him over to Andre the moment he had returned to New York. The truth was his own jealousy had colored his judgement. He was tired of fighting his feelings for her, but how could he tell her that now? And then expect her to do what he was about to ask of her?

"Preparations have been made for me to leave New York."

"You're going to leave everything, all this,"— she swept an arm expansively toward the busy shipyard with its scaffolds and workers. "Who will take care of your business concerns?"

He shrugged, already having prepared himself for what was to happen. "Everything will be confiscated. Bart will probably get most of it, including my house on Broad Street. That's what he's wanted all along."

"But that's so unfair!"

"Do you think I give a damn about that? I've already sent most of my ships to sea to be given over to our patriot navy, as meager as it is. I'll get my property back once we oust the British from our shores."

"When do you leave?" Her voice was full of dread.

"Within the week."

"Take us with you, Annie and me."

Her request was made with no sign of guile. He hesitated, but he knew that was impossible because of what they now required of her. "I can't, I'm sorry. I have an order for you, a strict one, so I want you to listen carefully and do exactly what I say."

Belinda's dark-lashed blue eyes riveted intensely on his face.

"I want you to betray me to Andre—" He got no further.

"No! I won't do it! I can't!"

"Listen to me, Belinda, if they think you're loyal enough to the king to hand me over, your position here in New York will be secured. Even Bart will be satisfied that you're on their side. With me gone, your closeness to Andre will be doubly important."

"No, I can't," she insisted, shaking her head. "What if they find you before you escape from Manhattan? They'll hang you, you know they will."

Gabriel took hold of her shoulders and forced her to look at him. She was fighting back tears. "That's not going to happen. If you play it correctly, I'll be gone before you incriminate me."

Her teeth caught at her bottom lip. "Where are you going? Back to the mill farm?"

"No. I'm going to march with the Continental Army. That's what I've wanted to do from the beginning."

"Will I get to see you again?"

"Perhaps. It's been decided that you'll stay here until you are no longer useful. If you need to transfer information, you're to get word to Dulcimer, and she'll relay it to me. She'll be leaving my house after I'm gone. Do you think you can persuade Andre to hire her on his household staff?"

She looked miserable, but she nodded. "I think so."

"That's what I figured. Tell him you need help with Annie if you must give him a reason. Do you have any other questions?"

She sighed heavily, obviously resigned, then lifted tearful eyes to him.

"Tell me, Gabriel, how do you want me to betray you?"

Several days later, filled with dire foreboding, Belinda walked with leaded footsteps toward Major Andre's study. She carried a silver tea tray in her hands, but she trembled with dread. She stopped, inhaling deeply, cleansingly, until she felt calmer. She did not want to do this, she thought. Every nerve and fiber in her body rebelled against turning in the man she loved. What if something went wrong? What if they caught him?

Her stomach rolled in topsy-turvy waves, and

she set her chin. Transferring the tray to her left hand, she slid open the doors. John sat behind his desk, his uniform jacket hanging on the back of his chair. He was poring over the sheets of parchment spread out in front of him. She forced a bright smile.

"I've brought your tea, Major."

He glanced up, returning her smile as he jotted down a notation. "That's very thoughtful, my dear, but I'm afraid I'm rather busy at the moment. Perhaps I will join you later."

Placing the tray carefully upon the marble-topped tea table, she hesitated, watching him work, but knew she had to get him to listen to her.

"Please, Major, I really must speak with you. It's . . . it's urgent, I'm afraid." This time when he looked up, she could see his surprise. "Besides, I baked a batch of molasses cookies this morning, like the ones my mother used to serve when you came to call on us in London. Do you remember?"

"Aye, I remember very well. Father and I could smell them the moment we climbed your stoop." He put down his quill and stood up, stretching his arms over his head as if his muscles were stiff. "I suppose I could finish these later."

As he sat down at the other side of the table, she concentrated on pouring the fragrant tea into gold-sprigged porcelain cups, but she was aware that her hands were still unsteady. No doubt Andre would notice, too. Gabriel was supposed to be off the island by now, but what if something had delayed him?

"What's upsetting you, Belinda?"

Belinda gazed straight into his eye. "It's Mr. Elliott, you know, the man who employed me before I came here."

His face grew quite still, as if he wanted to conceal his reaction to the name, and she knew then that Gabriel was indeed under suspicion. Here they sat, she thought sadly, old friends lying to each other, working against each other. How awful war was.

"What about him?" he asked casually, but he watched her face closely.

She handed him a cup and saucer and waited for him to take a sip. She mentally formulated the best words to incriminate Gabriel, amazed at how easily the falsehoods were beginning to roll off her tongue. She had learned well how to lie since Bart had brought her from Quebec.

"Are you in love with Elliott, Belinda?"

She hadn't expected him to guess that, but John had always been intuitive, even when they were younger. Still, he would never expect her to work against him. The sympathy in his eyes stabbed her with guilt.

"I am grateful to him," she admitted, but this time she was unable to meet his gaze. "He was kind to take Annie and me into his home. And he was generous to free us from our indenture and allow us to come here."

Major Andre seemed to relax. He leaned back and took another sip. "Then what is it?"

She had no need to manufacture the troubled expression upon her face. "I feel terrible about doing this to Mr. Elliott, but I feel I must, out of loyalty to you. You've been so good to us."

John Andre leaned forward. "What are you trying to tell me, Belinda?"

"I think, well, I have a suspicion that Mr. Elliott might be a patriot spy."

His cup rattled in the saucer. "What makes you think that?"

"I found a document when I was in his house. I've been afraid to show it to anyone, but if he's a rebel, then maybe I should."

"Do you mean you still have it?" he asked excitedly.

She nodded, retrieving from her apron pocket the paper that Gabriel had written for her to give to Andre. He snatched it from her, unfolded it, then quickly scanned the contents. She sat still, feeling sick inside. Spying was such a dishonorable thing, filled with lies and deceit. Even though she no longer bore love for her fellow countrymen, she felt horrible about manipulating an old friend, whose only sin was being on the other side of the conflict.

"You did the right thing, my dear. Bart's been keeping him under surveillance since he returned, and I suppose this proves he was correct all along in doubting Elliott's loyalties."

"What will happen to him, John?"

"He'll be arrested at once, and interrogated." He stood up and grabbed his coat. "Thank you, Belinda, you've done the Crown a great service."

After he took his leave, she moved to the window and watched until he had mounted his horse. He disappeared down the street and she turned, her eyes going at once to his desk. Her breath caught.

In his haste to catch Gabriel, he had inadvertently left his work spread out on the desk for anyone to see. He had never been so careless before, and she glanced outside again to make sure he had not returned to fetch something, then sat down and quickly skimmed through the neatly scripted documents.

Good Lord, she thought with growing excitement, the papers were written by his secret agents. The spies were identified by one initial, and there was mention of an American prison camp. She read further and found the British had a chain of safe houses across New Jersey.

Shuffling through the other sheets, she also found mention of hidden gunpowder stores. She finally had information that would help Gabriel, she thought with relief as she carefully rearranged the documents as she had found them. She hurried from the room in search of Annie. She had to leave word with Dulcimer. The sooner she did, the sooner she would see Gabriel again.

Twenty-three

In the early morning hours the front door to Crosby's Tavern had long been bolted for the night. Gabriel edged stealthily through the dark, empty taproom, gratified that Samuel Crosby, the West Indian mulatto who ran the place, or Black Sam, as he was called by close friends, had managed to rid the inn of lingering customers so that Gabriel could enter by the rear door without being seen.

The tavern was several miles inland from the New Jersey shore and isolated enough to make it possible for him to travel there undetected, but such meetings were not without danger, especially for Belinda, who would have to make her way out of the city. After he had obtained her urgent summons from Dulcimer, he had enlisted Namasset to guide her safely to the rendezvous at the tavern.

Despite his annoyance at her reckless insistence on meeting with him in person, he could not deny that he was eager to see her again. He had had plenty of time in the last month in

Washington's camp to view her actions with a more objective eye. He no longer faulted her for the choices she had made; she had made the best of the situation in which she had found herself. She had struggled to survive in a world over which she had little control, not only for herself, but for her little sister. Who could not admire the courage she had shown?

Behind the massive fieldstone fireplace there was a hidden panel that led up an enclosed spiral stair to a secret chamber, one built many years before as protection against French-led savages during the French and Indian War. The passage was extremely narrow, so much so he was forced to turn his shoulders to accommodate their breadth. Belinda should have arrived some time ago, so he rapped softly on the door at the top of the steps—once, twice, then once again.

He had to wait only an instant. Belinda threw open the portal, her face aglow with happiness. Gone was her reticence, her careful gauging of his mood as had been the case when they had met at social affairs in New York. She threw herself into his arms, and he shut his eyes, any vestige of doubt chased away forever. He forgot what had transpired between them in the past, forgot her close alliance with Major Andre. Every thought of danger, of war, of spies and enemy agents, all slid out of his mind, and he thought only of the way her mouth felt under his searching, trembling lips.

"God help me, I've missed you," he got out in a hoarse, muffled groan.

Belinda said nothing, smothering him with sweetly eager kisses, clinging to him until he laughed softly, mightily pleased by her passion. He dragged her off the threshold, shut the door, and threw the bolt.

Their mouths met, ravaging, hard, insistent, making up for lost time, and his fingers found the laces of her bodice, then jerked at them until they gave way, and her breasts swelled free for his pleasure. The gown fell into a heap on the floor. He crushed her soft body against him, struggling out of his shirt. He inhaled sharply as his bare chest crushed her naked breasts. Lifting her off the floor, his blood rushed with fire as she wrapped her slender legs around his waist.

There was little time for love play, for each was much too desperate for the other, two lovers separated too long, by too much, by distrust, by distance, by stupid jealousy. He was hard for her, excited beyond reason when he entered her, finding her ready, open, warm, her skin like soft, hot velvet. He heard himself groan as they joined together, his arms around her waist, holding her tightly against him; her arms clenched around his neck as if she would never let go. They clung to each other, joined as one, as he turned and carried her to the bed. Lips warm, fingers searching, tongues caressing in the sensual erotic dance that inflamed their bodies. He felt his own desire rising like a wave of bloodred sensation, heard her cry out with a shuddering climax that he could feel inside her, then he exploded into her with such wondrous force that he was left shaken and breathless in its wake.

His love for her swelled inside his heart, revealing itself as never before, as they lay together, breaths heaving, bodies still taut and quivering while they clung to each other.

"I had every intention of scolding you for coming here," he whispered when he was again able to speak. His fingers slid into the softness of her ebony hair, his other hand molding the curve of her hips and drawing her against him, breast to breast, thigh to thigh. Her skin was pure silk, her breath sweet, her eyes dreamy.

"I couldn't bear the way you left. I was miserable." She stopped, tenderly cupping his face. "I was afraid I'd never see you again."

Gabriel smiled, their noses nearly touching. He took her mouth, their kiss a beautiful, gentle mingling of lips. She smiled, her eyes like warm blue pools of pure love.

"You've forgiven me?" she whispered.

"I had nothing to forgive you for. I've acted the fool, but I can't resist you any longer."

"I love you, Gabe. Nothing will ever change that."

"And I love you," he admitted, finished with doubts and fears.

But she pressed herself closer, her arms tightening around him. "I've waited so long to hear you say that."

He lay back against the pillow, taking her with him, pleased at the way she cuddled up against him.

"You shouldn't have come, Belinda. Both British and American patrols ride these roads. What if you had been captured?"

"Namasset wouldn't have allowed it. He moves like a shadow in the night. No one will ever catch him."

"That doesn't mean they won't catch you. If you're intercepted, he won't be able to save you."

She leaned her cheek against the hollow of his shoulder, her fingers tracing down the middle of his chest. His loins tightened as she reached the flat plane of his belly.

"I had to come. I have important information I got from Andre."

"You could have sent word to me through Namasset."

"I wanted to tell you myself, though I did not expect such a delightful welcome from you."

"I doubted you when you didn't deserve it. I wanted to show you how much I regretted it."

"Well, you did." She smiled, her eyes as smoky and sated as his own. "I was afraid Major Andre would seize you before you got away."

Gabriel lifted a strand of her hair, wrapped the silken lock around a finger as he gazed down at her smiling face. "I suspect he was thrilled when you turned me in to him."

"Yes, he was." She smiled mysteriously. "In fact, he was so excited he left his intelligence reports lying unattended on his desk."

Gabriel shot up on one elbow. "Did you read them?"

She laughed happily and wriggled closer. "Of course, I did. I memorized every word. That's why I'm here."

"What did you find out?" he demanded eagerly.

"I found out that they've stockpiled powder stores on Gardiner's Island, but most of the report dealt with an American prison camp in Pennsylvania. It also mentioned Tory safe houses that stretch all the way across the Jerseys. Escaped British prisoners are hidden in them until they can get back behind their own lines."

"Did you get the name of the American prison?"

Again she smiled, a smug, totally charming curve of love-swollen lips. "Aye, 'twas at a place called Lancaster."

"Good God, Washington has been plagued by that problem. The prisoners seem to disappear like apparitions, despite their brilliant red coats. Our patrols completely lose them." His face became animated. "Did he name the Tories who are helping them?"

"A few initials, but no names, I'm afraid."

Belinda suddenly grinned, glancing at the floor where his buff and blue uniform lay discarded at the side of the bed. "I didn't have time to tell you earlier, but I think you look quite dashing as an American captain."

Indeed, neither of them had had time for pleasantries, he realized with not a little chagrin. A self-deprecating grin caught at his mouth, and he had a distinct feeling it would be this way often when the war was over and they could have a normal life together as man and wife. He didn't want to wait. He wanted to marry Belinda now.

He bent his head and touched her lips, thinking he would tell her so in time, but now he wanted only to make love to her, over and over again until dawn lit the sky.

The American prison compound at Lancaster lay in an open pasture surrounded by bushy undergrowth and thickets of red oak. The stockade itself was built from rows of upended logs, the tops carved into thick points, a full seven feet high. Inside, men in dirty red uniforms loitered in groups or squatted in the shade thrown by the outer wall.

Careful to keep to himself, Gabriel shuffled across the dirt enclosure and slumped against the wall of the prison barracks. He feigned sleep, feeling safer with his back protected. He had not been particularly thrilled when Washington had selected him to check out Belinda's intelligence about the Tory safe houses.

On the side of caution, Gabriel had decided to bring another man along with him, Andrew Lee of Poxtany, Pennsylvania, just in case one of them was recognized. He could see Lee now, wrapped in a blanket as if asleep. Both had disguised themselves well, and none of the guards had realized they were Americans, though several had turned out to be acquaintances of Captain Lee.

The scarlet coat Gabriel wore was tattered, the sleeves ripped, his shirt torn and blackened as if from smoke and grime of battle. He'd wrapped a blood-soaked bandage under his chin and around his head to hamper recognition. Now all he could do was wait. He watched the American sentry walk back and forth. Perhaps they were the ones engineering the escapes. Bribery was alive and well in this war.

The other captives were milling around the outer yard, and the stink of the open latrine saturated the wind. Propping his head back against the rough-hewn logs, he shut his eyes, bored after two days in the filthy clothes, sleeping on the hard ground.

He should get some sleep. It was unlikely anything would happen before sunset. It seemed that every missing British prisoner had vanished during the night. He tried to relax as best he could, able only to doze fitfully since he had entered the stockade.

A double shot of rum sounded damn good at the moment, he thought, but he craved something else even more. Behind his closed eyes, he saw Belinda's small, exquisitely beautiful face. It had only been days since she had come to him, wearing a blue dress, one he had veritably torn off her.

Mentally, he traced his fingertips down the curve of a satiny breast, then lower to her flat stomach. He stirred uneasily, well aware that, no matter how delicious were his fantasies of making love to Belinda, a prison was not the place to dwell on the body of the woman he loved.

Unfortunately, her face and figure were not so easily put aside. He smiled to himself when he thought of the way she had snuggled against him, her bare skin warm as she slept close against his side. How she had opened her eyes so dreamily when he had awakened her with soft kisses on her earlobe. He wondered where she was now, and if she was safe. Was she back with Major Andre, hostessing his parties?

The image of the good-looking British officer did not set well with him. For the first time he could ever remember, he found himself full of ugly, possessive thoughts about a woman, ones he feared would not go away until he got Belinda out of Andre's house once and for all.

He was going to marry her as soon as this mission was completed. She and Annie could stay at the Bronx farm until the war ended, then they could return to his house in New York. He'd been alone too long and found himself wanting a family more with each day that passed—a normal life with a wife who loved him, and with children, lots of children. He had never believed that he would ever want such things again, not until Belinda had come along.

"Someone's arriving. It may be the woman." The gruff whisper came from Captain Lee's bedroll.

Gabriel stayed where he was, but most of the other prisoners crowded forward. He watched covertly, wondering if it was the old woman whom they had heard came often to the compound. She was under suspicion, but no one could prove anything. A dozen or more British soldiers were congregating at the outer gate where the guards stood at their posts.

Gabriel's biggest fear was that he would run into a New York-born Tory soldier, someone who knew him. Fortunately, it was not a new batch of prisoners at all, but the old woman dressed in black. His eyes sharpened when he realized the guards had allowed her entry, surprisingly enough, and then he realized why. She had a market basket over her arm and was selling fruit to the incarcerated soldiers.

It was not unusual for the surrounding farmers to peddle their wares at prison stockades, but still he watched closely as she moved among the men. She appeared deaf and perhaps even slow-witted, but in time his suspicions rose when he detected signs of intense communications between the crone and some of the captives. She came closer, and Andrew spoke again as he turned toward the wall.

"I know her," he said, very low. "We threw her son out of the army a time back."

Giving her a good reason to work for the British, Gabriel thought, remaining alert to her progress.

The guards did not allow the woman to linger long, and after she left, he kept an eye on the soldier she had whispered with.

Darkness fell, a windy, rainy, miserable night typical of early April, and the prisoners took refuge inside the unheated barracks. Captain Lee slept while Gabriel watched, the Pennsylvanian's acquaintance with the woman making his efforts to infiltrate impossible, if she turned out to be the culprit they sought.

He dozed off a couple of times as the night wore on, the rain drumming on the roof in a steady hypnotizing rhythm, then was suddenly startled awake by he knew not what.

Glancing around, he saw a heavily cloaked figure had entered the barracks and was waking some of the prisoners.

Gabriel shook Andrew, then motioned for him to stay put. Lee could infiltrate the next group of escapees, in case Gabriel was captured.

Casually, he eased up to the silent group as if he belonged, and the man in the cloak motioned him forward.

"Come quickly."

To Gabriel's consternation, the door to the barracks was unbarred, and they moved stealthily across the dark building and beyond into the outside enclosure. Gabriel knew his patience was about to bear fruition. Excitement coursed through his blood, the rush of danger.

Outside, rain whipped against their faces as they huddled together near the south wall. Through the darkness he saw that a section of the barricade had been taken down. Where were the guards? he wondered as they were led outside to where the old woman was waiting for them.

Now the danger would begin in earnest if he was taken to the first Tory safe house. They moved softly toward a neighboring thicket where a male companion was waiting to guide them. Gabriel hung back to the rear, trying to note the twists and turns of their trail so that he could retrace his steps later. But if things went well, the chain of Tory safe houses would be out of commission as soon as he was guided through them.

Twenty-four

On the far horizon the afternoon sky spread out in layers of blood red, cobalt, and gold, rising into the darkening sky like steps to the heavens. Belinda admired the beautiful vista as she drove a lightweight, two-wheeled curricle west on a country lane toward Crosby's Tavern. She was in a mood as glorious as the sunset glowing over the trees because she had sent word to Gabe to meet her. She could not wait to see him again. The days had dragged by since the night of their reconciliation, and she worried incessantly about his welfare now that he wore a Continental Army uniform.

Very little had happened since she had returned to New York. Major Andre had been busy, unusually distracted by his military duties, and had left her and Annie pretty much to their own devices. But she had sketched the likenesses of several men who had come clandestinely to meet with Andre in the dead of night. She had brought the pictures with her, sewn into a secret pocket she'd stitched underneath her petticoat. She was petrified as she sneaked outside in the darkness and peered through the window where the meeting was taking place, but she had seen each conspirator quite clearly. Gabriel would be very pleased.

Her smile came unbidden, warming her as she basked in the new closeness with Gabriel. She'd felt completely safe in his arms, and their hours together, so brief but so tender, made her realize how deeply she felt for him. She had proven her loyalty, once and forever. He would not accuse her again.

And now she had something else to share with him, something so wonderful that a delicious pleasure filled her breast and slowly took possession of her heart. She was sure now. She was going to have his child. She must have conceived the night she and Konoc had gone into the icy pond, the very first time Gabriel had made love to her.

She had suspected for a while now, but did not dare think about it. But now that he had spoken of marriage, spoken of having a family, she longed to give him another daughter to ease his agony over Jessie's tragic death—or a son, many sons, many children during their life together. With precious little Annie, they would become the family she wanted and he needed, and they would live up in the quiet beautiful wilds of the Bronx River.

Her lovely daydream was dashed with the awareness of the danger he faced now that he fought with Washington's troops. But she knew he was happy, carrying a musket and marching alongside the other brave patriots. It was what he had wanted, to fight for the principles he believed in.

She had resigned herself to the reality that they could not be together until they had won the right to govern America. She was anxious to do her part to help, so she would stay on as a spy in Andre's house, at least until she began to show. Again, a blissful smile curved her lips and she could not wait to tell Gabe!

She slapped the reins, and the horses trotted faster, and she looked around at the trees lining the road, wondering where Namasset was. She knew Gabriel had ordered him to follow her whenever she sent a message through Dulcimer, but she never saw him except when he made himself known at the beginning of her journey. She had a small pistol strapped to her leg, another safeguard that Gabriel insisted upon, though she felt sure she could never bring herself to use it.

Major Andre was out of town, at least for a week, but he had been most mysterious about his destination. She had tried to find out so she could give the information to Gabe, but Andre had made it clear that he would not divulge his plans. She felt sure it had something to do with the men she had depicted in her drawing. Andre had hired Dulcimer as his housekeeper at her request, and now she felt comfortable leaving

Annie behind with her trusted friend to watch over her.

Not long after, she saw with alarm a narrow sentry box had been positioned on the road from the king's ferry upon which she had come from Manhattan Island. Though she had the necessary papers, traveling documents signed by Major Andre to give her leave to go anywhere she wished in British-held territory, she was always terrified they would search her person or accost her in some way.

But John's name usually tamed their manners considerably, and she felt a sharp stab of guilt to use the man's affection so heartlessly. Indeed, he treated her and Annie like little sisters, but even so, she considered him the enemy. She was a patriot, an American, and she would fight their cause as long as England tried to subdue them.

As she neared the striped red-and-white bar that had been lowered across the road, a single sentry stepped into sight. He stood tall and imposing in his red coat crisscrossed by white bandoliers, raising his arm and calling out for her to halt the trap. She obeyed at once and sat still as he lifted a lantern against the growing gloom and held it high enough to shine upon her face.

"Who goes there?" he demanded in an ugly tone that faded when he realized a lone woman rode upon the driver's seat. He immediately became less combative, his face settling into a polite expression. Belinda answered his overture with her own warm smile, desirous of charming him into a speedy pass-through.

"Good evening, mistress. I'm afraid I must examine your pass. Though we're honored indeed to have a lady of such beauty travel past our lonely outpost."

"You flatter me, sir," she answered, shyly lowering her eyes.

The man grinned, rapidly scanning her paper before he handed it back.

"Lift the bar and let the lady pass," he yelled to his comrades manning the barricade. "Allow me to warn you, mistress, the rebels have been active hereabouts of late. I urge you to proceed with caution and be safely behind locked doors before nightfall."

"Thank you kindly, good sir. I shall be more than happy to oblige."

Well pleased that he had given her no trouble, she glanced at the thick woods, wondering if Namasset watched them. She made haste, wishing to reach the tavern before darkness totally obliterated her way. Minutes later, her heart jumped into her throat when a small contingent of horsemen galloped into sight. Her papers signed by John Andre would not do well by her if the approaching men were patriots, she realized, but almost at once she recognized them as Tories, in the bright green coats they wore with such misguided pride. They, too, were mere puppets of King George and his ministers, but they strutted pompously as if they did not know it.

Sick dread congealed in the pit of her stomach when she recognized Bartholomew Smythe at the forefront of the riders. She pulled back on the reins, in no way eager for any kind of confrontation with the evil man. She had not seen him since Major Andre had taken her under his wing, and she was not sure what to expect. Bart was unpredictable, and she was afraid of him. He had a mean streak, one she had sensed from the first moment he had approached her at Lord Greenleigh's in Quebec. She had no choice, however, but to slow her horse and allow Bart's men to surround her curricle.

"Well, well, look who I found lurking about outside the confines of the city." Bart controlled his prancing horse expertly, one gloved hand holding the spirited mount in check. "My treacherous little serving maid from Canada." His pleasant tone and expression bore no resemblance to the anger she could detect in his dark eyes. She could not stop the shiver of fear worming its way up her spine. There were too many Tories for Namasset to intervene in her behalf.

"Major Andre signed my papers by his own hand."

"Of course he did, my dear. You've got Andre besotted with you just as Elliott was before you turned him in to us. I wonder, though, if you're quite the loyalist you proclaim so prettily."

Terror came in a cold flash, and she knew with crystal clarity that she was completely under his power, alone and so far away from the city.

He could do whatever he wished to her, and no one could stop him. No one would know. Be calm, she thought, lifting her chin. Namasset knew where she was. He would not forsake her.

"I'm in a great hurry, Mr. Smythe. Please examine my papers and allow me to go upon my way."

Bart leaned a forearm across his saddle, observing her in silence. "For your own safety, my dear Belinda, I believe you should allow us to ride escort. Major Andre is away for a time, as you well know, and I'm certain he would appreciate our taking good care of you. The rebels are active along this road. That's why we are riding patrol."

"I've seen no rebels in the area," she said at once, determined not to go with him. "I assure you I feel quite safe."

"On the contrary, you take your life in your hands to travel alone, especially with papers signed by Andre on your person. There is no way for you to return to the city, in any event. The rebels set fire to the ferry boat not an hour ago to keep Clinton's troops off the Jersey shore."

The look on his face, cold, measured, told her that he intended to make the patriots pay dearly for destroying the ferry.

"Then I will drive south to the next ferry crossing."

"I do not think so," he said with a look she remembered very well. He had struck her across the face the last time he had gazed upon her with such anger.

Belinda made no more protestations, sliding to one side as one of Bart's men climbed aboard and took the reins from her hands. A warning bell rang in her head as the wheels began to roll, and green-coated Tories fell in around her. One wrong move, one wrong word that would indicate her true allegiance, and Bart would gladly take her prisoner, perhaps even hang her. She quickly got hold of her rising panic. He would not dare harm her when she was under Andre's protection.

Perhaps Bart would lead her to more of his traitorous Tory friends, give her names she could pass on to Gabriel. She relaxed, relishing the chance to bring doom raining down upon Bartholomew Smythe's head.

Rain drizzled in a steady, vertical stream, miring the ground into a thick mud that sucked at every footstep. Gabriel trudged along behind the other silent escapees, their heads bent against the wind as they followed their two saviors to freedom. As he walked, he fought against his own anger, appalled at how damn easy the escape had been executed. Where had the guards been? Sheltering themselves from the inclement weather? Or had they been bribed? Whatever the reason, they would not fare well when he exposed them to their commander.

They had been on the move for nearly a week. After they had left the compound, they made their way swiftly to the old woman's house, about a mile from the stockade. There had been no alarm sounded by the guards as they entered the farmhouse where they had time to warm themselves by the fire, and even eat a bowl of vegetable stew. They had been warned in hushed tones to keep quiet and not to try to proceed to safety on their own.

He had been as eager as the others to warm his bone-cold body, and as they spooned the hot soup into their bellies, his fellow escapees bragged contemptuously about the easy flight and the stupid colonial clods who pretended to be soldiers. Gabriel held his tongue, pretending his speech was affected by the falsely bandaged injured jaw. No one pressured him to talk, and he ate slowly as if it were difficult, but he was as grateful as anyone for the warm, wholesome food inside his empty stomach.

In time an alarm gun had sounded from the distant American camp, and they hurriedly set off again through the awful weather. Their steady trek over soggy forest paths led them to one of the large stone barns common in south-eastern Pennsylvania. There, the first Tory host showed himself, an old man, his stooped form cloaked in a black wool cape. Bread was provided, and as Gabriel was handed his portion, he memorized the traitor's features for future arrest.

On the following day they stopped again, holing up in a cellar this time. Gabriel managed a couple of hours of restless sleep before they were rousted and trekked again east toward the banks of the Hudson. With each stop he identified more traitors, and as the odyssey continued uninterrupted, night after night, they made only a few miles between the caves or barns or hidden root cellars that served as sanctuaries.

It was hard to believe they could traipse through American territory so easily. He began to wonder how many British soldiers, how many spies, had used this chain of safe houses, owned and operated by men pretending to be loyal patriots.

Finally, they reached the haven for the night, a damp basement of a half-timbered house that Gabriel recognized. Certainly not a close acquaintance, but a man with whom his shipping company had done business before the war. John Blackburg was well known in Manhattan and thought to be a trusted patriot. In fact, Gabriel knew for a fact that he had even visited the Continental encampment. Damn the traitor, Gabriel thought furiously, but he would not continue his treachery for much longer. Blackburg would be the first man seized once Gabriel uncovered the rest of the secret Tories.

As the evening lengthened, he spent time lis-

tening to the talk among the other soldiers. He
had garnered more information from them than
he had dreamed possible. Throughout the journey they spoke openly of the strength of their
units and planned troop movements, had conjectured about potential attacks, and even identified a few secret British agents by name.

The old servant who had brought them food
was careless enough to mention houseguests
visiting from the city. Gabriel decided to find
out who the visitors were, and when his companions were snoring in peaceful oblivion,
wrapped warmly in thick blankets, he inched up
the cellar steps and eased out into the yard, as
if intending to relieve himself.

The house was large with stone fireplaces and
a look of prosperity to it. Most of the ground
floor windows were ablaze with light, and as he
moved stealthily through the darkness, he saw
that a small contingent of soldiers was biv-
ouacked in a pasture behind the barn. Their
campfire burned brightly, with perhaps a dozen
men lounging on the ground around it. He kept
down, pleased when it began to sprinkle rain.

Faraway thunder rumbled like a sheet of
metal struck by a mallet. He crouched down and
inched his way toward the dining parlor where
shadows moved behind the lace draperies. A secret meeting of Blackburg's collaborators? he
wondered as he crept through the thick shrub-
bery planted beneath the window.

A small party was sitting around the dining

table, John Blackburg and several other people.
He could not see their faces from his vantage
point, so he slowly made his way to the next
window, which had been opened to the cool
damp breeze. Slowly, he rose until he could
gaze over the sill. Bartholomew Smythe sat
across the table, a wineglass held idly in one
hand.

Shocked to find his nemesis there, Gabriel
ducked down again. It was no secret Bart con-
nived with the British—he was an admitted
Tory—but Gabe was surprised the coward
would venture off Manhattan where true patriots would take great pleasure in tarring and
feathering him. He pressed his back against the
wall and listened to the snatches of conversation
floating from inside.

"Mr. Smythe, I must return to the city. You
cannot continue to keep me here. Annie will be
worried about me."

Gabriel could not have been more astonished
to hear Belinda's soft, melodious voice. What in
God's name was she doing here with Bart? She
had returned to the city days ago.

"Now, now, my dear," Bart was saying, "you
know I am keeping you here for your own good.
The ferry will be restored soon enough."

It sounded as if Belinda was being held there
against her will. Why? And how had Bart managed to get her here in this nest of Tory spies?
She loathed him; she would never go anywhere
with him. In the back of his mind, the ugly ex-

planation began to gain momentum, one he hated, fought against, but nevertheless it struck him like a viper spitting venom.

Gabriel shut his eyes, sick at heart; then the anger came, hard, rolling almost uncontrollable. He clamped his teeth together, and forced down the groan that screamed for release in the back of his throat. No, no, he could not believe her to be so duplicitous. Despite how it looked at the moment, he had to believe she had good cause to be there. There had to be a plausible reason for her being with Smythe. Gabriel had been too quick to judge her before and had been dead wrong. But there was always the possibility that she had turned again.

The idea brought up red, rolling rage, and he fought desperately against his urge to barge into the house and confront Bart and all the other goddamn traitors where they sat dining so luxuriously. But he could not. He could not.

Instead, he sank down, bracing his back against the house. He took several deep breaths to regain control. He had to get out now before he was discovered. It didn't appear Belinda was in any kind of danger, and Bart could certainly identify him. Perhaps Bart was even the Tory link slated to lead the escaped prisoners to the next safe house.

He didn't want to leave her here, he thought, waiting a few moments longer. What if Bart was keeping her against her will? From what he had overheard, that could very well be the case, but he could do nothing to help her, alone as he was. He needed to get help, find a patriot camp and bring enough soldiers back with him to capture Bart, Blackburg, and their men.

Decision made, he delayed no longer, but made his way through the bushes to the other side of the house. He stopped and glanced toward the field where the soldiers were relaxing around the fire. He tensed when he heard a twig snap, then turned and saw a dark form, a brief flash of metal. Then the musket stock connected hard with his right temple. He crumpled to his knees, then hit the ground face first and knew no more.

Twenty-five

Belinda pretended to listen to Mistress Blackburg's boring account of the best method of preserving apple butter. She was on edge, restless, and furious Bart was keeping her with him for so long. For her own protection, he kept insisting, but she wondered if he had ulterior motives. What if he never returned her to Manhattan? She wondered if Namasset had followed her to the Blackburg farm. Would he have reported back to Gabriel at the tavern and told him why she had not arrived there to meet him?

She sighed deeply, glancing into the foyer. One of Bart's officers had summoned him outside, and by the man's excited demeanor, she was curious as to what had transpired.

Looking at the window, she saw that the rain had increased into wavy sheets of water sluicing down the glass. She hoped the bad weather would not strand them here even longer. She wanted to go home. She wanted to see Gabriel. She was worried since she had heard Blackburg telling Bart about several intense battles fought between the British and patriots on Long Island. Icy fear lay against her heart when she thought of Gabriel being involved. What if he had been killed? What would she do?

"Belinda, my dear, may I have a word with you outside, if you please?"

She jerked her eyes to the door and found Bartholomew standing in the threshold. He had been outside, his cape now soaked with rain. There was something about his smile, about the way he was looking at her that she did not like. Obediently, she excused herself to the Blackburgs and followed him.

What did he want now? He had been acting oddly from the beginning. Was he planning to arrest her? Was this a trick? She had been walking on eggshells around him, afraid she was going to incriminate herself. He was so dangerous and obsessive about hunting down Gabriel and the other patriots.

"Come along, Belinda," he told her mildly as they stepped out into hallway. "I've something very interesting to show you."

Warily, she drew up, unsettled by the bizarre smile painted across his face. "I'm very tired, Mr. Smythe, I'd prefer to retire upstairs."

"This will take only a moment."

Belinda nodded, though she sensed he was up to no good, then followed him through the kitchen to a covered back porch. Several Tory soldiers stood there, one holding a lantern. On the floor lay a man dressed in a British uniform, the red coat tattered and splattered with mud. His head was partially bandaged, and he was groaning and trying to get up.

"What's wrong with him?" she asked Bart in concern. "Has he been wounded?"

"Aye, I'm afraid he took a severe blow to the head. He was trying to escape."

A queasy feeling ballooned in her stomach because they were all grinning at her now, expectantly, full of self-satisfaction.

"I don't understand. He's a British soldier. Why aren't you helping him? Why did you bring me out here?"

Bart's face was shadowed by the flickering light, carving hollows and glinting off planes, but his expression was triumphant.

"Because, my dear, the plan you and I initiated so long ago in Quebec has finally come to fruition. I told you I wouldn't give up until I got my dear cousin in irons, did I not?"

Bartholomew's meaning hit her with the impact of a doubled fist to the forehead. Her gaze darted back to the man on the floor as the soldier with the lantern grasped a handful of hair and jerked up his head.

Too horrified to speak, she stared at Gabriel's battered face. A huge bruise darkened the side of his head, his right eye blackened and grotesquely swollen. Blood matted his hair and ran down his cheek. She felt sick and had to fight not to fall to her knees and take him into her arms. Somehow she stopped herself, though she trembled from the effort.

"We got him," Bart was telling her now. "Impersonating a British officer. That's a hanging offense."

Belinda fought down her emotions, knowing she could not let Bart see her distress. If she was to help Gabriel, she had to pretend she was unaffected by the capture of a rebel spy.

"Major Andre will wish to interrogate him. He told me so himself." She spoke quickly, but could not stop her bottom lip from quivering.

"You've turned quite white, my dear. Surely you aren't feeling compassion for our old friend, are you?"

"He's hurt, of course I do. Let me tend to his head."

Bart laughed. "I really don't think he'd like that since you're the one who turned him over to Major Andre."

He turned to his men and jerked his head toward the barn. "Lock him up, and we'll hang him in the morning. Come along, my dear."

Belinda forced herself to walk away, to not look back when every fiber in her body urged her to run after Gabriel. Bart left her at the bottom of the steps before seeking out Blackburg, but he stood waiting long enough to watch her ascend the stairs and enter her bedchamber.

Belinda shut the door, turned the key in the lock, then sank to the floor amidst the billowing folds of her skirt. She covered her mouth with both palms, shaking all over, stomach rolling, sick at heart. What was she going to do? What *could* she do?

For several minutes, she could do nothing but weep, great, racking, silent sobs. Bart had threatened to hang him, and she knew he would. How many times had he told her how he yearned for the day he could watch Gabriel swing from the gibbet? She had to do something, she thought frantically, now, while Bart was preoccupied with Blackburg. She stood up, clasping her hands together to steady herself. Then she lifted her petticoat and retrieved the pistol strapped to her thigh. She had to go now.

Gabriel fought to fling off the anvil bearing down on the top of his head. He couldn't seem to do so, couldn't seem to think where he was or what had happened to him. He only knew his head was hammered with an awful, never-ending sharp stake. Struggling desperately, he forced one eye open, but the other seemed solidly fused.

The odor of dust, manure, and horseflesh filled his nostrils. He blinked, coughed, tried to swallow. The rusty tang of blood was in his mouth. Slowly, by force of will, he focused his bleary vision. A man was sitting at the open end of the stall—a man wearing Tory green. He shut his eyes, too weary to hold them open any longer.

A moment later, he sought to move his limbs,

found it impossible, and realized he was tightly bound. He remembered getting clubbed, seeing Bart. Anger revived him, and he opened his eyes again, slightly more alert. The guard was unmoving, his head propped back against the side rail, his eyes closed. Gabriel pulled at the knots binding his wrists, but could not loosen them.

When he looked back at the guard again, Belinda was standing beside him. *Belinda?* She was holding some kind of club. With dull eyes, he watched her raise it over her head and bring it down hard atop the unsuspecting man's head. He had to be dreaming, but no, he had seen her with Bart, hadn't he? He couldn't quite remember.

"Gabe? Gabriel, darling, can you hear me?"

Her voice was low, soft against his ear. He could smell the scent of gardenias, sweet, so sweet, one he had dreamed about more times than he could remember.

"Come on, Gabe, we've got to get out of here."

She was working desperately to loosen the cords binding his wrists. He shook his head, still dizzy and disoriented.

"Why're you here with Bart?" he forced through stiff lips as she finally found success with the rope.

"He stopped me on my way to meet you at the tavern. The ferry was out, so he made me come with him." Her whisper intensified. "I don't have time to explain. Can you stand up?"

Gabriel grunted, pain knifing through his head as he forced himself into a sitting position.

His brain began to clear as Belinda thrust something heavy into his hand. "Here's the guard's gun. Come on, there's a window in the back."

He felt better once the familiar shape of the weapon weighted his palm. He curled his fingers over the top of the stall, pulled himself up to his feet, and stumbled after Belinda.

The window was high up on the wall, but he was revived considerably by the cold rain gusting down into his face.

"Where's Bart now?" he asked, for the first time actually comprehending the danger they were in.

"Inside the house with Blackburg. They're going to hang you in the morning."

Gabriel was thinking of Belinda's danger. They'd hang her, too, if they caught her helping him escape. "Go back inside with him, Belinda, so you'll get out of here alive. I can make it on my own."

"No. You're hurt. You need me." She was already climbing atop a bale of hay to gain access to the windowsill. She jumped clumsily, and he boosted her the rest of the way and watched her leap outside. He followed swiftly, landing in the mud beside her. The rain beat already sodden ground around them, and he could hear the hollow drum of the downpour on top of the shingled roof. Despite the discomfort, they were lucky the night was stormy and would shield their flight.

Gabriel took her hand and began to run toward the woods, to the east, veering away from the Tory soldiers. His head pounded as the exertion sent blood thudding through the veins at his temples. There was no way to outrun Bart's riders, no matter how far they got on foot. They'd have to find a hiding place and hole up until Bart got tired of looking for them. He hoped to God Belinda could hold up that long.

They traveled hard through mud and thick bracken until Belinda began to slow down. He slipped an arm around her waist and supported her as they moved ahead, but he knew he was going to have to let her rest. The gloom of night was rapidly being dispelled by the sun slowly rising somewhere behind a gray and overcast sky.

He had to find them somewhere to hide. He had considered taking refuge at a farm they passed a few miles back, but discounted it as a possible nest of Tory vipers. Now his adrenaline rushed like boiling water, and he knew Bart would never let them get away. He glanced behind them through the mist-shrouded woods and saw nothing but a smoky, surreal silence.

"Gabe, please, I'm sorry but I have to rest."

Gabriel searched their surroundings for a suitable hiding place. His gaze fell upon two giant white oaks growing close together. A hollow was formed between them, large enough to accommodate both of them, and he headed for it. If nothing else it would conceal their presence from pursuers. He backed into the tree and eased into the hollow, bringing Belinda down onto his lap. She was cold and wet and shivering. Wan with exhaustion, she laid her head against his shoulder and looked up at him. Tears formed in her eyes, and she reached up and touched his swollen eye.

"What did they do to you?"

"Shh, I'm all right," he whispered, staring intently out through the trees in the direction from which they had come. He propped the pistol on his bent knee.

"Leave me here," she said, sitting up suddenly, her eyes pleading. "Bart won't hurt me, but he'll hang you if they find us."

"He'll show no mercy to you now that you helped me escape. I'm not leaving you."

She sighed tiredly and was quiet.

Gabriel shut his eyes, so tired he could barely think, much less function. *Maybe they'd get lucky, maybe Smythe wouldn't find their trail through the mud and wet leaves of the forest floor, maybe the rain would obliterate it.*

Some time later, he came awake with a jerk, every muscle alert. He froze, his eyes locked on Bartholomew Smythe's face where he sat astride his horse, leaning over the saddle.

"I suggest you put down that pistol, Elliott," he said conversationally, "unless you want me to shoot Belinda before I hang you."

Belinda awoke then, gasping when she saw they were surrounded. Gabriel tossed his gun onto the ground, looking around at the six other horsemen accompanying Bart. All had pistols out and pointed at him.

"Get up, Belinda," Gabriel said softly, "and move away from me."

"No, please, Bart," she cried as Gabriel pushed her up, then rose behind her. He grasped her arm, and though she tried to cling to him, one of Bart's men dismounted and jerked her away.

Bart smiled, lifting a coiled rope off his saddle. A noose had been fashioned at one end. He stood in the saddle and tossed the rope over a sturdy branch just above his head as one of his men took the other end and secured it around the tree trunk. He smiled as the noose dangled in front of Gabriel's face.

"I suppose I should thank you, Elliott, for choosing a suitable tree for your hanging."

Twenty-six

"No, Bart, don't, you can't!" Belinda cried, fighting against the soldier's hold on her. His grip tightened, and he locked her against his chest. She struggled impotently, sobbing, her horrified eyes on Gabriel as they bound his hands behind his back.

Gabriel's face was impassive, so battered he was hardly recognizable. Only the muscle in his jaw jumped as Bart ordered him hoisted atop a saddled horse.

"Oh, God, no, no!" Belinda collapsed to her knees in utter despair as one of the men secured the noose around Gabriel's neck.

Bart took hold of the horse's bridle. "Anything you want to say, cousin, before you meet your Maker?"

"I'll see you in hell, Smythe," Gabriel ground out through clenched teeth, then his eyes found Belinda's terrified face.

"Gabe!"

Belinda's shrill scream echoed hauntingly through the trees, but did not give pause to

Bart's intentions. He brought down his riding crop hard across the horse's flank, and the mare skittered, then lunged forward leaving Gabriel kicking in the air.

Belinda recoiled in sheer horror, then jerked free and ran toward Gabriel. He was still fighting, twisting at the end of the rope. She had to get him down!

Bart laughed, then grabbed her arm and swung her around. She clawed at him, trying to scratch at his eyes, then faltered in her fight when he suddenly went still. His mouth opened, and she heard a whoosh of air as his breath left him. A bloody arrowhead protruded from the center of his chest. Shots rang out all around her, and she saw riders bursting through the undergrowth toward them. Namasset, she realized, but her only thoughts were for Gabriel.

She ran to where he hung, and though only a matter of seconds had passed, he barely moved as she frantically clawed at the knotted rope attached to the tree. She couldn't get it loose, and instinctively she hugged his legs, trying to lift him, desperate to free his weight from the tight noose. She sobbed helplessly then cried out in relief when Namasset appeared at a run and brought his tomahawk chopping down on the rope. It snapped, and Gabriel fell in a limp, lifeless heap. She went down with him, trying to break his fall, oblivious to the shots still whizzing around her, hysterically working the rope loose and lifting it over his head.

"Gabe, Gabe, please, please don't die," she moaned, choking at the sight of his throat. The rope had cut deeply into his neck, and she saw raw flesh oozing blood, but when she put her ear against his chest, she could hear a heartbeat. He was still breathing. *Oh, thank God, he was still alive.*

She cradled his head against her breast, weeping in relief, then realizing she had to stanch the flow of blood. She stripped off her shawl and blotted desperately at the open slash.

Then Namasset was kneeling beside her. "Does Gabe live?"

"Yes, but he's badly hurt! Look at his throat!"

Namasset began to wrap the shawl snugly around Gabe's neck, and Belinda glanced around, for the first time realizing that Bart's men were dead, their corpses scattered around on the ground. Patriot soldiers were searching their bodies.

Belinda lifted Gabriel's hand and held it against her cheek. It felt cold and weak.

"Thank God, you came in time, Namasset, but how did you find us?"

"I followed when Bart take you to house with stone barn. When he keep you there, I went for men to help me get you. At dawn when Bart rode out, we follow. We not know Gabe with you."

"We must hurry, Namasset, and get Gabe to a doctor before the rest of the Tories come looking for us."

"There's a patriot camp to the east," Namasset told her, leaning down and lifting Gabriel over the saddle of Bart's horse. He climbed up behind him, then waited for Belinda to mount before he kicked the horse into a gallop, leaving the other patriots to follow them into the safety of the forest.

Belinda used her fingertips to idly push ajar the window. She inhaled deeply. Below she could see Willamette walking across the front yard from the mill. Annie was with her, holding her hand, skipping and dancing along in her usual high spirits. Childish laughter, faint, so sweet as to bring tears, floated up on the soft twilight breeze. She was glad that Namasset had smuggled Annie out of New York. She was happiest here with Willamette and the boys. Sighing, she tried to remember the last time she had laughed, or even smiled. Not since the day they had strung Gabriel up like some mangy dog. She pressed her fingers against her closed eyelids, but the ghastly vision would not die, would never die, not as long as she lived. She would never forget the look on Gabriel's face. It was burned forever into her memory.

Turning quickly, as if physical movement could rid her of the nightmare imprinted indelibly in her brain, she moved to the bed. Gabriel lay there, his arms lifeless atop the coverlet. She picked up his hand and pressed it to her lips. It had been over two weeks now, and he still lay unconscious. His eyes were closed, his blond eyelashes sweeping down upon his cheeks. She kissed his long brown fingers, fingers that had touched her with such tenderness, that had brought her body alive.

Oh, Gabriel, my love. She hadn't expected this long period of unconsciousness when she had huddled in the bottom of Namasset's canoe with Gabriel's head in her lap, the journey north seemingly endless as they tried to get him to safety. At that point she had only been glad he was still alive, that the noose had not worked well enough to snap his neck. Now she waited, watched him lie in a living death, and wondered if he would ever awaken again. He rested so still in the bed, so large and strong, so normal-looking, as if he were sleeping, yet he did not move, did not even open his eyes.

She knelt beside the bed, pinching her lips as tears threatened for the thousandth time, reaching out to gently brush back a lock of his hair. It was soft against her fingers, and she remembered the night when she had clutched handfuls of his fine blond hair in her fingers and cried out his name. *Oh, Gabriel, please come back to me.*

Lovingly, her eyes moved over his handsome face, the strong angle of his jawline, the lean planes delineating his cheeks where stubble grew a shade darker than his hair and shadowed his skin with a beard in a way he had never allowed it to do when he was aware. *Do you want me to shave your beard, Gabe? Would it make you wake up?*

She smiled down at him, but her expression changed when she saw the terrible angry gash that cut around his throat. The rope had penetrated deep into his flesh before they had gotten him down, had come very close to killing him. *Bart's dead, Gabe. And I'm so glad he is. Namasset killed him, but I wish it had been me. For what he's done to you.*

He seemed so peaceful, lying motionless, as he had been when they'd spent the night at the inn. He seemed as though he were trapped in some strange unnatural netherland. She had fed him broth a drop at a time, and water, squeezed from a cloth, determined that she would bring him back, that he would not die. He seemed almost content to sleep there, unmoving, forever. *Well, I'm not content, Gabe. I want you back. Our baby wants you back.* In her mind the words came forth as screaming, shrill shrieks of despair, of loneliness, hopelessness, but still he did not move. He did not hear her pain.

His face never changed, his breathing quiet, regular. She rested her head on his bare chest, listening to his heart, the beat steady and solid beneath her ear, as if nothing was wrong. She shut her eyes and listened to it, took strength from the constant rhythm that promised he was strong enough to wake up someday. *But when? Why didn't he just open his eyes? What stopped him?*

Sitting up again, she put her palm on her lower belly, but felt only a slight hard mound, barely noticeable. She wanted desperately for him to know about their child. *Please, God let him wake up long enough for me to tell him. Tell him now,* a voice within urged, and she picked up his hand and sandwiched it flat between her palms.

"Gabriel, darling, listen, you must try to hear me. I'm going to have your baby. You must come back because there's so much we have to decide. We have to choose a name, don't you see? And we have to get married . . ."

Her voice clogged into silence, hot tears burning until she thought her lids would turn to flame. She hadn't wept hard but one time, after a week had gone by without his awakening.

This is my fault, Gabe, if I had stayed behind as you told me, you would have made better time. You would have escaped. This never would have happened. I've done something terrible, and now God is punishing me. Please God, don't punish Gabe for my selfishness. She felt her strength ebbing, felt her defenses wobble and start to come down. *Stop,* she told herself, *you must be strong. You must reach down in that dark quiet place where Gabriel floats and make him want to take hold of your hand.*

Gently, with all the love aching within her heart, she ran her fingertips lightly down the contour of his cheek, pallid now under his dark skin. "Can you feel my touch?" she whispered.

"Can you hear my pain? Come back, Gabriel, fight for us, fight to see us again."

She put his hand to her mouth. "Feel my breath, Gabe, feel my lips and my heartbeat. I'm here for you. I'm waiting for you."

Gabriel did not move.

For a long time she talked to him as if he sat up against the headboard, smiling in the old way, teasing her, caressing her hair between his fingers the way he liked to do. She chatted on and on, told him everything that had happened since he had been unresponsive. She told him that Bart had died, that he would never hurt anyone else. She told him that Henri had come the day before with news that Charleston still held off the British siege, that the French were sending a fleet to help the Americans.

"Isn't that wonderful, Gabe? We're going to win now. You've got to come back so you can see the British thrown out of New York." She told him how Timon had caught a trout as long as her arm, how Annie had drawn a picture of him smiling, his eyes wide open. She squeezed his hand and talked on and on, watching the full moon rise higher and higher in the sky outside the window, until her throat was hoarse and there were no more words.

Then, with a sorrow pressing down on her spirit like a boulder lodged atop her chest, she snuffed the candle and slid into bed beside him. She snuggled close and laid her cheek against the smooth warm skin of his shoulder. "Good night, my love. You will wake up soon. I know you will."

Gabriel swam just under the surface of lucidity, through eerie dreams, dark, frightening, confusing. He struggled to find a way up out of the murky depths where voices reverberated like submarine echoes that hurt his head and made him want to sink to the bottom of his black ocean, to bury himself in the deep, thick, cold mud, where it would be safe and quiet as a grave. He let himself sink, deeper and deeper, until the voices stopped and he was finally at peace.

For a long time he lay like a stone at the bottom of a well, then slowly, against his will, he began to rise like bubbles in a cauldron. Up, up, higher, higher, faster, faster until he burst out of the blackness and into the bright light.

Gabriel opened his eyes. He saw wood beams, dark knotty pine. He heard a voice, a woman's voice, and he tried to comb the cobwebs out of his fuzzy mind so he could understand what she was saying.

"That's right, Gabriel, I'm sure he's going to be a boy, a big healthy baby with blond hair and a strong jaw like yours. We'll need to choose a name, but not until you wake up to help me."

Belinda's voice, he thought, aware instantly that something terrible had happened, but not sure what. He turned his head slightly, blearily focusing on the blurry movements beside him. Eventually, Belinda's finely chiseled profile became clear.

She was darning a sock, had it tucked over her left fist as she worked a needle through it with her right hand. She never stopped talking.

"I wanted to tell you about the baby, but I wasn't sure yet. But now I am, my darling. I'm so happy, but I want to share it with you, Gabe, I want to tell you how pleased I am—"

Her voice caught, and her hands stilled, the long needle poised in the air.

Gabriel opened his mouth to speak, but found he could not. His throat felt as if he had ingested a straight razor that was still lodged deep in his larynx. He tried to swallow, and the blade slashed with pure agony. He groaned, a muffled, torturous sound.

Belinda froze. Her head jerked toward him. She stared in shock, eyes wide, the only movement in her face the tears suddenly trickling down her cheeks.

The needle fell from her fingers, and she came to her feet. The wicker sewing basket in her lap fell, bounced, and sent balls of yarn rolling in every direction. Then she was on her knees beside him, his hand in hers. He tried to smile, but even that hurt like hell.

"Oh, Gabe, Gabe . . ." She burst into a full flood of tears, her forehead against the back of his hand. He reached out and put his palm atop her soft black curls.

Her head came up, and she dashed the wetness from her eyes with her fingertips. She still had on the sock. "Gabe, how do you feel? Are you in pain?"

Her eyes were worried, staring at his neck. He touched his throat where it hurt the most, wincing when his fingers found a bandage.

"Waaa . . ." Nothing but a croak. He tried to think what had happened, but his mind wouldn't cooperate any better than his vocal cords.

"Don't talk if it's painful for you," she whispered, gently stroking his face. "You've been unconscious for three weeks, my darling, and you've barely eaten. You're very weak."

The revelation stunned him, and he tried to rise up on his elbow, but found himself too feeble. He fell back, head spinning, brow knitted. He couldn't remember anything. He knew he was at the mill farm, but how did he get there? How could he have lain unconscious and survived for nearly a month? Why was Belinda so distraught? She looked unwell herself, with dark violet-colored crescents underneath her eyes. And she couldn't seem to stop crying.

Shutting his eyes, he steeled himself to swallow. Pain ripped like a hot poker into his throat. Belinda had a spoonful of water now, urging it at his lips. Somehow he managed to let it slide down.

"I was so scared for you, Gabriel," she murmured as she carefully fed him more, "but now you're back with us, and you're going to be alright. You'll just have to be patient while your throat heals." She was kissing his left hand. He motioned as if to write with his other hand.

"Do you want paper?" she asked, turning at once to rummage through the drawer of the bedside table. She came out with a piece of her drawing paper and a lump of charcoal.

What happened? he scribbled as best he could.

Belinda turned it around and read it. "You don't remember anything?"

Trying to think what was the last thing he did remember, he drew a blank. Then a picture formed slowly in his mind's eye. The prison stockade at Lancaster. The old woman leading them through the night, the Tory safe houses then all the rest came barreling down upon him. Smythe at the Blackburg house, Belinda helping him in the barn, then with him in the wet, dark night, stumbling and tripping, on the run, but then his mind rebelled, got tangled up, indistinct as seaweed in murky water.

He gestured at his throat and shook his head.

Belinda's face flitted through various expressions like a trapped moth—surprise, fear, horror, then reluctance. Through it all she held tightly to his hand, gripping him like a lifeline. Once more her eyes filled with tears that ran over her lashes and wet her face. Gabriel was surprised. Belinda rarely wept for long. She had always been strong.

"It was Bart," she was whispering, though emotion was making her voice thick. "He tried to hang you. If Namasset hadn't been following us, if he hadn't come in time . . ." She seemed unable to proceed. ". . . I couldn't stop him. They were holding me back, and it was so awful . . ."

Gabriel frowned as she buried her face against his chest. He stroked her hair soothingly, thinking it must have been a horrible thing for her to endure. Fear gripped him in that instant, and he scribbled another message.

"No, he didn't hurt me," Belinda replied after reading it. "Namasset and a patriot patrol found us in time. They killed Bart, Gabe."

Gabriel felt no regret on that count, and he fingered his throat again, trying to recall, wondering if he ever would.

He put his arms around Belinda and pulled her down until she lay beside him. Determined to talk, he turned until he could look into her eyes. He put his hand against her belly, felt the slight curve.

"Bay . . . beee?"

For the first time Belinda smiled through her tears and put her fingers against his lips to stop him from speaking.

"I'm with child, darling." Her eyes searched his. He could see the love, could almost feel the warmth of it against his skin. "Willamette says it will come in the fall, when the leaves are red and gold."

"I . . . love . . . you," he croaked out.

"I love you, too," Belinda said with a happy sigh, then relaxed in his arms, pressing her face against his chest. He held her tightly, and they lay quietly together, savoring each other's warmth. They said nothing more. No words were necessary.

Twenty-seven

Gabriel dipped the straight razor into a bowl of water, sloshing it back and forth to rid it of lather. He stared into his own face in the mirror, hardly recognizing himself now that the heavy dark beard was gone. He looked gaunt, his cheeks deeply sunken. He had lost a lot of weight in the past month, his injured gullet unable to tolerate much in the way of solid food.

Lifting his chin, he toweled off the rest of the shaving soap, then leaned forward to examine the long raised weal left by the constriction of the noose. The wound was better, though still red and raw, it had finally begun to heal. He still couldn't remember exactly what had happened. Not the hanging, not Bart's death at Namasset's hands. But Belinda remembered. He had stopped asking her about it because every time he did, she wept as if she could not bear to relive it.

He could see her now, behind him in the mirror. She had been gathering up their clothes for washing, but she had stopped at the window, still holding several garments in her hands as she gazed out over the river.

Tenderness welled up, seeping deep into his heart, warming him with a contentment he had never before had in his life. She had been through so much since she had been drawn into the intrigues of his rebellion. He had subjected her to a lot himself when he had used her as a pawn against the enemy. He was as guilty as Bart in that respect. She had shown loyalty, love, and commitment in more ways than he could name.

Suddenly, he wanted to touch her, wanted to hold her in his arms. Naked from the waist up, he picked up a shirt of soft white cambric and slipped it over his head. Belinda had made it herself, a Christmas gift she had started long ago and finished stitching while he lay comatose in the bed. It fit him perfectly.

When he slipped his arms around her waist and pulled her back against him, she dropped the shirts and bodices she held and laid her hands atop his, her head dropping back against his chest. She sighed, so contented a sound that he smiled. He slid his palms down over her stomach to where their child formed inside her womb. Whether it was a son or daughter, he did not care. And he was going to marry her as soon as he could make the proper arrangements. Their baby would have his name, and they would have each other, forever.

"What are you looking at, my love?"

"I was watching Annie and Konoc," she said softly. "See them there skipping rocks near the shallows. I was thinking that in a few years our own child will be playing with them. And so will Willamette's new baby."

Gabriel looked out the window to where the children were playing in the warm May sunshine, laughing and splashing the water with their feet. While he watched, Annie darted up toward the cabin and Konoc pursued her, practicing his war whoops.

"And we'll be married by then, too."

She turned her head and smiled up at him. "Much sooner than that, I hope."

"As soon as I can persuade a preacher to come up here."

"I don't care how long it takes. As long as you are safely here with us and healing fully."

Gabriel said nothing. He would have to return to the army soon. Though he had not told Belinda yet, he felt well enough to travel now, and he intended to fight again. Slowly but surely he had begun to recall the precise locations of the different enemy's places on his journey from safe house to safe house. He had wasted enough time while British prisoners continued to escape. He could shut down the Tory route across Jersey once and for all, and he meant to do it.

He put his mouth against the side of her throat, and she turned her head and guided his mouth toward hers with her hand against the back of his head, but their burgeoning desire was interrupted when Annie and Konoc suddenly burst into their room.

"We wanna draw, Bee. Can we have some of your papers?" Annie's face was flushed with excitement.

Reluctantly, Gabriel released Belinda, but decided he wouldn't let her escape what they had already started. He wanted her again as he always wanted her, and feared he always would.

Belinda was pulling open a dresser drawer and retrieving some of the sketching pads Gabriel had brought from Savannah. He remembered suddenly, and with a pang of regret, the day he had accused her of spying on him and made her angry enough to toss her Christmas pictures into the fire. He would make that up to her, he told himself. When the war was ended, after they were man and wife, he would give her everything she ever wanted, everything in his power.

As Belinda picked out several clean sheets of paper and handed them to the children, Gabriel's attention fell upon several sheets that had been folded in half and then into quarters.

"What is this?" he asked Belinda as she doled out lumps of charcoal to Konoc and Annie.

"I made sketches of some of the men I'd seen with Major Andre while we lived in his house. I was bringing them to you when Bart forced me to go with him." Her face changed, and he saw her bitter reaction at the mere thought of Smythe.

"He's dead, Belinda. He can't hurt any of us anymore," he told her as he picked up the papers.

As usual her drawings were excellent, and he marveled at her talent as he scrutinized one after another. Unfortunately, he didn't recognize the men depicted until he reached the last one. He went completely rigid, staring down at the man's face in absolute disbelief. Slowly, he turned incredulous eyes to Belinda.

"Did you see this man with Andre?"

"Yes," she said, coming back to him and peering down at the picture in his hands. "He came very late one night, and I was immediately suspicious of him because Major Andre asked me to remain upstairs with Annie. I sneaked outside and peeked in the window." She smiled, then sobered instantly at the serious look on his face. "Why, Gabe? Do you know who he is?"

"Aye, I know him well. He's an American general."

"A general!"

"His name's Benedict Arnold, and he sits in the meetings of our command. That's where I met him. Good God, it can't be Arnold. Are you absolutely sure this was the man?"

Belinda nodded, her eyes wide. "I took great pains to memorize his face because the major was so secretive about him."

Gabriel frowned, anger rising when he realized just how disastrous Arnold's turning would be to the American Army.

"There have been rumors floating around for some time that some of our generals were being courted by Andre, but I never would have suspected Benedict. For God's sake, Belinda, General Washington considers him one of his top aides, and a good friend. He's given him command of West Point—oh, Christ."

Their eyes met, and Belinda read his intentions at once. Her face openly reflected dismay. "You're going back, aren't you."

"I have no choice, Belinda. If this is true, General Washington's got to be warned."

She flew into his arms, and he held her, stroking her hair, but over her head, he stared down at Benedict Arnold's visage, comprehending all too well the magnitude of the defection of such a high-ranking American officer.

His jaw went hard, determination molding his expression. If it was true, he would do whatever it took to see the traitor uncovered for the villain he was.

We hold these truths to be self-evident, that all men are created equal, that they are endowed by their Creator with certain unalienable Rights, that among these are Life, Liberty and the pursuit of Happiness. . . .

Belinda paused in setting the type and stared down at the words written by the leaders of the Continental Congress. Gabriel had told her about the American leaders before he had left, about how a committee had drafted their Declaration of Independence, though one man by the name of Thomas Jefferson had written most of the eloquent words. *Pursuit of Happiness*, she thought, staring down at those words, realizing that she had never thought of happiness as being a right to pursue. After her mother had died, she had only sought to struggle through life and survive its ordeals as best as she could in an unjust world. She had not known real happiness until Gabriel had given it to her.

Sighing, she sat back in her chair and looked around the hidden mill room. Ink covered her fingers, and her cheeks were smudged with black where she had pushed back straying strands of hair. It was early afternoon, and everyone else was outside, including Namasset, who usually helped her when she printed copies of the patriot documents and newsletters. She could hear the children calling to each other on the landing. She was tired because she hadn't rested well since Gabriel had returned to his unit. He had been gone several weeks now, and they'd had no word from him.

At first she had watched the river incessantly for his canoe, praying daily for his safe return. Then as the days dragged on, she had thrown herself into the printing work so she wouldn't have to think about him so much.

Outside, she heard a sudden commotion and wondered what game the children played, but their excited shouts soon faded. They would all head up to the cabin for the midday meal soon, she thought, and she would join them. First, she would finish the first page of the document. She started again.

That to secure these rights, Governments are instituted among Men, deriving their just powers from the consent of the governed. . . .

Bending over the letters, she was concentrating hard when the creak of a floorboard brought her head up. She stared at Gabriel where he stood leaning a shoulder against the ladder. She dropped the metal letter she held, and it landed with a clink in the tray in front of her. Then she was up and running into Gabriel's arms.

"Lord help me, but I'm glad to be home," he muttered as he held her fiercely against him.

Belinda said nothing, could not, so overcome with relief and joy. She had been so afraid, but she didn't want to think about that now. She only wanted to touch him, look at him.

"Are you all right?" she asked when at last he released her. "Is your throat healed?"

"I'm fine. Except that I'm exhausted."

He sat down and drew her onto his lap. She knew he was very tired when he laid his head against her breast and closed his eyes. She stroked his fair hair, so happy to have him back.

His hand moved to her stomach. "And you, my love? Have you been well? I've worried about you and the baby."

Belinda smiled and moved his hand over her abdomen. "He's growing, can you tell?"

"Aye, he'll be a big one."

They shared a smile then a tender kiss, but his face grew more serious, and she was frightened again. "I'm afraid I have bad news. I was too late to foil the intrigues perpetrated by Benedict Arnold and Major Andre. Fortunately, though, the plot was discovered before I returned to the camp with your etching."

"Someone else found out?"

"Actually . . ." he paused as if he hated telling her, and Belinda frowned, as if not wanting to hear what he might say. "It was John Andre who made the mistake. He had dressed as a civilian and crossed into patriot territory to meet with Arnold, but luckily he was captured. He had papers on him identifying Arnold as his contact, but somehow word didn't reach Washington until too late. Benedict got away. He's in New York now, and rumor has it the bastard's ready to openly take up a British command against us."

Belinda could see the anger in Gabriel's face, and she smoothed her fingers over the tight lines at the corners of his mouth. "I'm so sorry, Gabe. Did no one suspect him?"

"No one. Washington is furious, and determined to hang him if we can get him back."

"What happened to Major Andre?" she asked, and knew at once by Gabriel's expression that things had not gone well for her old friend.

"I hate to tell you this, Belinda, but he's dead. Hanged as a spy. Washington tried to exchange him for Arnold, but Clinton wouldn't agree."

Belinda's heart twisted because it hurt to think that John Andre was gone. He had been a good friend to her and to her family, even if he was on the wrong side. Emotion rose to clog her throat, but she did not cry. It was war, and terrible things happened to the men fighting it. She didn't speak, but she mourned his passing, and would never forget him.

"We did get Blackburg and shut down the safe houses, thank God," Gabriel was saying now, but his eyes were full of compassion for her suffering.

"I'm glad. You nearly gave your life to uncover them."

"I'm sorry about Andre, Belinda, I truly am. He was a good soldier, and he died honorably. Even Washington was reluctant to execute him, but he had no choice since he was not in uniform when he was caught."

"I understand. I just wish it was over, all the killing and hangings. How long must it go on?"

"Until we win," he answered simply, hugging her close again.

After a moment he drew back and smiled. "I do have some good news to share with you."

"What?"

"It's a surprise. Come outside and I'll show you."

Belinda laughed as he pulled her up and drew

her toward the ladder that led up into the mill. She wiped her inky hands on her apron as best she could, then preceded him, his arms supporting her as she climbed.

When they descended the staircase outside, she could see that Namasset, Willamette, and the children all stood awaiting them on the landing. Henri was there as well, beaming a wide grin, with another man she did not know. Annie was jumping up and down with excitement. Willamette held a bouquet of red roses from the trellis behind the cabin.

Gabriel took both her hands. "I love you, Belinda. Would you do me the honor of becoming my wife?"

"Now? Today?" she said, but her heart was singing.

"Right now. I've dragged one of the army chaplains all the way upriver, and Henri is here to stand as witness."

Belinda could not stop smiling as Annie ran up and thrust the roses into her hands.

"Yes, yes, of course, I will!" she cried, putting her hand in Gabriel's.

Gabriel led her down among their friends, and they all gathered around on the landing, smiling as the young chaplain spoke to them of love, hope, and commitment. Then it was over, and Belinda was Gabriel's wife. The joy within her was beyond anything she had ever known, and Gabriel shared her happiness, staying beside her every moment as if he did not want her out of his sight. Willamette prepared the wedding feast, and they smiled at each other and held hands while the others chatted and mingled, content to sit quietly and look at each other.

"Are you happy?" Gabriel asked her later that night when they finally were able to hold each other in bed, their bodies entwined, their hearts as one.

"Gloriously happy," she murmured, then closed her eyes as his lips touched hers, gently, so unbelievably tender.

Epilogue

Belinda rode in the open carriage, her smile so broad, her heart so joyous that she could not find her voice. Gabriel handled the reins, and his face was full of the same unbridled pleasure as he waved greetings to the throngs of people dancing in the street. Annie was hanging onto the backseat, laughing at the way everyone was yelling and dragging the British flag through the streets. The British fleet had sailed from the city that very day, and the celebrations were only just beginning.

Even her darling little Will was clapping his pudgy hands and giving his chortling laugh where he sat in her lap. His thick black curls blew about riotously as they turned the corner of Beaver Street onto Broad, and his blue eyes, as azure as her own, danced with merriment. He was a good little boy, but a handful to catch now that he had learned to walk. It seemed impossible that he had turned two the previous month. For the first time, he would see his father's house, where they would make their lives together now that the long, terrible war of rebellion was over.

When Gabriel drew the coach to a stop at the curb, Dulcimer flung open the front door and ran down the steps. Lizzie came right behind her, and they clapped and cried out welcomes as a small parade passed on the street beside them—returning American soldiers marching to the drums and fifes that led them back to their homes and families.

Gabriel jumped down, grinning widely, then reached up to take his son. Will went quickly into his father's arms as he always did when Gabriel was anywhere nearby. The toddler held onto the fringed epaulette of his father's buff-and-blue military jacket and gurgled down at Annie, who had already scrambled out on her own and was clutching Dulcimer around her waist.

Belinda put her hand into her husband's as he assisted her to the ground. He squeezed her fingers, then looked up at the house.

"We're home, my love," he said, his voice thick with emotion. "At last, we're at home to stay."

Belinda nodded and walked proudly at his side, up the steps and into her home, her heart warm with love, for she knew that now they would have the most wonderful life together. One of peace and harmony with all the rights for which Gabriel had fought so long and hard—life, liberty, but, she thought with an inner smile, there was no reason any longer to pursue happiness. She had found more than she could ever have dreamed of with Gabriel and their beautiful son.

If you enjoyed
Forever, My Love,
be sure to look for
Linda Ladd's
next historical romance,

A Love So Splendid

Coming soon from Topaz Books.

Turn the page
for a special preview. . . .

Palmetto Point Plantation, 1765

With his elegant, silver-buckled shoes dangling well above the intricately swirled designs adorning a lush crimson and navy blue Chinese carpet, Lord William Remington sat in the massive, well-worn depths of a burgundy-colored leather wingchair. Spine stiff, hands folded respectfully in the fashion required by his exceedingly proper, disciplined father, he waited as patiently as any active young boy could.

It was, however, an immense personal struggle not to squirm forward so that he could catch a glimpse of his friends through the opened French doors just behind the desk where his father sat writing with a quill pen. The whisper of a summer breeze invaded the draperies, billowing the thin panels of soft white lawn. The air smelled good, laden with a mingling of perfumes— the cloying sweetness from the pink blossoms on the spreading mimosa tree that shaded the pillared gallery, the spicy aroma of scarlet geraniums in the pots outside the door, and the purple bougainvillea that entwined the marble stair, and now and then, and most fragrant of all, a faint whiff of yellow tea roses.

Far across the lawn where a towering row of ancient magnolia trees formed a natural barrier between the grassy lawn and the cobbled stableyard, William could hear his little brother yelling. Stephen's cry was excited, and William squirmed restlessly, craning his neck to peer past his father's broad shoulder.

All the boys who'd come in their parents' carriages to attend William's wedding were out in the yard with Stephen. Probably planning strategies for tonight's acorn battle. They'd be choosing a new captain of the guard about now, he figured, since he was no longer available to lead them. Maybe they'd chosen Stephen, maybe that's why he'd given that glad shout. Frowning, mad as fire, William balled up his fists. It wasn't fair! He was the oldest, after all, and yesterday they'd voted him as the best leader.

Twisting impatiently in the confines of the big chair, he grit his teeth until he felt a sharp pain dig into his temple. Why'd he have to be the one inside sitting so still? Listening forever as his father droned on about duty and honor? Sometimes he wished he hadn't been the firstborn male. It was fine, of course, that he'd be the Duke of Thorpe someday when he grew up, but sometimes he wished Stephen had been the eldest. His brother was barely three years younger than he, and Stephen was never called upon to closet himself with their father, or worry about getting some rich, suitable heiress for a bride.

The truth was William didn't care whether he ended up the duke or not, and he didn't even know what a member of Parliament did. He wanted to be a soldier! With a long musket that had a glossy, oil-polished stock of carved wood and a sharp bayonet affixed at the end. Or even more exciting, he could be a blood-crazed pirate like the infamous Blackbeard Teach, who'd sailed the seas and plundered ships in William's grandfather's time. Back then, the planters around Charleston had pooled their gold and put out a price on his head. And they'd got it, too, cut it off and put it up on a pole to warn off other pirates. But William'd be too good a pirate to get executed.

But now, here he sat like he was already a prisoner, bored and uncomfortable in the grandest crimson frockcoat he'd ever owned, and a white neckcloth edged with fine Nottingham lace, waiting and waiting so he could repeat the dumb wedding vows. It didn't seem fair, not at all, that not one of his other friends had to be a husband so young! He'd just turned eleven, hadn't he, was still a lad, not even sent off to school yet? But worst of all was that his father was making him marry up with Geoffrey Kingston's little cousin, Trinity. And she was just four years old!

He sniffed at the idea, pure disgust puckering his mouth. Trinity Kingston acted like a spoiled little baby, wailing and blubbering and pestering him and Geoffrey until they had to sneak off and hide so she couldn't find them. Yesterday the brat even grabbed his wooden sword and stabbed him in the leg. What kind of wife was she going to grow up to be?

Outside, a loud yell drifted from the magnolias. Geoffrey, this time. William braced his wrists and raised himself up an inch or two off the arms of his chair so he could see better. His father didn't pay him any mind; his dark head bent in concentration as he put a few finishing flourishes on the wedding document. The scratching of the quill plume was the only sound as Geoffrey shouted out something about Blackbeard Teach and the way he stuck burning matches in his beard.

William's mind floated away from the boring study, and formed that frightful image. A thrill went through him when he imagined himself grown up with a long scraggly black beard that reached to his knees. He'd set lots of flames in his beard someday, so many that the ladies would swoon and the governor would quake in his fine high-heeled shoes. Maybe he'd even have a peg leg, if he got injured somehow in a battle. Smiling, enthralled with fantasies of derring-do, he sobered instantly at the sound of his father's deeply resonant voice.

"I'll remind you, William, that this day is most momentous, an occasion that will shape your destiny from this moment forward. There's no place for levity. I do trust you'll retain a dignified demeanor throughout the entire ceremony?"

Lord Adrian paused, his piercing eyes fastened upon his son and heir. His stern features softened a bit as he continued. "Your bride is hardly more than a toddler, and you a bit younger than is usual for a husband to pledge his troth. I'm certainly aware of that. I'm afraid, however, I've little choice since I'll be living in England while you and Stephen attend school. 'Tis a wise course of action to get this affair finished and done with, so Eldon Kingston and I can begin the task of consolidating Trinity's future inheritance with your own holdings. Do you have any questions you wish to ask me, son?"

William avoided his father's inquisitive gaze but there was something that had been plaguing him a good deal. "Does Trinity have to tag along with us? I mean, live at our house in London, and all that?"

A rare smile softened Adrian Remington's taciturn face. "No, William. In fact, you'll have little opportunity to see the child again until she reaches the age of sixteen. At that time you'll commence a normal courtship and become acquainted, before a second, more formal wedding is held in Charleston. I daresay our voyages back to the Carolinas will be few and far between until you come of age. Your mother will stay in the colonies for a portion of the year at Trenton Hill, but she'll be at Thorpe Hall in England the rest of the time."

"I understand, sir." Inside, William thanked the saints that Trinity wasn't going with them. The truth was that William couldn't bear the sight of her. She was such a bother.

"Anything else that concerns you, boy? The ceremony itself, perhaps? Do you understand what exactly will be required of you?"

"Yes, sir. I'm ready to do my duty as the future Duke of Thorpe."

"Most commendable, William." Adrian Remington nodded approvingly as he waved the parchment back and forth, allowing the freshly inked notations to dry. "This union will nearly double our land holdings here in the colonies, and since Trinity's the only child, she'll own this great plantation house and the thousands of acres of rice and indigo harvested annually here at Palmetto Point."

William nodded, smiled brightly, as if any of that actually concerned him, but he really wished everything was over so he could play soldiers with his friends.

"Now, William," his father said, rising, taking a moment to adjust the lace-edged sleeves that peeked from the wide, dark blue, turned-back cuffs of his gray silk brocade frock coat. "I suspect it's time for us to join Trinity and her father in the chapel. Our guests will be waiting. Straighten your stock, son, stand straight and proud, and remember to comport yourself as a gentleman and lord of the British realm. Someday you'll inherit a dukedom and you must never, ever forget your duty to your family and to your King. Do you understand how important you will someday become?"

"Yes sir."

"Then come along. I daresay dear little Trinity's becoming a tad restless. It'll soon be time for her nap, I understand."

Dear little Trinity, William found several minutes later, was more than restless, she was screaming her head off. He could hear her awful yelling all the way down the corridor. He hazarded a wary glance at his father, alarmed by the muffled din filtering out from the sanctity of the chapel. Adrian's stern mouth had thinned even more, now a stitched line of disapproval. As William well knew, Adrian Remington would never allow one of his children to behave in so shameful a fashion.

As they opened the double doors leading into the long, narrow chapel, they were immediately confronted with the full effect of his bride's eardrum-piercing shrieks. At least fifty pairs of relieved eyes turned to watch them make their way down the center aisle toward the raised altar. His mother was there at the front, holding his baby sister, Adrianna, in her arms. She smiled at him, and made him feel all warm and calm inside. He wished she'd be in England with them all the year through.

His tardy arrival did not lessen Trinity's angry cries or even modify the shrillness of their pitch, and William's green eyes widened in disbelief at the sight of her. She was all dressed up like a pint-sized angel in rows and rows of white ruffles and had on a little lace bonnet that had fallen from her head and hung off one shoulder by its pink ribbons because she was in the middle of throwing the worst hissy fit that William had ever beheld.

Eldon Kingston, the child's unfortunate father—

imagine having to be around the awful little girl all the time!—had her by the hand but she would have none of his soothing. Why, she looked like a fighting rooster caught by the feet, the way she was twisting and turning, and falling down on her back and kicking her white slippers at the priest's long black robe.

William considered it the funniest thing he had ever witnessed and wished Geoff and Stephen could watch her roll around and screech like a piglet caught in the handle of a slop bucket. But he dared not betray even the hint of a smile. No one else seemed to think Trinity's behavior was amusing, not in the least. All the guests watched from the pews, openly aghast and mightily concerned. William couldn't fathom why they were so shocked at the spectacle. Everybody in Charleston, and even out in the surrounding plantations, knew Mister Kingston spoiled his only child rotten and had given the little girl everything she had ever wanted since her mother had succumbed to yellow fever two summers ago. She threw similar tantrums almost daily, did she not? And wherever she happened to be, too. It didn't matter to her, no, it sure didn't.

By the time William and his father reached the foot of the high mahogany altar, Mister Kingston had managed to get his daughter up off the floor, at least, and had her under his arm, her feet off the ground. She was kicking and flailing her arms, and his round face had turned the color of a ripe cherry, and his loose jowls were flopping all over the place with exertion, but all William could see was how Trinity's curly red hair was flying all around in a big wild tangle, like a drawing he'd seen of Medusa's head with all the snakes writhing on it when Perseus held it up after he'd chopped it off with his sword. That was William's favorite Greek myth.

"There, there, Trinity, dearest, don't take on so. Young Will's here at last. Don't you want to be a good girl and hold his hand? You like the boy, now, don't you? You said you did, after all."

To everyone's surprise, not to mention relief, especially William's, Trinity stopped her struggling, yowling tantrum long enough to raise her freckly face and latch her weird eyes on him. They were the color of gold coins, old ones that were burnished and not as shiny as freshly minted ones, and seemed absolutely enormous in her tiny heart-shaped face, sort of glowing and peculiar against cheeks as flushed as fire and mottled from her hysterics. Then, to his shock, she outstretched her arms in his direction as if she wanted him to hold her.

A surge of hot blood crept up William's neck, making him burn all over and so horribly embarrassed that he couldn't move. He tried to swallow, had to force it down with a gulping sound that even he could hear. He refused to look directly at her, attempted to remain where he was instead of fleeing back down the aisle, but it was difficult with so many people staring at them.

Boy, was he ever glad his father was taking him off to an English boarding school. At least he wouldn't have to put up with being around Trinity and watching her throw maniacal fits and knowing he was stuck with her as a wife until he died. He wished he were far away somewhere—on the levee that overlooked the sea would be good, searching the ocean swells with a sea captain's brass spyglass for skulls and crossbones.

"Now that's a good girl, dearie." Trinity's father set the wild child on her feet, gingerly, as if any sudden movement might set her off again, like a cocked and loaded flintlock. He was crooning now in some strange voice, hopeful and gruff and sort of scared almost. William had heard other grown men resort to that queer tone when coddling recalcitrant children. William had never heard such conciliatory appeasement from his father. He'd have got a caning instead.

The moment Trinity's little slippers clicked down atop the shiny marble floor, she lit out for William like a fieldmouse fleeing a hungry tabby. William took a step backward, flushing crimson and gazing helplessly at his father as the frizzy-haired tot barreled at him with the energy of a whirling dust devil. No help was to be had and a second later she hurtled herself up against his chest so hard that the impact staggered him backward.

Somewhere in the audience he heard some lady's voice say "oooh" and another woman breathe out "aaah," as if Trinity's jumping on him and nearly knocking him on his back was a real cute thing. William groaned out loud in utter humiliation as the little girl clutched thin arms around his neck in a stranglelock that cut off his breath, then to his horror, clamped ruffled, pantalette-clad legs around his waist.

Above the heads of all the gawking, whispering onlookers, he caught a glimpse of Stephen and Geoffrey, their faces visible through the diamond-shaped panes of the arched chapel window. They were out there laughing at him, he realized with a rushing wave of shame, and then he got mad, and even more mortified, and tried to unpry the awful little urchin from his torso.

His efforts were in vain; she was stuck as tight as a bolted door, and holding on so hard that she was wrinkling up the smooth silk of his white waistcoat and pulling loose all the neat folds in his neckcloth that he had worked so hard to get just right. She smelled like she'd been eating strawberries all day long, and she was making him look as silly and babyish as she was.

"Quit acting like a ninny, Trin," he whispered close to her ear, making his tone vicious and harsh enough to make her shudder in her beribboned little pumps. "Or else Geoff and I will sell you off to the pirates and you'll never get to see your papa again!"

The threat settled her down quick enough, he thought with smug triumph as he untangled her skinny arms from around his neck and got her off him and on the floor again. She grabbed his hand, though, and then he found out why she smelled so fruity. Her fingers were so sticky with syrup that she must've eaten out of the jam pot with her hand!

But at the moment at least she was holding relatively quiet as they listened to the priest mumble lots of Latin words William couldn't understand. Unfortunately, her niceness didn't last very long. When she began to balance on one foot and tug on his hand so that he had to hold her up to keep himself from stumbling into the front pew, he gave her a hard pinch on the arm. She yelped shrilly just as the priest got to the end of the marriage ceremony and smiled benignly at the two children before him.

"Now William and Trinity, I declare the two of you

to be joined together as husband and wife, forevermore, under the eyes of these good witnesses and with the sacred blessing of God Almighty."

The ensuing applause and cheers of congratulations were loud and enthusiastic, and fortunately so, because they drowned out poor William's groan of pain as his baby bride sank sharp little white teeth deep into the side of his hand.

Palmetto Point Plantation, South Carolina, July 1781

"Truly, William, I'm surprised Trinity hasn't come yet to greet you. I suppose she misunderstood when I told her you were arriving from Charleston before the noon hour."

Sir William Remington, lord of the realm and heir to the fourteenth Duke of Thorpe, turned a skeptical glance upon Victoria Ballantine Remington where she sat on a high-backed, gold-and-white-striped silk settee facing the opened doors of the rear gallery. He had not seen his mother since he had last visited the Carolinas, a journey which had occurred nearly eight years ago, and in far better times, a good three years before the Americans declared their independence.

With faint surprise, it dawned upon him that he hardly knew Victoria anymore. He'd remembered her as a younger version of herself with the rich chestnut hair he'd inherited from her, not as she was now, an aging woman with wings of gray fanning out from her temples and a fine etching of lines at the corners of her eyes. And he knew even less about Adrianna, his raven-haired little sister who was seated beside their mother.

Little wonder, since his father had insisted that both he and his younger brother, Stephen, obtain their education from English masters. His mother had obstinately refused to spend much time in London, and they'd returned to the Carolinas so infrequently that they'd veritably missed Adrianna's entire childhood. He swiveled his regard to Adrianna, a serenely pretty, pleasant young woman, who'd had precious little to say to him since he'd arrived earlier that day.

After open hostilities had commenced between British regulars and American rebels, further visits had been forestalled for half a decade due to the fact that Charleston had been held by patriot troops until of late when the English had finally managed to reoccupy the city. Now that the town was filled with enough soldiers to maintain order, William had come home, his safety on the war-ravaged continent relatively assured. Sometimes, however, he couldn't bring himself to believe the Americans' political grievances against King George had deteriorated into such fierce fighting and bloodshed.

Good God, the colonists were Englishmen, after all, shared mutual ancestors, were distant cousins, and in his case, bore even closer familial ties than that. He was used to fighting the French, England's nemesis in war, trade, and conquest, but to destroy other Englishmen was a harder task to stomach, be they rebellious, or not.

When minutes ticked by without his offer of a suitable response to his mother's lame excuses for Trinity Kingston's deplorable behavior, Victoria fixed him with a disapproving, expectant stare, one elegant eyebrow arched in censure. A look he well remembered from his childhood and which finally spurred him to reply.

"I can't pretend I'm surprised by Trinity's display of ill manners, if that's what you want me to say," he said, not really bothering to hide his dislike for the damned girl. "I'm sure you'll remember, Mother, the last time I visited here at Palmetto Point, she foolishly forced her mare up the portico staircase like some bloody Mongol horseman."

William dropped into the cushioned depths of a peach and green floral armchair, crossed his legs and tried without success to disguise a grimace chock-full of distaste. He was thoroughly disgusted at the girl's outlandish lack of propriety, and had been for a long time. True, Trinity had only been twelve or so when she'd shown her recklessness on the stairs, but not so young she shouldn't have known the curved marble steps were slick and treacherous and no place to endanger expensive horseflesh. The image of the way she'd looked then was exceptionally vivid, even now, eight years later. She'd sat astride one of the most beautiful white mares he'd ever seen, her frizzy reddish hair flying all around her freckled face flushed blood red.

Lord Almighty, what an undisciplined hoyden she'd been! But she'd always had a wicked, troublesome streak, and apparently hadn't learned a blasted thing about being a proper lady. If she had, she wouldn't be out gallivanting around the countryside while he, the next Duke of Thorpe, sat waiting for her. But worst of all, and the most galling part, to be sure, was that he'd been married to the little chit the day she'd pulled that stunt.

William grimaced, clamping his jaw with frustration, as he did every time he thought of the ridiculous marital alliance. Scowling, he tossed back the remainder of his brandy then looked up sharply when his heretofore silent sister suddenly came alive and raged a quick, impassioned defense against his assessment of Trinity's character.

Surprised, he stared at her. How the hell old was Adrianna, anyway? Seventeen? Eighteen? Her future was another less than coveted task facing William on this trip. He and his father had made all the appropriate decisions; all he had to do was tell her what was expected of her. Until now he had assumed her well trained enough to cause him no unnecessary problems. But as he listened to what she was saying, he wasn't quite so sure.

"I daresay, brother," Adrianna had paused dramatically after that opening, for effect he decided since she slanted him a haughty stare before continuing, "that poor Trinity is little desirous of meeting up with the cad who jilted her so heartlessly before the whole of Charleston society, and not so long ago, I might remind you."

A bolt of shock coursed through William that the girl dared criticize him aloud, and in front of their mother. He was in a black enough mood already without having to dress down his sister. He remained calm, deceptively so, lifting one shoulder in a casual, dismissive shrug.

"I had little recourse, sister, as well you should

know. Father reneged on the marriage contract when Trinity's father openly declared allegiance to the Continental Congress. Blatant defiance of the Crown is not looked kindly upon by the King, especially from the in-laws of the Duke of Thorpe."

"But you were such a coward about it! Canceling the wedding by courier was an appalling thing to do, even you must realize that. Trinity told me she felt like one of those thoroughbred fillies you and father are always acquiring, one you didn't want anymore because she'd gone lame or something, and so you cast her off with impunity like you would any other unwanted trinket. Trinity was most indignant, being treated so shabbily by you."

"Adrianna, dear, I believe that's quite enough on this subject." Victoria's reproof, though steely under her soft voice, did little to eradicate his sister's open hostility toward him. Adrianna was not finished voicing her opinion, it seemed.

"Well, really, Mother, 'twas just abominable the way it all happened, seeking an annulment out of the blue in such a way. Thank goodness that Trin loathes you so much, William, or she might've been utterly devastated over the awful insult."

William tented his fingers and calmly eyed his little sister over them, annoyed with her, to be sure, but his interest was piqued by her last revelation. "Trinity loathes me?"

"Why, of course, she does, and has ever since that last time you visited us when you were so cruel and critical of every little thing she did. Don't you remember how mean you were to her when she showed you how she'd taught Moonbeam to ride up the gallery steps? You compared her to a stableboy and humiliated her in front of her father and everyone there. After that I'm sure she was secretly quite pleased to escape the horrible fate of having you for a husband."

Oh, yes, a horrible fate indeed, William mocked inwardly, resisting a contemptuous laugh. Trinity Kingston would do well indeed if she found another husband who would make her a duchess. Especially now that her family wore the brand of rebel.

Still, Adrianna's outspoken, defiant attitude rankled

William, and made him worry that his sister had been exposed to Trinity Kingston's unsavory habits too long for her own good. Or were all American women willful, disobedient harridans?

"You'd be wise, Adrianna, to support the actions of your family and your King instead of pleading the case of known rebel sympathizers."

Adrianna bristled like a hungry mastiff hunched over a rack of ribs. "Trinity's my dearest friend, and will always be so, despite her father's politics. Besides, no one can prove she's guilty of any crime. The British command has no shred of evidence to support their accusations against her."

"Almighty God," William said, sitting up straighter and staring at her in dismay. He turned an incredulous gaze onto their mother. "Is she saying Trinity's an accused criminal?"

His mother evaded his gaze, suddenly inordinately fascinated with the view outside the open door. Completely uncharacteristic for her to evade a subject. She'd always been one to meet obstacles head on. He drooped back against the cushion with sinking heart, already knowing full well that Trinity was indeed involved in something that could bring down doom on the entire family.

"Well, madame? What pit of mire has Trinity Kingston dragged our good name through this time?"

Under the sting of his open sarcasm, his mother's eyes found his face without the hesitation of the moment before. He was slightly subdued by the forlorn expression in their soft nutmeg depths, a deep, abiding sadness that startled him. She was disappointed in him, he knew it as well as if she had said the words out loud. Uncomfortable with that knowledge, he shifted in his chair like a schoolboy who'd skipped lessons to go fishing.

"As Adrianna mentioned, there have been no charges proven against Trinity."

"What kind of charges, mother?" he persisted, scandalized that a young woman her age was even under suspicion, though in truth nothing Trinity did should shock him. Her father had been a widower for years, had adored his only child, had spoiled her incessantly and unconscionably since the day she was born. No wonder she'd grown up feeling free to comport herself in any fashion she desired. Hell, the last time he'd seen her she'd paraded around in male breeches and had looked just as he had described her that day—like the meanest of stable hands.

Victoria's sigh was a deep, chest-heaving inhalation that intensified the following silence. She took her time smoothing out a wrinkle in her shiny black bombazine skirt. "Cornwallis feels she might be riding courier for the rebel, Will Washington. You've heard of him, I'm sure, he's the brother of General George Washington who commands the Continental Army."

William certainly did not need an explanation about the hierarchy of the patriot leaders. He'd heard enough of them throughout the halls of Parliament. He tried to school his incredulity. "Heaven help us, are you telling me she's actually riding with the enemy?"

Anger soon pushed the shock from William's mind. Distress, annoyance, embarrassment all came together like tributaries surging into the sea. What could possibly happen next? London was still buzzing about Trinity's father, Eldon Kingston, formerly a wealthy man of class and stature smiled on by His Majesty, now imprisoned for treasonous acts.

"You're rather nonchalant that you might be harboring a suspected spy in your household," he clipped out curtly, and in a tone so pregnant with scorn that his mother stiffened and lifted her chin.

"I'll remind you, William, that we're sitting this very moment in a house that rightfully belongs to Trinity, though the King's soldiers have confiscated it and given it to your father in recompense for the destruction of our own property. And I might add this, so that you won't continue to exhibit such contempt for Trinity. She and Eldon were the very ones who took pity on Adrianna and me at the beginning of the war when zealots burned Trenton Hill out from under us. Not only did they face patriot censure for harboring us but they protected us from harm." She paused, her regard set uncompromisingly on his face. "I will show her the same courtesy, whether it meets with your approval or not. Furthermore, I'll inform you in no uncertain terms that I've no use for masked Tory riders who use their loyalty to King George to viciously attack their former friends and neighbors, as happens in these parts nearly every night of late."

"Then I will be equally blunt, Mother." William chose his words with utmost care. "Your remarks could very well be construed as traitorous. Perhaps you should guard your tongue to better degree when speaking against allies of the Crown."

His mother did not back down from her convictions. "Eldon Kingston and his family have been friends of my heart since many years before you were born, William. I'm pleased to say it's not a flaw of my character to forget my past associations." She gave him a significant look, the meaning of which he was able to read only too well. "Nor could I, or would I, ever forget my pride in my colonial heritage."

William felt her rebuke with the impact of a balled fist to the stomach, though she had couched the blow quietly, with her usual silken civility. Supremely irritated that he had allowed himself on his first day home to become embroiled in base arguments with both his mother and his sister, he pushed himself to his feet and sought out the brandy decanter kept behind a glass door in a cabinet alcove.

Concentrating on pouring the cognac into his snifter, a goodly proportion to calm his anger, he decided that—considering the disloyal undercurrents threading through the previous discourse—his father was absolutely inspired to order his wife and daughter back to England where they belonged. The way they came across at the moment, it was only a matter of time before they were openly aligned with the Americans.

He shouldn't be so surprised, because, as his mother had openly admitted, she was, after all, Victoria Ballantine Remington, a Charlestonian, and distinctly proud to be so. For generations her family had cut fortunes from the Carolina swamps, and William's father had married her strictly for those same financial considerations.

And indeed the Duke of Thorpe had gained much wealth from his American heiress—the immense profits from Ballantine indigo and tobacco had refurbished the ancient walls of their massive ancestral edifice known as Thorpe Hall where it lay nestled in vast deep parks fifty miles north of London, as well as funding the acquisition of the magnificent townhouse near Hyde Park where William himself kept his residence.

Stepping across the plush designs on the gold and navy blue carpet, he paused in the threshold to enjoy the faint breeze. He'd forgotten how damnably hot and humid South Carolina could be in the summertime. In front of him, the grassy lawn spread out into the distance for a good three hundred yards then ended where the raised levee edged the first watery field of rice. Beyond those crop-filled lakes lay the sea where palmetto palms lined wide sandy beaches.

The view brought back memories of the days when he and Stephen used to come here from Trenton Hill to play. They'd been very little then, and Trinity had followed them around and pestered them relentlessly. Trinity's older cousin, Geoffrey, had been William's best friend for the first decade of their lives, and William still thought of him fondly, though they hadn't seen each other in years. William had heard Geoffrey, too, had become a rebel, but he hoped to God his old friend would come to his senses and pledge loyalty to the Crown before it was too late.

His relaxed stance revealed nothing to the ladies in the room behind him. But within his stoic calm, he was becoming more and more angry with Trinity, and the longer she made him wait, the more incensed he became. The whole affair was a difficult business at best, and all he wanted was for the farce to be over and done with. And as rapidly and painlessly as possible so he could get back to England and wed Caroline, if and when he decided she was the right woman for him. In any case, she was infinitely more suitable as his duchess than Trinity Kingston ever had been.

Bloody Zeus, his father would succumb to apoplexy at the mere hint of Trinity's collusion with the enemy. Under no circumstances could such intelligence get out among their comrades in Parliament. His father was openly and outspokenly, and despite his Carolinian wife, a staunch anti-American hawk, and had carefully hidden any kinship with Eldon Kingston. If any of his political enemies learned the truth, the newspapers would have a heyday with his credibility.

"There," Adrianna said from outside on the gallery where she'd retired in a huff only moments before. "Trin's coming now, just as I told you she would."

Still cradling his glass, William moved to the smooth marble balustrade and watched three riders leave the distant levee and set out for the house. The road edging the lawn was a straight white strip against the green grass, paved with the crushed oyster shells so prevalent on thoroughfares in and around Charleston.

The last time he had laid eyes on his hellion bride, he'd been standing approximately in the same spot, and he could still remember the unadulterated astonishment he'd felt when she'd guided her horse unerringly up the precarious marble stair. He glanced at the graceful winding steps off to his right. If he hadn't been there, hadn't watched her accomplish the feat, he'd declare the tale a lie. As the riders reached the flagstones below in a clatter of shod hooves, he wondered if Trinity was still fool enough to do such a thing. Would she now? Brazenly? Just to annoy him?

"Come out here, Mother, Trinity's arrived." Adrianna called inside to Victoria. "Not to see William, of course, but because you bade her to make an appearance."

His sister was becoming more than adept at looking him in the eye while she boldly insulted him, William noted as their mother joined them on the pillared gallery. He caught a faint whiff of the bougainvillea climbing the balcony, mingled with the lemon verbena toilette water which was his mother's favorite perfume.

Buried memories awoke and stirred in his mind as she moved up beside him and her wide skirt brushed his pantleg, resurrected from days long past and nearly forgotten. He looked down at his mother, his affection dimmed considerably by many, many years of separation, and now complicated by different loyalties. Victoria remained unaware of his tender thoughts as she stood, erect and dignified, watching the trio of approaching riders.

William suppressed a sigh and turned to refocus his attention on Trinity, perversely dreading to confront the girl but at the same time curious to see if she had changed from the wild thing she'd been when last they'd met.

FROM A CLOISTERED CONVENT

Ainsley Campbell was raised as an orphan and an outcast within the harsh confines of Kilchurn Abbey. She was condemned for her shame-shadowed birth and haunting beauty that could only have been bestowed on her by the Devil to tempt the lust of men.

TO PASSION'S OPEN ARMS

When dashing Rodric MacDonald took her from the convent, Ainsley was still an innocent, but she knew enough of her native Scotland to understand that his clan and hers were deadly enemies. And she swiftly learned enough of her weakness and his strength the first time he touched her. She had to guard herself against surrender to desire . . . or give herself to a daring man whose love could lead them through dangerous intrigue and dark secrets to emerge in dazzling fulfillment. . . .

Lilacs on Lace

DRIVEN BY DESIRE

Stuart Delaney, a notorious Civil War adventurer, has traveled across land and sea to rescue a lovely young Englishwoman, Anjelica Blake, and bring her home to an arranged marriage. Stuart has been paid well for his trouble—but the real trouble begins the moment he lays eyes on this woman who is promised to another.

BOUND BY LOVE

Anjelica must decide if she will remain loyal to the kind-hearted gentleman she hasn't seen since childhood, or continue the delicious, scandalous alliance with the mysterious American who has recklessly risked his life for her and who promises her nothing but the heated passion of his love . . .

White Orchid

A VICTORY OF THE HEART

With hair as bright as flame and eyes as cool as silver, Cassandra Delaney is changeable, unpredictable, and a perfect spy. Her brother, Harte, has sided with the hated Yankees, but Cassandra is the notorious "White Rose," risking her life and honor for the Confederacy in a desperate flirtation with death. . . .

Derek Courtland, rakehell Australian blockade runner, possesses an uncanny ability to perceive danger, but on this mission his every sense is taut, his blood on fire. His job is to abduct the mysterious, sensual woman known as "White Rose" to Australia to save her pretty neck. Only she is fighting him, body and soul, to escape his ship and the powerful feelings pulling them both toward the unknown. . . .

Now, under star-splashed skies, the ocean rising and plunging beneath them, a man who can see through deception and a woman who is an expert at lies are being swept way on a perilous voyage to a distant, seductive land . . . and to the far more dangerous territory of deep, fathomless love.

White Rose

THEY CAME TOGETHER
IN LOVE AND WAR

Ravishing, golden-haired Lily Courtland is both blessed and cursed with the extraordinary gift of second sight. But even she can see no way to escape from the men who have abducted her—and from the nightmare of sexual slavery awaiting her.

Harte Delaney has conquered countless women with his virile good looks and braved many dangers as secret agent for the North in the shadowland of intrigue during the Civil War. But he has never met a woman as magically mysterious as this beauty for whom he risks all to rescue and possess.

Amid the flames of war and the heat of passion, this woman who knows all and this man who fears nothing find themselves lost in the heart-stopping adventure with their own fate and the fate of a nation hanging in breathless balance. . . .

White Lily